The Con

Rachel Rosato

ISBN: 979-8-9902897-0-3 (paperback)
ISBN: 979-8-9902897-1-0 (ebook)

Cover art by Rachel Rosato

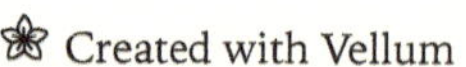 Created with Vellum

Author's Note:

To avoid drawing comparisons to any real convention, this story takes place in a fictional city in Indiana, USA.

This story contains references to mild violence, including kidnapping, as well as emotionally abusive relationships, substance abuse, and severe depression.

Rule #1: Never underestimate someone.
You do not know what they are capable of.

- Princess Serafina of Lorg

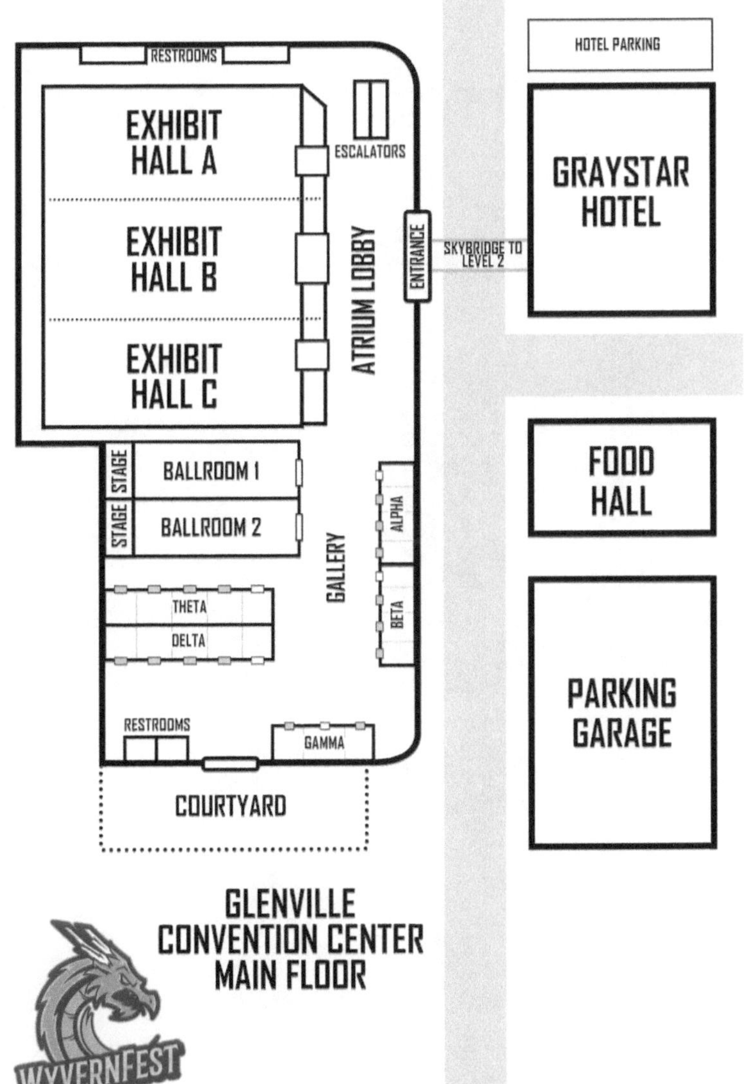

RESTROOMS
EXHIBIT HALL A
EXHIBIT HALL B
EXHIBIT HALL C
ESCALATORS
ATRIUM LOBBY
ENTRANCE
SKYBRIDGE TO LEVEL 2
HOTEL PARKING
GRAYSTAR HOTEL
STAGE
STAGE
BALLROOM 1
BALLROOM 2
GALLERY
ALPHA
BETA
THETA
DELTA
FOOD HALL
RESTROOMS
GAMMA
PARKING GARAGE
COURTYARD
GLENVILLE CONVENTION CENTER MAIN FLOOR
WYVERNFEST
GLENVILLE

1

It's ironic how pretending to be someone else can help you figure out who you really are. As if somehow by trying to live out your delusions and escape reality you actually discover your truth.

But such is the life of a cosplayer.

If I can even call myself that anymore, considering I haven't been to a convention in over a year. Even longer since I made a costume, or even sketched a design. I guess that explains why I don't really know who I am anymore.

Parking my car in the nearest open spot of the Graystar Hotel parking lot, I take a breath and look down at my Star Wars pajama pants and faded *Reading Rainbow* t-shirt. The same clothes I slept in last night.

My bushy, copper red hair is in absolute shambles, I haven't worn makeup in months, and these ratty old sneakers are fighting for their lives. My wide-rimmed glasses sit low on my nose like a disappointed librarian until I push them up again with a sigh.

Grabbing the rearview mirror and angling it towards my face, I assess the damage, regretting it instantly. "Looking good there,

Elsie," I say to myself with mock enthusiasm, wiping some crust out of the corner of my eye.

Honestly, it's a miracle I even managed to get myself out of the house at all.

Outside my car window, the bright morning sun is warming up the surrounding city, and the birds are merrily chirping away without a care in the world. The maple trees lining the side-walks are clinging to the last breaths of summer, as their various shades of green prepare for a slow fade to yellow and orange.

I pull my unruly hair up into a messy top knot, finishing off that homeless chic look I've perfected these past few months, still needing a few more minutes alone to compose myself before I open this door and have to face everyone.

They're your friends. They love you. They want you to be here.

Maybe if I repeat it enough, I'll actually start to believe it.

I cross my arms on the steering wheel and rest my head over top, trying to calm my mind and think about all the reasons why I should get my ass out of this car.

I've been coming to these cosplay conventions for years with my twin brother, Ethan, and our two best friends, Jade and Damien. It's kind of our thing. We get dressed up in costume, drink way too much, and nerd out with thousands of other people all weekend.

Nothing else compares.

We all look forward to WyvernFest every year here in Glenville, Indiana, and spend a lot of our free time designing and building costumes, buying supplies, making props, and perfecting our characters. Attending conventions is our chance to show off all the work we've put into these costumes and reconnect with friends who share the same interests as us.

But honestly, it's so much more than just dressing up; it's transforming yourself into someone else and embodying an entire character inside and out. They become an extension of you.

Some might dress up to honor a character they love and relate to on a deep level, or maybe they just like the way their outfit looks.

To let yourself become someone else entirely is empowering and thrilling.

And also, it's really fucking fun.

I look down at my phone after yet another buzz.

ETHAN (9:01 A.M.)

Els you here yet?

we're not starting without youuu

Ethan has been blowing up my phone for the past hour, making sure I'm still coming. I get where he's coming from, but even with my train wreck of a personal life, I was not going to miss it this year. If anything, I have never needed this more in my entire life.

I look up at the Graystar Hotel, where we'll all be staying this weekend for the convention. The beautiful seven-story building reminds me a lot of the hotel Jared and I were supposed to get married in almost three months ago.

I slowly and mindlessly scratch at my throat.

I can't help but think about my favorite aquamarine necklace, which I managed to lose that beautiful spring morning — my something blue. If I hadn't lost it, I wouldn't have gone searching around the hotel for it, and ultimately wouldn't have found my fiancé nestled between the thighs of our friend, Tegan, before the ceremony.

It's hard to convey what happens to someone in a moment like that. The best I can describe it is like someone ripping you open and dousing your insides with acid.

I had known betrayal before, but not like this.

I honestly don't remember much about what happened after that. I don't know who broke the news to the 207 guests patiently waiting for the ceremony to begin — it certainly wasn't Mom or Dad, since they weren't even there. I don't know who canceled the DJ or who collected all the gifts people had graciously brought for us. I don't remember changing out of that stupid fucking wedding dress or how I even got back home.

Well, what I *used* to call my home with Jared. That expensive monstrosity he loved showing off. At some point, Ethan moved my shit out of there and let me move in with him.

I went into a pretty deep depression, as one might imagine. I stopped coming into the office, so obviously they fired me. Not like I even wanted that job anyway, working for his father.

Spiraling into a very dark place, I basically just stayed in bed with the curtains shut, binge-watching all the shows and movies Ethan and I grew up on and playing video games until my eyes popped out. It's my usual trusty coping mechanism, to do all the things we did as kids, back when life was still good and simple.

Ethan checked on me regularly, making sure I was still eating and staying hydrated. But he never pushed. He always knows exactly what I need, and it's usually just being around him. Our twin bond is strong, and I honestly don't know what I would do without him, or if I would even still be here.

Another buzz pulls me out of my spiraling thoughts.

ETHAN (9:07 A.M.)

nevermind you're taking too long

we're all here waiting!!!

ME (9:08 A.M.)

just parked, see you inside

ETHAN (9:08 A.M.)

ordered you a drink, let's goooo

A smile tugs at my lips. Three days of partying and geeking out with my brother and our best friends is just what I need to recover and start getting on with my life.

I drain the last of my coffee, adding the Styrofoam cup to the mountain of trash on the floor of the passenger seat. I prepare myself for the onslaught of Midwest humidity as I climb out of my run-down Honda Civic and grab my hefty luggage from the trunk.

Making my way down the sidewalk towards the hotel entrance, I stop to admire the Glenville Convention Center across the street, where WyvernFest is held every year, and where we'll be spending most of our waking hours this weekend.

There are other hotels nearby, but Graystar is where most convention-goers will stay, mainly because of the easy access to the rooms thanks to the skybridge connecting the two buildings at the second level. After spending half the day walking around, carrying props in a heavy costume and uncomfortable shoes, the last thing anyone wants is to trudge down six blocks in the thick, sweltering heat.

Walking through the sliding glass doors that lead into a pristine, open lobby, I readjust the enormous duffel bag over my shoulder and pull my two oversized, wheeled suitcases behind me through the entrance.

"Good morning!" a woman greets from the front desk. "Checking in?"

"Oh, no, my friend already checked us in, thank you."

"Not a problem, enjoy your stay!"

"You too!" I reply before I can stop the words from spilling out. "I mean...yep." *Why am I like this?*

The receptionist returns a polite but confused smile as I walk away in shame.

I had thought about leaving my bags at the front desk to have someone take them up to our room, but now I can never have a conversation with that woman again for the rest of my life. Also, the thought of inconveniencing someone to do a task that I'm fully capable of makes me sweat just a little.

I know I need to work on my people-pleasing tendencies, because right now I have a lot of baggage — I mean, luggage.

The lobby is bright and beautiful with its polished black and gold marble floors, rock waterfall along the side wall leading to the elevators, and a spacious lounging area with plush evergreen sofas and leather chairs. The familiar calming aroma of lavender fills the air, reminding me of so many years past, standing in this very spot, readying myself for an epic weekend ahead.

I make a bee-line to the hotel restaurant just past the lobby and pause at the entrance.

I immediately spot Ethan, Jade, and Damien in the dimly lit space, sitting at our usual corner booth, laughing and making jokes. A pang goes through me, realizing in this moment just how much I've missed spending time with them. Well, Ethan not as much, considering we live together now, but all four of us together. Like we used to.

We all live in the same city two hours from here over the Illinois border, so there really is no excuse for not hanging out more often.

Well, that's not entirely true. The excuse is me and my poor life choices.

I only drove here separately because I had to work last night, and like many attendees, they wanted to arrive a day early to get a head start on partying, and to be ready for the events on day one. My new job at our local bookstore graciously let me have Friday through Sunday off for this, and considering I just started there two weeks ago, I'm not in much of a position to demand more time already.

I talk and text with Jade all the time, when we're not hanging out. Besides Ethan, she is my best friend, and has been since we were five years old. She's been amazing these past few months, listening to my whining and self-loathing without judgment.

Although I never did tell her the worst of it.

The one person I am nervous about seeing is Damien. I

haven't talked with him all that much since I got engaged — the reason I missed last year's WyvernFest — but I know they've kept him updated on everything that's happened. So I don't expect him to bring up Jared or the wedding.

The wedding he was not invited to because Jared didn't like me having any guy friends.

Guilt sinks into my gut. I hope Damien isn't too pissed at me for how I treated him while I was with Jared. Anything he has to say to me about how shitty of a friend I've been, I totally deserve.

I just hope he can forgive me one day.

2

I still haven't moved from the doorway of the restaurant, shifting nervously from one foot to the other as I fiddle with the handle of my luggage. I was hoping to have gathered the courage to walk inside by now, but I can't bring myself to move from this spot.

I have to at least pretend I've gotten my shit together, or they may decide they don't even want me here. I wouldn't blame them. No one wants to be around the sad, mopey girl.

They deserve so much better than what I can offer right now, and I don't want to ruin their con weekend. Maybe this was a mistake.

I shouldn't have come here.

I should just go back home.

I readjust the duffel bag on my shoulder, turning to leave just as I hear, "There she is!"

Jade.

She jumps up and runs the short distance to me, past a few empty tables, wrapping me fully in her arms, nearly knocking me over as the duffel bag falls from my shoulder onto the floor. She refuses to let go, forcing me to lean into her even more as I try to keep a check on my emotions. It's like she knew I was second-guessing myself just now and, without any words, was reassuring me that she did, in fact, want me here.

Jade releases me as Ethan and Damien approach with warm, genuine smiles. Maybe a little shock mixed in there too, as if they really weren't sure I'd crawl my ass out of bed for this.

"About time, sis," Ethan says as he shoves a mimosa in my hand. "You look like shit, by the way."

"Thanks, jackass. You sure know how to make a girl feel special." I punch his arm playfully, and there's nothing but affection in his eyes as he pulls me in for a quick side squeeze. After everything I've been through, it's actually quite comforting that Ethan continues to treat me the same way he always has — with love through relentless teasing.

Like nothing ever changed.

Damien steps up beside Ethan, leveling me with an unreadable expression, his chestnut brown eyes pinning me in place.

"Hey," I say softly.

I hold my breath, unsure of what he's going to do. My heart begins to pound as I ready myself for him to tell me off. To yell at me for being such a terrible and disappointing friend. Because I deserve it.

When he leans down for a hug, wrapping one arm over the top of my shoulders and the other down my back, pulling me close, my breath catches. It's so unexpected I forget how to move. Convinced he'd be upset with me, that our interactions this weekend would be strained at best, a hug was the last thing I was expecting.

Relief floods me as I wrap my arms around his robust frame and bury my face into his shoulder, fighting back tears.

Dammit, pull yourself together, Elsie.

Ethan and Jade grab my bags and walk back to their seats as Damien keeps me held tightly in his arms, his head gently leaning on mine.

Breaking the silence, he whispers in my ear, "I've missed your sweet scent of blackberries and fig leaves."

I snort. Loudly.

I had almost forgotten one of our favorite inside jokes, poking fun at all the fantasy/romance novels I read that, for whatever reason, always include someone's scent being made up of two or three of the most random smells. Coming up with new combinations of ridiculous scents became our go-to greeting, to the sheer annoyance of our friends.

"And yours, of pomegranate and wintergreen and...something else I can't quite place." I would never admit out loud that he actually smells like a sweet bouquet of fresh flowers on a warm spring morning.

I pull away with a wide grin, and the intensity of his stare forces me to turn my head and finish my drink in one go. Damien's dark eyes stay on me as we walk back to the table in awkward silence, and I feel a flush creeping up my neck at the attention.

"What?" I ask nervously, pushing my glasses back up my nose.

Jade and Ethan observe us from the booth with curious grins.

He shakes his head slightly like he's pulling himself out of a trance and takes a deep breath. "Nothing. It's just...it's really good to see you."

I can't help but soften at his words and his growing smile. The smile that produces two dimples on either side. "It's good to see you too."

My brother and my best friend are still staring up at us from the booth, eyebrows raised. Ethan has his chin cradled in his palms, both elbows on the table, and a shit-eating grin on his face.

He's enjoying this way too much.

I clear my throat, needing to break the silence as we both

take a seat in the booth — me scooting in next to Jade, and Damien taking Ethan's other side. Jade slides a plate full of my favorite breakfast foods in front of me with a wink, and I elbow her softly in thanks. They're all about halfway finished with their own plates.

"So…what's up? What were you all talking about before I got here?" I motion to the waitress, pointing to my empty glass in a silent plea for another mimosa.

"Oh God, please don't get them going again," Jade sighs.

"Mouthfeel!" Ethan and Damien proclaim at the same time.

My face contorts. "What…the hell is mouthfeel?"

"It's a measurement of something you're eating or drinking," Ethan explains. "Not the taste or anything, but how it actually *feels* in your mouth."

"And you made this up?" I ask with a raised eyebrow, taking a bite of scrambled eggs.

Both of their faces light up, but Damien is the one who says, "No, it's a real thing! You can look it up!"

"Please don't," Jade says. "These idiots have been discussing mouthfeel for the last twenty minutes and rating all their favorite foods. But now that you're here, we can discuss con business."

I can't help but smile. I don't care what we talk about, as long as I'm here with them. I'd be content to just sit and listen to them all day. "What's the plan anyway?"

Ethan pointedly rolls his eyes at Jade as he answers, "Today, of course, we have Tamara's Q&A at three o'clock, followed by her signing at four."

"Ahh, I can't wait!" I clasp my hands together. "Then tomorrow is the panel with her costar and the showrunners, right?"

"Yep, same times — three for the panel, then they'll be signing together afterwards," Ethan replies without even looking at the con schedule. Of course he would have her events memorized already.

Tamara Jenkins is one of the headlining celebrities this weekend, and the up-and-coming star of the TV show *Serafina*, playing warrior princess Serafina of Lorg. It was a huge win when WyvernFest landed her as a guest this year, considering it's only a mid-sized con with an average of 20,000 attendees and around twenty-five guests, including actors, voice actors, and other artists. However, with Tamara being the biggest name they've ever had, they're expecting a record-breaking attendance this year.

The waitress brings me my drink, and I take a sip, slowing down to savor this one, as the conversation continues around me. I mostly stay quiet, as I'm used to doing these days, savoring my eggs, bacon, and buttered toast, and think about the fact that I'm finally getting to meet Tamara Jenkins after all these years.

Ethan and I grew up reading the wildly popular fantasy books, and then watched religiously when it was made into a TV series a few years ago. One of my absolute favorite costumes that I have ever made is Princess Serafina. The sketch I made for the design is framed and hanging up on my bedroom wall.

The story follows a seemingly ordinary girl who is raised by her grandmother, never knowing who her real parents are. She learns the truth about who she is and goes on wild adventures to discover that she is heir to a magical kingdom and must fight to save her people from a powerful and evil ruler. Of course, there's a love interest in there too, but it's certainly not the main focus of the story. The heart of *Serafina* is that she is finding her true self along the way.

Plus, it has seriously fun Scottish Viking vibes, as well as magical dragons and mermaids.

Serafina was the first character I really connected to on a deeper level. Aside from having the same wild, red hair as me, she made me believe that I, too, could be destined for greatness and that nothing could hold me back from fulfilling my higher purpose in this world. Tamara brought her to life beautifully on screen and it filled a part of me I didn't even know was missing.

Despite Serafina's humble past and not knowing her parents, she went on to do great things. World-altering things. It was hope I felt. Hope that I was actually in control of my own destiny.

Tamara Jenkins quickly became my idol, and though I know she is just an actress portraying a character, I still feel a great connection to her. I pretty much know everything about her, from her shoe size — 7.5 — to the name of her five-year-old golden retriever — Benjamin — to her favorite breakfast cereal — Count Chocula. I could run my own unofficial Tamara Jenkins superfan group at this point if I wanted to.

"That season finale was incredible!" Jade says as she leans forward and sets her drink on the table.

"Right? The final battle at the shores of Lorg was a masterpiece," I reply. "So well done."

"What do you think about those rumors that they might be trying to write Tamara out of the show?" Damien looks around the table. "They're saying she's difficult to work with."

I slam my drink down on the table so hard everyone flinches. "There's *no way!* She *carries* that show, no one could ever replace her. They might as well just cancel it." I put a finger up and continue, "*And,* I hate how they're starting to stray so far from the books. They're just making shit up at this point."

"Yeah, why do they always feel the need to change things? Most people just want to see the story they fell in love with in the first place." Jade shakes her head.

"They won't write her out. She's making them too much money." Ethan finishes his drink with a satisfied sigh and sets down his empty glass.

"So what else do we want to do today?" Damien asks.

"Vendor booths maybe?" Ethan shrugs and looks around the table. "I'd love to pick up some new d20s."

"Same. And I want to see what new games they've got."

As Ethan and Damien continue talking, Jade looks over at me and gives me a reassuring squeeze of my hand. She doesn't have to say anything. We've known each other practically our whole lives.

I force a fake smile as I lean my head on her shoulder. She knows me so well, and knows I have a lot of shit to work through, but I don't want to think about all that right now. I am here to have fun and to move on from emotionally unavailable, narcissistic, cheating ex-fiancés.

With that thought, I finish drink number two.

"How's the family?" I ask Jade.

"They're great," she replies with a smile. "They'd love to see you sometime. You know you're always welcome."

I return the smile. "I know. I'd love to see them too. It's been too long."

I extract myself from Jade and start to scoot out of the booth to stand up, wiping my hands on my thighs. "Do you all mind watching my bags while I run over to registration to grab my badge and get my props approved real quick? Then maybe we can all go get dressed?"

All prop weapons need to be inspected and approved by the convention's Weapons Master, giving you a special designation on your badge stating they've been cleared. They are very strict on this, and people have been kicked out for not having properly approved weapons.

"We'll all come!" Ethan proclaims as he nudges Damien out of the booth.

"No, you guys really don't have to. I'm fine." I put up my hands. "Stay and enjoy your drinks." *Without me.*

"It's not up for discussion. We're not letting you out of our sights all weekend," Jade says with a grin, snaking an arm around me.

My heart sinks a little. The last thing I want from them is pity.

"You don't have to stop having fun just for me. Really, I'm *fine*."

They're not going to let me go alone, I already know that. It's why I love them…but I don't deserve them.

"You keep saying you're fine, yet you look like—" Ethan motions at me up and down, scrunching his nose, "—that."

I roll my eyes but can't suppress the growing smile. "Jackass."

Damien flashes that warm smile as he grabs my duffel bag. "Stop being ridiculous, Els. Being with you *is* fun."

3

After picking up my badge from the convention center registration booth, and getting my prop weapons approved by the Weapons Master, we cross back over the 100-foot skybridge connected to the hotel. The walkway has windows on all sides, allowing a breathtaking view of the outside without having to cross traffic or brave the heat. Once we are on the hotel side, we aim for the elevators and ride up to the fifth floor to our rooms.

"See you fools in a bit!" Ethan says cheerfully as we reach rooms 531 and 533.

Jade and I are staying together in one room, and Ethan and Damien are next door.

The moment we enter the bright, spacious room, I take a deep breath. The rooms here are sleek and modern, way more expensive than I could afford on my own. While I'm genuinely proud of my friends and happy for the success they've had in their careers already, it does serve as a reminder that, at twenty-five, I'm nowhere near where I thought I would be in life, and still don't even know what I want to be doing.

So, while I know it's not intentional, sometimes their constant support and generosity can end up feeling a bit like charity.

Jade and I fall back into our familiar routine, having done these conventions for nearly a decade together. I always take the bed closest to the bathroom, and Jade likes to be by the window, which she has already claimed.

I abandon my duffel bag on the floor and pull the suitcases off to the side next to it. Needing a moment to collect myself before getting started, I sit on the plush white bed and lean forward, resting my elbows on my knees, and let out a long breath.

I need to hurry up and pull myself out of this insufferable funk so I can start having some fun.

Jade walks over, stopping in front of me. "I'm not going to ask if you're okay, because I know you hate it…"

I sense a "but" and raise my eyebrows.

"But…" she continues with a growing smile, "we are not allowing thoughts of *him* anymore. He is quite literally the worst, and I am not going to let him ruin this weekend for us like he did last year."

She doesn't even know the half of it.

I can't fault her for it, seeing as I never let any of them know just how bad it had really gotten with Jared. They knew things weren't great towards the end and that he was insecure, but I became an expert at pretending things were "good enough" while we were together.

She is staring at me with her arms crossed and no room for argument in her face.

So I sit up straight. "I know, I'm sorry. I just…I don't know what to do. It just feels like I don't even know who I am anymore." I look back down at my hands in my lap.

After the utter humiliation of being cheated on *at my own*

wedding, I spent a lot of time going over old memories and moments with him, trying to pinpoint when exactly things changed, and when I started changing for him. It happened so gradually I never even realized what was going on.

I still get flashbacks sometimes when I'm overwhelmed, but my therapist said that's normal when dealing with the aftermath of an emotionally abusive relationship. A term I never thought applied to my situation until she tossed it in my lap like a grenade.

"Exactly. He was a prick. He never deserved you, and you lost sight of who you were and what was important." She squats down to my eye level, forcing me to look at her. "But that's not your fault, it's his. Nobody blames you for all the shit he did."

"But you should!" My eyes start to sting. Everything I've been holding in is forcing its way to the surface. I squeeze them shut, willing it all to stay buried deep down. "I was a terrible friend, and I put him before all of you. I hate myself for letting that happen."

"Look at me." Jade grabs my hands, and I meet her gaze, blinking away a stray tear. "Nothing you could say or do will ever make us hate you. Ever. You went through a tough time, but now you're here with us, where you belong, and we're going to get you back to your old self again. And that starts with getting in costume so we can go downstairs, where you can finally meet Tamara Jenkins."

Jade doesn't wait for a response before squeezing my leg and standing up to go get ready. I can always count on her for her brutal honesty. She is really one of the most amazing people I've ever known, and I'm so lucky to call her my best friend. She's not going to let me wallow in my feelings this weekend, and it's exactly what I needed to hear right now.

Side by side, we look like complete opposites. Her rich brown skin, jet black curly pixie cut with burgundy streaks, along with being unfairly tall and gorgeous, next to me — pale, freckled, bushy red hair, and a totally average five-foot, four-inch frame with the odd curves here and there.

We make quite a pair.

Back when we were kids, Jade lived in the house next door to us. Her family was wonderful. Welcoming and warm, they were everything a child could ever want or need. She was the youngest of six kids, so there was always plenty of delightful chaos over there at any given time. Her incredible mother knew things were rough for Ethan and me at home, even if she didn't know specifics, and always kept a spot open at the dinner table for us.

She is pretty much the reason we even survived as kids.

In high school, Jade and I mostly went unnoticed by the rest of the student body. She was immersed in band, and I was in theater club, so it was easy to fade into the background while the rest of our peers were preoccupied with fitting in and getting laid.

Something else I didn't figure out until much later.

I push up my glasses and peel myself off the bed with a groan. Despite how I must look on the outside, I really am excited about this weekend with our friends, even if thoughts of Jared keep hanging over me. But I no longer want him to have any power over me, and that starts now.

It's time to find myself again.

I walk over to my suitcases and open up the one containing my Princess Serafina costume pieces and makeup bag. In years past, when I used to make more elaborate costumes, I might have brought as many as six suitcases to a convention, but this year, I kept it down to just three to make sure I didn't overdo it.

Depending on the complexity, a costume can take months or even years to make. It's an all-consuming and rather expensive hobby, but we wouldn't have it any other way.

We are actually somewhat known around our little cosplay community for our detailed costumes and dedication to the art.

Jade has a decent following on social media, where she show-cases her elaborate costumes, as well as tutorials on how she makes them. My strengths lie more in my illustrations and drawings of the costumes.

We try to hit the major cons every year if we can, and even though WyvernFest is not as big as the others, it's definitely our favorite.

There is something about a smaller con I just love. It still has so much heart and is put together with the fans' best interests in mind, allowing for genuine interactions and experiences. Some of the larger ones have become pretty corporate over the years, prioritizing profits over everything else. With those cons, you end up losing a lot of the magic.

WyvernFest was the first convention Ethan, Jade, and I ever went to when we were thirteen, after we convinced Jade's mom to take all three of us that summer on a one-day pass. A day that ultimately changed our lives forever.

Then, five years later, it was where we met Damien.

So it definitely holds a special place in our hearts.

I think back to being that young and being overwhelmed stepping into a place so electric for the first time, where everyone was accepting and fun and creative. Where no one judged you for being a little — or very — weird and over the top.

I saw a diverse and beautiful community, and I knew deep in my bones that I belonged there. Anyone who ever felt like an outcast or a misfit could find their place there, and nothing in life can compare to finding where you truly belong.

After laying out all my costume pieces, I start my transfor-mation into Princess Serafina.

I step into the emerald green armored skirt made of sixteen long foam strips, sprayed with metallic paint and held together with a leather belt. Next, is the matching sleeveless top with gold trim around the neck, and intricate designs flowing around the torso, tucked into the skirt, seamlessly blending them together.

With each new piece I put on — slowly and carefully, so nothing gets pulled or snagged — I pause to look in the mirror. So far so good.

I attach the matching breastplate over top, also metallic green with gold trim. The remaining arm pieces are smaller, but they really pull the whole thing together. Dragon scale pauldrons adorn each shoulder, arm bands with intricate matching gold designs on each bicep, and gauntlets covering forearm to wrist.

I slip my feet into thick, comfy socks before putting on the matching slouchy leather boots. A shining gold holster is attached at my waist, which holds my small satchel for carrying any essentials I might need throughout the day: snacks, lip balm, bobby pins, makeup, you name it.

To top it all off, I place the gold crown with twisting spikes atop my straightened, oil-infused hair. This is the only costume I have where I don't have to wear a wig, only a few extensions for length.

"Are you at a stopping point?" I shout to Jade as I swap out my glasses for green-colored contact lenses.

"Ready for hair?" she asks without hesitation.

"Whenever you are."

Jade exits the bathroom as a nearly complete Ahsoka Tano from Star Wars. All she has left, it seems, is the orange body paint. She braids my hair into the gold crown and down my back as I start on my face makeup. We've been helping each other with these costumes for years; it's become such a natural part of our routine together.

The final touch of my costume is the long, gold-painted sword with a twisting hilt, and a blade forged with a blood red center flowing down from guard to point: Lightbreaker. I sheath it at my back in a simple leather scabbard, since it can be a real pain to carry around all day.

I take a look at myself in the mirror, my Princess Serafina costume completely transforming me and providing the confidence I wish I could have in real life.

I help Jade apply the last of the orange body paint to her arms and her back before we prepare to leave our room for the day. The room is a complete wreck, but we've managed to get our process of getting dressed, made-up, and props assembled down to about an hour.

Making our way down the hallway towards the elevators, Jade walks alongside me wearing a black and grey tunic, slouching black trousers, and a belt to hang her two white lightsabers. Above her elbows are linen arm wraps leading down to fingerless gloves and plates of silver armor.

The headpiece — called a "lekku" — is an absolute marvel, made of several large pieces of carefully cut foam, glued together, draped in spandex, and painted with blue stripes down the front and back. Her face has also been painted orange, with white markings down her forehead and cheeks.

Her normally dark hazel eyes, now a bright blue thanks to colored contact lenses, make her a carbon copy of Ahsoka.

ETHAN (1:09 P.M.)

we're in the atrium, you coming?

Of course they're over at the convention center already. They don't have to spend a half hour on hair and makeup alone, like we do.

We step into the elevators with a few other female cosplayers. One is dressed as Tifa from *Final Fantasy VII*, with long black hair, a white crop top, black miniskirt and suspenders, and red boots and gloves. The other is Zelda from *Breath of the Wild*, wearing a blue and white top with gold trim, black leggings, brown boots, and a long blonde wig with pointed ears poking out.

We make chitchat with them, admiring each other's costumes until we get off together on the second floor, walking towards the skybridge that will take us over to the convention center. As we get closer, the noise crescendos and the busy crowd comes into view.

WyvernFest has officially begun.

4

The Glenville Convention Center is stunning and bright with its two-story atrium and floor-to-ceiling windows, colorful banners hung throughout, and unique, modern sculptures suspended from the ceiling.

The main floor is comprised of three enormous exhibit halls — A, B, and C — two large ballrooms, and several smaller meeting rooms that can be joined together or sectioned off as needed. For this weekend, the rooms are joined and opened up to their maximum size, leaving five blocks of meeting spaces — named Alpha, Beta, Gamma, Theta, and Delta — perfect for hosting panels, workshops, and other various activities throughout the convention.

I lean over the railing to get a better look at the hallways and common areas below, packed full of people, some in large, elaborate costumes, others just in regular attire enjoying the festivities.

The buzz and excitement at these conventions is difficult to put into words. It's just a feeling. There is something so special about being surrounded by thousands of other people with just as much passion as you for movies, shows, games, and stories that transport you into another world.

While you're here, you can meet some celebrities and geek out about your favorite things without the judgment of others. Obviously we all have lives outside of conventions, but for this little slice of time, this is our reality.

I've learned there's nothing wrong with needing to escape real life for a bit, and in fact, cosplay can be a very healthy medium for creative expression and exploring different aspects of yourself. Jared certainly didn't understand it though. He dismissed it as "nerd stuff," but for a lot of people here, this "stuff" helped shape who we are today, and it can be hurtful when people diminish it.

"There they are." I point down to the crowd.

Jade and I take the escalators down to the main floor after spotting Ethan and Damien taking photos with various friends and attendees. There are a ton of people here, but I've seen Ethan in his enormous Doc Ock getup more times than I can count and could spot him a mile away. Not to mention he looks just like me with the same fair skin, freckles, and red hair, except his is cut short on the sides with perfectly styled layers on top. And at five foot eight, he's only a few inches taller than me.

"God, he's such a show-off," Jade says with a laugh.

"Insufferable jackass. Gotta love him."

He spent ten months building and perfecting this costume. The device that controls each six-foot mechanical arm splayed out in every direction, expanding and retracting with the buttons on his right glove, he built from scratch. He's always loved building gadgets in his spare time and figuring out how things work. No surprise when he went on to become a mechanical engineer.

He chose the dark brown trench coat look from the Spiderman movies rather than the original Doc Ock from the comics. His reasoning is that no one wants to see him in tight green spandex, and quite frankly, I agree. Though, I wouldn't put it past him to do it just to get a laugh.

Regardless, this costume is a big hit every year.

Damien is wearing his Force Ghost Obi-Wan Kenobi costume, another favorite. Dressed in tan and brown linen robes, his hair slicked back and sprayed white with temporary hair dye, and a press-on white beard and mustache, he is the spitting image of an old Obi-Wan. A light blue translucent tulle is draped over top, gently conforming to the shape of his body and giving him that ghost-like appearance from *Return of the Jedi*.

Simple, but so well done.

We hang out among the crowd for a while, reconnecting with friends we see every year, and taking pictures. Luckily, there are always several professional photographers floating around taking photos of cosplayers.

We love the photographers here because it really is a mutually beneficial partnership. You could spend months creating a single costume from scratch — sewing, soldering, 3D printing, gluing — not to mention spending hundreds of dollars on supplies. So after pouring your blood, sweat, and tears into it, you want to get plenty of great-looking, professional shots where you can pose and really show off your hard work.

Jade, especially, maintains close relationships with them so she can repost their photos on her social media.

We finish mingling around two thirty, when I motion to the group that we should start heading inside the ballroom where Tamara's Q&A is being held. I'm immensely grateful that Ethan built his mechanical arms in such a way that they could fold back in, close to his body, without taking up too much space.

"E, did you say Ballroom One or Two?" I shout over the deafening crowd noise, sheathing Lightbreaker down my back.

"One!" He points towards the door ahead of us. "Number

Two is being used for a Settlers of Catan Tournament most of the afternoon."

We enter the ballroom, and the four of us gently push our way up as close to the stage as we can, but it's packed. Beige and dark brown panels line the towering walls, and glimmering lights hang overhead, but my focus stays on the cream carpet at my feet as the unease of being surrounded by so many people simmers beneath my skin.

Most con guests have their Q&As in one of the five room blocks, but this is definitely one of the most popular events going on all weekend, and people are anxious to get a glimpse of Tamara up close and ask her questions about the show.

Force Ghost Damien sidles up to me as we settle into our spots, nudging me playfully in the arm. "So...how you doin', Els?"

I let out a breath. "I'm fine! I just wish everyone would stop asking me that!" I wince at my harsh tone and immediately wish I could take it back.

I know Damien is only looking out for me, but I'm really getting tired of people asking me if I'm okay. It's hard to move on when people keep reminding you of how fragile they see you.

I don't want to be seen that way, especially by him.

Damien gives me a sad half-smile under that ridiculous blue tulle, like he already knows what's going on inside my head. His eyes are wide and kind as he turns to me, placing his hands on my dragon scale pauldrons and squaring me up so I'm looking directly at him.

"Elsie Graham," he starts, using my full name and not just *Els,* so I know to pay attention. He pauses and chews on his lower lip, while I hold my breath. "I want you to listen to me. I've barely spoken to you or seen you in over a year."

The reminder sends a wave of guilt through me.

"But you know me. I'm not asking you out of pity or anything like that. I just want us to talk again, like we used to.

I've been worried about you, you know? Not leaving your house or anything…"

I look away, embarrassed, heat creeping up my neck. I wasn't aware he knew about that part.

"Ethan kept me updated," he says softly, as if reading my thoughts.

His hands drop from my shoulders, and I can only nod, not knowing how to respond to that. I get the feeling he has more to say, so I just wait. Wait for the angry words he no doubt has ready to pelt me with.

The ones I deserve.

So I steel myself for them and meet his gaze, ready to take it.

His eyes are still warm, but a line etches his brows. "I asked if you are okay because you're one of my favorite people. And if there is something I can do to help, I just want the chance to be there for you." He tugs at the braid draped over my shoulder. "I've missed you."

My eyebrows scrunch together. I must be mistaken, because this sounds kind of like forgiveness, which I don't deserve from him. Not yet.

"And if you don't mind me saying," he continues, "I'm *really* glad you didn't marry that guy. He never deserved you."

My stomach flutters at his words.

Damien is a genuinely kind and caring person, always looking out for others. It's just who he is. When he was studying to become a nurse, his parents were disappointed that he chose not to be a doctor, even though he graduated with honors from his master's program and now works for one of the top hospitals in the state for critical care.

For him, his true passion is getting to know someone at their core, and making sure they are happy and taken care of. Helping them heal so they get back to feeling like their true self again.

I shut my eyes and lean into his warmth without saying a word as he wraps a blue tulle-covered arm around me.

When we first met, Damien and I got along right away and became very close, maintaining an easygoing but meaningful friendship. Nothing romantic ever developed between us, especially since one of us always seemed to be dating someone else at any given time. Not to mention the type of girls he dated were always these highly successful, intellectual, gorgeous women — nothing like me. So we just stayed really good friends.

Then, I started dating Jared.

I look up at Damien and muster up the courage to finally apologize and take responsibility for how I treated him. I've been dreading this moment for so long, but I have to do it.

My heart picks up speed as I pull away from him. "Damien, I'm—"

"Oh whoops, one of your extensions came loose," he says as he inspects my head. "I got you."

Probably got snagged on that damn tulle. He reattaches the clip behind my ear with the bobby pins, tucking it back under my hair and smoothing out the loose strands.

"Thank you," I say softly.

Before he can say anything else, Ethan comes up behind us and puts his arms around our shoulders, announcing loudly, "Not much longer now! God, Tamara is so hot. Do you think she'd ever go out with me? I should ask her if they call me up."

Jade looks at me from my other side, and we both roll our eyes.

"Go for it, Doctor Octavius, I think you have a real shot!" I say with a wink and a thumbs up.

Not surprisingly, Ethan became obsessed with Tamara shortly after the series started airing. The beautiful, twenty-nine-year-old actress was fairly unknown until the role of Serafina projected her to Hollywood stardom. The series became a hit, and images of her in tight-fitting, curvy armor and long, intricately braided, copper red hair weaved into that gold, spiky crown were suddenly everywhere.

I start bouncing on my toes. This is really happening. The anticipation is killing me.

Any minute now, Tamara Jenkins will be on that stage, and I will finally get to see her for the first time with my own two eyeballs. Damien shoots me a quick glance and a smile from my side, and I playfully elbow him in the ribs.

We'll have to finish this conversation another time, then.

A short, plump man comes out on stage with a microphone to thunderous applause.

Holy shit.

It's time.

"Hey, all! How we doing today?" he asks, and the massive crowd answers with more applause and cheering. "Ohh, come on, I think we can do better than that! *How we doing today?*"

The crowd returns with cheers even louder than before.

"Alright! Yeah! So we thought we'd kick this off with a little fun first! Who wants to play a game, huh?"

A smattering of confused clapping follows. No one wants to play a game. We're here to see Tamara. Who even is this guy?

"You there!" He points to someone near the front, waving him up. "Come on up here!"

He proceeds to do some kind of magic trick or game or something. Most of us aren't even paying attention anymore. This is not what we came here for.

We suffer through nearly a half hour of this, while the crowd grows restless. Some people outright leave, knowing time is precious around here, and no one wants to waste it on this dude riffing if they've got other events to go to.

Something is off.

This guy looks nervous, and he's clearly stalling. Tamara's Q&A should've started by now, and she is notorious for being punctual. It was once reported on gossip sites that she fired an assistant for making her five minutes late to an interview. Stories like that were always reported through the lens of *she's difficult to work with,* but I actually thought it spoke volumes about her professionalism and projecting an image she worked hard for.

But the fact that she's a woman means she gets labeled as "difficult" or just an outright bitch.

"Where is she?" Jade mutters as she adjusts the lekku on her head. "This is weird, right?"

We all exchange confused looks and shrugs, unsure of what to do at this point. I turn around and get on my tiptoes to scan the room and notice two tall men dressed in all black walking along the side of the room towards the back, where a dark grey cloth panel is rigged up for privacy.

They're both gesturing frantically and having an animated conversation as they step behind the panel. Me being a busybody, I casually step away from our group and walk through the crowd towards the back of the ballroom. Looking as if I'm simply trying to find a friend and pretending to scroll on my phone.

I get as close to them as I can without raising suspicions, trying to make out what they're saying, still keeping out of sight.

"We're going to have to make the announcement soon, but we can't raise any alarms. We don't want to cause a panic," one of them says in a hushed voice.

"Did they tell you anything else?" the other one asks. "I mean, maybe she's just sick or being a prima donna. Everyone always says she's difficult."

I roll my eyes.

"Nah, man, it's complete chaos up in HQ right now. They did a wellness check when she didn't show up, and she wasn't in her hotel room. Not answering her phone or nothin'. They said no one can find her. She's fucking missing, dude."

<h1 style="text-align:center">5</h1>

I suddenly feel my heartbeat pounding in my ears.

Panic courses through me.

Did he really just say that? She's missing?

When the con workers step away, I head back over towards our group to spill what I just learned.

"Hey!" I whisper-yell as I motion them away from the crowd.

They exchange confused looks but follow me over to the side of the ballroom.

Once we're all together I continue, still mindful of my volume. "She's missing! Tamara's missing!"

They all just stare at me like I have two heads.

"What are you talking about?" Ethan asks with pinched eyebrows.

"I just heard two guys over there saying that no one can find Tamara. She's missing!" I repeat, trying to make sense of this information that refuses to sink in.

Just then, a clean-shaven man dressed in a nice suit walks with purpose onto the stage towards the fumbling emcee and reaches for the mic, mercifully putting him out of his misery.

"Good afternoon, WyvernFest friends. I uhh...regret to

inform you that today's Q&A and signing with Tamara Jenkins has been canceled."

The room erupts in grumbles and disappointment as the man tries to continue, speaking louder over the crowd. "We are working to reschedule these events as soon as possible, so stay tuned. We apologize for any inconvenience!"

The room is in an uproar, but the four of us just look at each other with wide eyes.

"Huh…" Jade says, looking around the room.

"Els, she's probably just sick, or being difficult," Ethan says, echoing exactly what the con worker suggested. What everyone suggests about her.

"She's not difficult! Stop saying that about her!" I practically yell.

A memory flashes through my mind.

"You were with him again? Elspeth, why do you have to spend so much time together? You know how I feel about him. Is it too much to ask that my fiancée doesn't spend all her time around other guys?"

"But…Damien is one of my best friends, I've known him for years." I reached for Jared's arm. "There's nothing going on with him."

He slammed down the TV remote on the kitchen table so hard the back plate came off and the batteries went flying. The silence fell over us like a heavy blanket.

Why was he getting so mad? Didn't he trust me?

"I'm sorry. Jared, we're just friends. You know you are always welcome to come hang out with us but…you never want to."

A muscle ticked in his jaw. "I don't want you seeing him again." The anger in his eyes made my heart pound. I can't believe he just said that.

"What? Are you serious?"

"Does it look like I'm joking?" He jumped to his feet. "God, why are you being so *difficult* about this? Why do you keep pushing me? I swear, Elspeth, do you ever even consider how this makes *me* feel?"

I looked down at my feet.

It wasn't often that he raised his voice, but it always left me with a sinking feeling in my stomach. Like my body physically couldn't bear it.

I didn't realize being friends with Damien would hurt Jared this way. Maybe I should have considered his feelings more, even if there really was nothing going on between us.

Maybe someday I could convince him that Damien wasn't a threat. Once he started dating someone else, this would all blow over and we could hang out again.

But for now, all I wanted was to make this dreadful feeling go away and go back to how it was supposed to be with Jared.

Jade — Ahsoka — puts a hand on my shoulder, snapping me back to the present. I have to shake my head to rid myself of those awful, lingering feelings.

"Okay, babe, let's say for argument's sake that she's missing. What exactly are we supposed to do about it?" She puts up her hands and shrugs, looking to each person in our circle. "Why don't we just go back out there and enjoy the rest of the con. There's probably a reasonable explanation for all of this, and she'll be back for tomorrow's events. Come on, let's go get another drink!"

She starts to walk out towards the hallway, Ethan and Damien a step behind. I'm suddenly at war with myself over what to do next.

My palms are sweating, and I'm terrified of ruining their con weekend, but something is telling me not to back down on this. For whatever reason, this is important.

I made myself quieter and more agreeable with Jared for far too long, and it cost me everything. So I summon the courage to speak my truth to the people I know will listen.

"How can you guys not want to know what happened to her? What if she was taken or something?"

They stop walking and turn back to me.

"If something bad happened, maybe there's something we could do to help. Come on...all I'm asking is that we look around for a little bit. Please?" I lay it on thick and add a pout for good measure. "Come on, when was the last time we had an adventure together? I really need some excitement in my life!"

They all look at each other with the same pitying expressions.

Ethan finally puts his hands up in defeat. "Fine. But this is the last time you get to pull the depressed card. We all love you, and this is us *taking pity on you*," he adds, knowing that last part will annoy me. "So let's go 'find Tamara Jenkins.'" He uses air quotes for emphasis.

"What's the plan, Veronica Mars?" Damien teases with a smirk.

He means for it to sound like an insult, but in actuality, finding clues and solving mysteries is my jam, and I love *Veronica Mars* (we, the fandom, prefer to be called Marshmallows, thank you very much).

I'm suddenly energized, my stomach fluttering. How long has it been since I've actually felt excited about *anything*? The thought is so depressing I refuse to acknowledge it right now. Denial is another effective coping mechanism, by the way.

Doesn't matter.

We're doing this.

"Okay, first we need to assess what we know." I put up a finger to start counting. "Tamara was scheduled to be down here at three p.m. for her signing, right? It's now…3:50," I say as I look at the giant clock on the wall.

Silence.

They're all looking at me to continue, but I realize in this moment, with a lone finger hanging out there and their eyes boring into me, that this is all we have to go on.

Shit.

My cheeks flush.

Ethan claps. "Wow, Els. You know, I think you might've just cracked this case wide open!"

"Shut up." I jab him in the side. "Obviously, we need more information. So come on, think! This can't be any harder than our Tomb of Annihilation campaign, right?" I add with a smile as I look to each of their faces.

Back when we used to play Dungeons and Dragons, Tomb of Annihilation was the last campaign we ever did together. Not only did it take forever to finish and nearly ruined our friendships, but not long after that is when I started dating stupid Jared, and I haven't rolled another die since.

I instinctively scratch my throat at the memory.

"Well, that's because Ethan was a subpar DM," Damien offers with a grin and a clap on my brother's shoulder.

"That's right. I'm running this show." I tap my chest for emphasis. "So, our first quest is for information. Let's start by getting away from the crowds here and checking out the hotel where there will be fewer people."

That at least earns some nods. I've got them on board, now we just need to work on their enthusiasm.

I lift my chin a little. It feels good to take charge for once. Not to ask for permission, but to lead. It must be the Serafina costume, allowing me to channel this newfound courage.

We take the escalator up to the skybridge and cross over, taking in our surroundings for anything unusual or out of place.

On the hotel side it's fairly quiet, except for some chatter coming from the lobby. We approach the grand curving staircase that leads from the second floor down to the lobby and notice a small group of police officers at the front desk, talking to staff and some other people.

Police officers.

That means…it's true.

Tamara Jenkins really is missing.

6

"See!" I smack Ethan's chest with the back of my hand. "They called the cops. Obviously, something is up. I was right!"

Everyone stays quiet for a beat, exchanging glances, but it's Damien who breaks the silence.

"Els...if the police are here, doesn't that mean it's already being handled? I mean, if there's something sketchy going on, we should probably stay out of it and let them do their job. There's no need to put ourselves in danger for...someone we don't even know."

I huff out a breath and start to protest, when one of the officers steps to the side, revealing a tall, lanky man with toffee brown hair, who looks agitated and distressed.

A man Ethan and I know.

"Holy shit. Ethan, look it's Andy." I point down towards the group gathered at the front desk. "Do you think he knows something about Tamara's disappearance? Or...maybe he's involved somehow?"

The thought puts me on edge.

"Are you kidding? Andy's like our nerdy older brother. You know he'd never hurt a fly."

We all walk down the staircase until we reach the landing.

Damien says, "I forgot you guys knew Andrew Locke, that's so cool! He's got signings every day. I was hoping to make at least one of them."

With all that's been going on, I totally forgot we'd be seeing Andy this weekend.

Ethan and I met him about five years ago at LA Comic Con after he approached us and complimented us on our cosplay. He's a fairly well-known comic book writer, who created a popular series called The Quantum Protector, and was especially impressed with Ethan as Forge from X-Men that day. We talked with him and all got along so well that we ended up hanging out the entire weekend.

Eventually, he kind of took us under his wing, stepping in as, not quite a father figure since he's only about ten years older, but as someone we greatly admire and look up to. Like a protective big brother.

We all exchanged contact information and continued to stay in touch over the years. Ethan was more than happy to help Andy with various projects, especially once he got his 3D printer and started sending him miniature models of Quantum Protector characters.

Andy stomps away from the group of officers in a huff and shoves a hand through his shaggy hair. He nearly walks past us before he registers our presence, immediately changing course to come talk to us.

I give him a half-smile and a wave as he approaches.

Ethan says, "Hey, Andy! You alright?"

"Hey, guys. Fucking great, just having the time of my life over here talking to these clowns. In case you've never had the pleasure, Glenville cops are the absolute worst."

He pulls Ethan in for one of those half hugs with a back slap guys love to do but has to awkwardly maneuver his way around Ethan's large mechanical arms.

"Hey, Andy."

"It's great to see you, Elsie." Being nearly a foot taller than me, he has to lean way down for a hug. His entire body is tense.

As he pulls away, I notice his slate grey eyes are dull and distant. Creases line his pallid face — normally tanned and glowing from the LA sun. He gives Damien and Jade a small wave before putting his hands in his pockets.

"So what's going on? Everything okay?" Ethan asks as he glances back towards the police at the front desk.

Andy takes a moment before answering, looking at all four of us, as if trying to assess how much we might already know, and how much we need to know. His eyes land on my Princess Serafina costume and his entire face droops.

I cut right to it. "Is it about Tamara?"

He flinches ever so slightly, and his eyes go wide. "What do you guys know? Did you see something?"

"Elsie heard some con workers say that she's missing, just before they made the announcement to cancel her events," Ethan replies. "Do you know her?"

Andy sighs and looks away, scratching the back of his head. "We're...friends, actually. I was with her today before she..." He trails off and takes a breath. "We were hanging out a few blocks away just before the Q&A. Her con handler picked her up from the restaurant to bring her back to the convention center, but no one has seen her since. That was over two hours ago. She didn't answer my earlier texts so I assumed she just got tied up in work stuff or was busy hiding away from the crowds...but then she never showed up for the Q&A."

Damien asks, "Did you say *handler*? Is that like an assistant?"

Andy shrugs a shoulder. "Sort of. Guests of the convention are usually assigned a handler — or multiple handlers — throughout the weekend. Someone to usher them around, make sure they get to all their scheduled events on time, helping them navigate crowds and such. They're supposed to help keep things running smoothly, being the eyes and ears for the con and getting guests where they need to be."

"So...the handler took her somewhere?" Ethan asks. "Can't the hotel or whoever's in charge track the handler down?"

"That's the thing, no one knows who it was."

This earns confused glances from all of us.

"The person originally assigned to her this morning reported that he was reassigned to someone else at the last minute, but the asshole in charge said they never reassigned him. It's all a big clusterfuck."

We all look at him as he rakes a hand through his hair again.

I ask gently, "So what did the cops say?"

He scoffs. "They're fucking amateurs. Said they can file the missing person's report now, but they're not going to start an investigation yet, because there's no evidence of foul play." He shakes his head, more to himself. "But I know Tamara, and she wouldn't just leave without saying anything. And her phone goes straight to voicemail. This is so messed up. I've walked the entire hotel and convention center, and no one has seen or heard *anything*. She's just...gone."

My insides are churning. I can't believe this is actually happening.

"Where were you and Tamara when she got picked up?" Jade's using her professional lawyer voice now.

After graduating at the top of her class in just two years, and being courted by some of the best law firms in the country, she's notorious for making people crumble under questioning. If anyone can help uncover the truth about Tamara's disappearance, it's her.

"A few blocks away at Melvin's Diner. She was due for her Q&A shortly after and was hoping to stay hidden from the crowds for a little while. When it was time to go, she got a text that her handler was out front. She got in the car that was supposed to bring her around to the back of the convention center, through the hidden entrances and service corridors, to avoid being mobbed by the crowds. But no one knows what happened after that."

We're all silent as we try to process everything.

After a minute, Andy lets out a long breath and scrubs his hands down his face. "Okay. Fuck. I've got to go get ready for my signing in an hour. My agent said he can't get me out of it, otherwise I'd still be out looking for her. Right. I'll see you all around."

Before he walks away, I reach for his arm. "Wait. We want to help if we can. What can we do?"

"I really don't know. You guys know a lot of people here… maybe see what you can find out? I don't want to start any rumors, but maybe you can feel out the people you trust and see if anyone knows anything, or saw anything?" He snaps his fingers. "Oh, and the car she got into was a dark blue Pontiac. If that helps."

"You got it."

He gives a stiff nod and walks away, leaving us all standing there in silence. We watch as he steps through the sliding doors towards the convention center with his hands in his pockets. I remember him always being so positive and full of life. It's hard to see him like this.

But…as I watch him cross the street, there's also something different about him that I can't quite place. I go back through everything he told us about Tamara, but something doesn't add up, and I can't help but wonder if there's more to Andy's relationship with her than he's leading us to believe.

7

We decide to split up into two groups to gather more information around the con. Ethan suggests that Damien and Jade team up, since they are both dressed as characters from Star Wars and they might get more people wanting photo ops together, giving them a chance to casually bring up Tamara without too much suspicion.

Ethan and I will stick together like we always have. Our bond only having strengthened after a difficult and lonely childhood when our dad left us at eight years old. Our mom got sole custody, but she was never the same after their messy divorce. Having to take on a second job, and being in various states of depression, she left us alone a lot and eventually turned to alcohol and pills to cope. We had to find ways to entertain ourselves, and even ways to get by, just the two of us.

Since then, we've always had each other's backs. Our matching line-drawing Luke and Leia tattoos on our wrists are a reminder of our unbreakable bond.

"Nothing in the entire galaxy could keep us apart," Ethan once said to me in a rare moment of vulnerability.

While our friends journey across the street into the belly of the beast, Ethan and I decide to walk to the restaurant where Andy and Tamara were before the Q&A, to get a sense of the space in which she was last seen. Maybe see if we can find any clues.

We'll have to play it cool though, in case someone actually did take her, and they decide to return to the scene of the crime. We really just don't know what we're dealing with here.

Stepping out into the sweltering August heat, the humidity thick enough to swim through, we are both suddenly and painfully aware of our large, heavy costumes. Perhaps we should've gone back upstairs to change, but really, that would take more time than it's worth. Luckily, just about everyone within a few blocks is also in costume, so it shouldn't look too suspicious that we're out here looking like this.

Con weekend really is its own reality.

We follow the map on my phone to make the eight-minute walk down several short blocks. Mostly down tiny side streets with cracked sidewalks and a few dirty alleyways.

"So…" Ethan starts.

"I swear to the gods if you ask me how I'm doing, I'm going home."

"Okay, that's fair." He looks sideways at me, squinting against the bright sun, even with his oval-shaped sunglasses on. "Just worried about you, you know? I know you don't like other people making a fuss over you, and you'll deal with it like you always do, but I want you to know I've really enjoyed having you stay with me these last few months."

My chest tightens. "I know. Me too."

"Not to get too sappy on you, but it kinda felt like old times. Except it was me taking care of *you* for a change."

That pulls a smile from me. "I'm not sure I like that role reversal as much, but…yeah. I don't know if I ever really thanked you for all you did for me." I sniffle. "I'm not so sure I would've made it through these last few months without you, E. So…thank you."

He reaches out and pulls me in closer as we continue walking. He doesn't have to say anything else. We have always needed each other, ever since we were little kids, too small to understand the big, scary world around us. Our parents were going through their own drama, too involved in themselves to worry about how it was affecting either of us.

He lets me go as we cross the final street. We spot the weathered sign for Melvin's Diner, walking over a few empty parking spaces to get to the front door. It's a hole-in-the-wall, unsuspecting place to hang out.

Ethan opens the creaky, weathered door for me to enter first, and I am instantly hit with the comforting aromas of freshly brewed coffee and sizzling, savory meats on the grill. My mouth waters.

"I can't believe in all our years coming to WyvernFest, we've never eaten here," Ethan says as we both look around the place.

It's filled to about half capacity with a few open booths, as well as some seats at the counter. It's not dirty by any means, but it has that old, worn-out, vintage vibe to it.

"Sit anywhere ya like!" a young waitress with an armful of plates and a pot of coffee yells to us with a smile as she walks by.

We pick one of the booths near the front window and relieve ourselves of some of our cumbersome costume pieces before sitting down. The worn, cracked vinyl seats squeak as we slide in on opposite sides, Lightbreaker resting on the table, and his Doc Ock machinery in the space next to him.

"Man, Andy is a mess. I didn't realize he even knew Tamara Jenkins," I say, grabbing a menu from the edge of the table. "Did he ever mention anything to you about her?"

"Not at all. I would've remembered something like that. I wonder why he didn't say anything."

"Probably because he knows you're a horny superfan and would never stop hounding him to arrange a meetup." I ignore his look of pretend shock as he grabs his own menu. "Honestly, I don't blame him."

"This isn't really the kind of place I'd expect them to hang out in."

I look around, nodding. It's just a regular run-of-the-mill diner, nothing fancy. Though, I find it oddly comforting that Tamara Jenkins would hang out in a place like this, just like a regular person.

The waitress comes by, and I order a coffee and a chocolate chip cookie. Ethan asks for a Cherry Coke.

I fold my hands over the table to get down to business. "So, they were here, eating or hanging out or whatever. She was hiding out a bit from the crowds before the Q&A, or else they probably would've gone to the food hall."

Ethan nods. "Andy said she got a text that her handler was out front." He jabs a thumb towards the window. "So they left the restaurant and went their separate ways."

I twist my mouth to the side, trying to put it all together. "So she got in a blue Pontiac...I guess they might not have known what the handler looked like?"

"Or someone *pretending* to be the handler."

The thought makes my stomach churn. "I guess they wouldn't have any reason to assume they weren't from the con, if they were texting her and knew where she was and where she was supposed to be. There would be no reason to suspect anything was amiss."

Ethan drums his fingers on the table. "I wonder if she could have been taken during the walk from the back entrances through all the secret hallways, if there was enough of a commotion or a distraction."

"But what if she didn't even make it to the convention center? I can't remember what Andy said. If that's the case...the *handler*, whoever they were, had to have taken her somewhere else, straight from here."

We sit and think about it, but something else doesn't seem right.

"Shouldn't she have had, like, a bodyguard or something? Being an up-and-coming star, don't you think her team would have sent someone here with her?"

"I don't know," Ethan replies, picking at a chipped piece of the linoleum table. "Maybe since this is a smaller con, they didn't think it was necessary. If they thought the convention could manage with their handlers? But I don't know how all that works." He sighs.

I still can't believe this is all really happening. I'm still clinging to hope that there's a reasonable explanation behind all of this, but the more we talk it out, the less likely that seems.

The waitress comes back with our drinks and my cookie. "Great costumes, by the way. I love your Princess Serafina."

I look down at myself before saying, "Oh thanks, she's my favorite character of all time."

She leans down and lowers her voice as I reach for the sugar packets. "Well you shoulda been here earlier. The actress who plays her was eatin' right here at this booth! She was tryin' to blend in, wearin' this green baseball cap to hide her face a bit, but I knew it was her. I was so starstruck!" She squeezes her eyes shut and squeals. "I had to stop myself from askin' for an autograph."

Ethan and I just stare wide-eyed at her.

A witness.

"Was she with someone?" Ethan asks.

"Yeah, some guy. Not that handsome costar everyone says she's datin' though. I woulda recognized him anywhere." She swoons.

I fight the urge to roll my eyes at the mention of Mitchell Brantley. "Did you see them leave?"

Her wide grin falters. She's getting suspicious and is probably wondering why we're asking so many questions. Like she just realized that maybe she shouldn't be divulging too much information to Tamara Jenkins superfans and risk getting herself in trouble. I busy myself with stirring my coffee and casually taking a sip.

"Yeah…they left together. Didn't see anything after they drove away."

Ethan turns his head to me and narrows his eyes. I can see the gears turning in his mind. "Wait." He looks back up at her. "They left *together*? Like in the same car?"

Now she's downright annoyed with us. "I don't really know," she answers before looking off towards the kitchen, desperate for an out. "Look, I gotta get back to work. Let me know if ya need anything," she says, already walking away.

We sit in silence, both of us working through the information the waitress just dumped on us.

One: She was here with a "random guy." Andy. No surprise there.

Two: She's rumored to be dating her costar, Mitchell Brantley, from the show. Of course, I've heard that one too, but I never actually believed it. He seems like a slimy dude, so at least I hope it's not true.

And three: She said they "left together." Did she actually see them getting into a car together, or did she just mean they left the restaurant together? She must mean the latter because I don't see why Andy would lie about that.

"You know what this reminds me of?" I say to Ethan as I finish the last bite of my cookie. "Do you remember that woman who went missing around here a few years ago?"

His eyes light with recognition. "Oh yeah, that's right. And they never found her, did they?"

"Nope." I take another sip of my coffee. "It was like she just vanished into thin air."

The thought sends my insides churning again. I desperately hope this situation ends a whole lot better.

We have to find Tamara.

After finishing up and paying, we step back out into the stifling heat, taking note of our surroundings: a paved area big enough to pull a car through, with the parking lot snaking around to the side and back. Right now, the lot is empty and nothing looks unusual.

We take a different way back, down a few smaller roads and alleyways. I'm a little disappointed we didn't get any answers, just more questions. I wipe my sweaty brow with the back of my hand.

About two blocks from the convention center, we approach a dirty, dingy alley. We decide to backtrack and take another way around, not wanting to get murdered in this absolutely murdery-looking space between two brick buildings, that also smells like piss.

Until something catches my eye.

I take a few steps back into the alley and crouch down low to the ground, as best I can in this costume, to get a better look.

Crumpled up on the ground…is a green baseball cap.

8

"Ethan?" I shout over to him as he enters the alley behind me, his scrunched-up face indicating that he clearly doesn't want to be here either.

Until he sees the hat.

His baby blue eyes go wide in shock as I pick it up to inspect it. Written inside the lining are two letters: *TJ*.

He and I share a knowing glance. After twenty-five years together, we have definitely mastered the whole twin telepathy thing. It annoys the hell out of our friends, but we can have entire conversations without making a sound.

I give him a look that says, *This shit just got real. We need to go back and find Andy*. He nods in confirmation.

Ethan and I quickly walk the rest of the way to the convention center with Tamara Jenkins's hat tucked away safely in my satchel. Under normal circumstances, I'd be thrilled to have a piece of clothing from my idol, but nothing about this day has been normal.

Walking through the main doors, we are instantly overwhelmed by thousands of attendees and thunderous commotion. Pure con chaos. My heartbeat picks up at the sight of so many people in one place.

"Holy shit. This year's turnout is insane!" I shout as we start to weave carefully through the crowds.

"Everyone wanted to come and see Tamara!"

I can barely hear him over the noise. Finding anyone in this crowd is going to be next to impossible.

"Hey, do you want to message Andy to meet up when he's finished with his signing?" I ask. "Tell him we have something."

"On it."

I pull out my phone to text Jade and Damien in our group chat, Browncoats — named after the rebels in *Firefly*, one of our favorite TV shows.

BROWNCOATS

ME (5:44 P.M.)

hey where are you guys?

we have a major update…

If this was any other con year, we would be having the time of our lives with the friends we've made over the years, attending events, taking pictures, and drinking the day away.

Instead, we are investigating Tamara Jenkins's disappearance…or more likely her kidnapping. This is not how I expected this weekend to go.

We make our way through the massive, stifling crowd in the atrium lobby, and down the hallway towards the gallery to begin our next mission. On the way, we pass by hordes of amazing costumes, ranging from inflatable dinosaurs to intricate, detailed fantasy characters; from unique and spectacular hybrid creations, to simple and understated outfits. There really is no wrong way to cosplay, as long as you're having fun and being respectful to everyone around you.

I try to take note of all the costumes I see and appreciate all the amazing creativity. Just from this vantage point, I see characters from video games like *Halo*, *Metal Gear Solid*, and *Final Fantasy*; comic book superheroes and villains; and plenty of anime characters, which I'm not as familiar with as Jade or Damien, I'll admit. But I can appreciate the remarkable costumes all the same.

We pass by the costume repair station run by volunteers whose sole mission this weekend is to help fix costumes and parts so people can keep having fun when something breaks or falls apart. I have had to use their services on more than one occasion in the past. It makes me so happy to see people out here supporting one another.

I give them a wave and a smile and remind myself to go back later and catch up with them, once we sort out some of this craziness and get back to enjoying our con weekend. Whenever that may be. Maybe I can find out if they've seen anything suspicious that might help us out.

"Elsie! Over here!"

I spot our friend Kat, who we see at just about every con. Right now, she is cosplaying as Hela from *Thor: Ragnarok*, surrounded by a number of excited attendees taking turns getting photographed with her and asking her to pose.

She looks incredible in her tight-fitting black bodysuit with shiny emerald green trim, bare shoulders, and a matching green cape billowing effortlessly behind her thanks to a battery-powered fan built into her boots.

She spots us approaching and breaks from the group to come greet us. Her tall frame swallows me whole, and I fully embrace her as much as I can around each of our costumes, angling my head in a way that does not disrupt her large, spiky headpiece.

God, I have missed being with my friends far too much, so I hold on for a few extra seconds.

Her piercing green eyes study my face as she pulls back.

"What have you been up to, El? I've missed you. It's been a while!"

Ethan patiently waits for her attention at my side, standing idly by like a fan waiting for an autograph. Kat gives him a quick wave and a smile but immediately turns back to me.

I notice a small flicker of disappointment in his face, but just as quickly, it's gone.

We first met Kat eight years ago, just after her transition. When she came out to her parents as transgender, they disowned her and kicked her out of their house. Luckily, she was able to move in with her amazing, supportive aunt, who saved her in every way possible. Kat is incredible, and her talent for making costumes is unreal.

I search for the words to answer her question about what I've been up to, as if it didn't entail reliving all the horrible details of my embarrassing breakup and depressive spiral.

Instead, I scratch at my throat and say, "Oh you know, little of this, little of that…" I look to Ethan for a lifeline, but he still has that weird look in his eyes. I nudge him with my elbow to snap him out of it.

What's up with you?

Nothing!

I turn back to her, desperate to change the subject. "What's new with you? Ready for some fun this weekend?"

"Hell yeah! Though I'm guessing you're a little bummed after Tamara's events were canceled." She waves a hand at my costume.

"Yeah, hopefully it's just today. Maybe they can keep her other events and reschedule the Q&A." I cast out the line to gauge her reaction, hoping for a bite. Any indication that she might know more about the situation.

"Hope so! I know you're, like, her biggest fan. Wonder why they canceled though. Maybe she got sick or something," Kat offers with a shrug.

I deflate a little, knowing she doesn't have the answers I seek.

We continue to talk and catch up for the next few minutes or so. Her awaiting admirers are looking a little impatient and fidgety, but they're still being respectful, so we hug one last time and part ways to continue our search.

When we're far enough away, I look over at Ethan and punch his arm. "Why were you being so weird with Kat just now?"

He looks at me and scoffs a little too quickly. "What? Me? I mean...I wasn't being weird, you're weird."

"You got a thing for her?"

"What? Jesus, Els, I barely know her. Leave me alone."

I drop it, knowing how he gets when he's like this. But I can't help the smile dancing on my lips as we walk through the crowd. We pass by some Trekkies, Rufio from *Hook*, and a sweet-looking couple holding hands dressed as Sally and Jack Skellington.

Walking hand in hand through the park after yet another elegant, romantic dinner, I could tell he had something on his mind. I smiled up at him and leaned my head gently on his arm as we continued to walk. "What are you thinking about?"

"I was thinking..." He stopped walking and turned to face me. "Look, we've only known each other a few weeks, I know, but... gosh, I've never felt this way about anyone before. You make me so happy, and it's probably too soon to tell you this, but...I guess what I'm trying to say is...I'm in love with you, Elspeth."

The butterflies in my stomach went wild.

"Oh wow. Jared, I...I love you too."

He kissed me so hard I nearly toppled over. His strong arms held me up, and he laughed softly against my lips as I smiled so wide my cheeks hurt. No one had ever said those words to me, romantically.

This man, who swept me off my feet, who made me feel safe, and desired — he chose me.

I did love him. From the moment I saw him at Tegan's party last month, I finally understood what people meant by "love at first sight." I was drawn to him instantly, unable to stop myself from approaching him. We talked all night long about everything from movies and books, to travel, to our wildest dreams, and by sunrise, I knew I wanted to marry him.

He cupped a hand over my cheek and pressed his forehead to mine. "You're the girl of my dreams. I'm never letting you go."

9

After about a half hour, neither Andy, Jade, nor Damien has responded to our texts, so we decide to take a break for dinner.

There's an amazing two-story food hall situated across the street from the convention center and next door to the hotel, where most people eat during con weekend. It has six restaurants, two bars, and two gourmet treat shops. Enough variety that everyone can find something they like and not have to eat or drink at the same place twice.

BROWNCOATS

ME (6:18 P.M.)

meet us at the food hall

We cross the street and head inside. Instantly the aromas of several different cuisines hit me all at once in a delicious medley of flavors. Pizza, sizzling fajitas, curries, barbecue, burgers. I didn't realize how hungry I was until this very moment.

It's fairly packed in here, like always, but the space is large enough to fit everyone comfortably. The second level is visible from down below through an open space, accessible by escalators in the center, like in a mall. Some of the restaurants have their own seating, but the entire center space is lined with rows and rows of tables and chairs for people to gather. Perfect for when each member of your party wants something different.

Ethan puts his sunglasses on top of his head as we both gravitate toward the Mexican food place, El Rodeo. I look forward to coming here every year for their savory chorizo queso, spicy beef tacos, and their famous 2-for-1 margarita special.

We order our food and drinks, taking it all to one of the center tables, so we can be visible if any of our friends finally decide to show up. Just like at Melvin's, we take off the excess costume pieces and place them on the seats next to us, so we're able to sit and eat comfortably.

Now that we're able to rest from a long day of being on our feet and walking around looking for clues, I finally realize how much my feet hurt. I may not be able to stand up again for a while.

The first bite is an explosion of flavor, and I'm unable to stop my eyes from rolling in the back of my head. "Mmm, damn that's good."

"Should I give you a moment alone?"

"I wish you would."

"Bitch."

"Jackass." I grin and Ethan shakes his head, taking a bite of his own food.

About halfway through our meals, I pull out Tamara's hat from my bag and place it on the table between us. It just sits there, taunting us. It may be loud and buzzing all around us, but at our little table, in our own silence and stillness, the reality of the situation sinks in.

I gently rub the bill of the cap between my fingers. "Do you think we should've called the cops? It feels kinda wrong that we took this thing in the first place."

Ethan runs a hand over his face and nods, leaning back in his chair. "I was thinking the same thing."

"What do we do now?"

He pauses, like he's struggling to find the right words. "Andy made it clear the cops weren't taking it seriously, so I was hoping we'd find him right away and...I don't know, maybe he would have an explanation or know what the hell to do." He leans forward again, bracing his hands on the table. "This whole thing is fucked."

"I'm trying to understand though. How did it get in the alley, blocks away from Melvin's? How would that even happen?"

"I guess if they took her out of the car? Maybe they moved her to the trunk and it fell off her head?"

The trunk? Jesus.

The tacos turn sour in my stomach.

"You don't think she could be in one of those buildings, do you?" I ask quietly.

"I mean, it's possible, but those are all stores and restaurants. It's not like they're abandoned or anything. Whoever took her would probably want to take her far away from this area."

We sip on our margaritas in silence, trying to make sense of it all.

Looking around the food hall, it's like nothing has changed. I was a little worried after missing last year's WyvernFest that I would come back and everything would be different. It's comforting knowing some things are exactly the way I remember.

Ethan finishes the last of his drink, slurping up the dregs. "I am concerned about Andy though. I've never seen him like this, but...I don't know, I also can't help but feel like he's not telling us something."

"Right?" I lean over the table. "Something felt off when we were talking to him earlier. Maybe it's just stress over a friend missing, but he was acting really strange."

I hope we can help figure out what's going on.

Ethan nods in agreement but then freezes as he stares over my shoulder with wide eyes.

When I turn to look, I see Andy quickly approaching, his eyes unblinking as he navigates between tables.

"Where did you get that?" He swipes the hat off the table and holds it up, presumably looking for her initials written in the lining. It looks like he's about to lose his cool, when suddenly his shoulders sag and he squeezes his eyes shut.

"We found it a few blocks away, in an alley. This is hers, right?" Ethan asks. "Should we give it to the cops? It could be evidence of foul play, don't you think?"

Andy just stares at it without saying a word, his thumb mindlessly rubbing over the *TJ*. He narrows his eyes like he's thinking about what to do next.

"Andy?" I gently put a hand on his arm.

He shakes his head and snaps out of whatever thought he was in. "Yeah, okay." He pauses and looks around. "I'll call them now and see if they'll come back. Maybe they will finally take this seriously." He pulls out his phone and tucks the green hat under his arm. "Can you both come back to the hotel in a bit?"

"Of course, Andy. We'll be there," Ethan says.

Andy walks away, putting his phone up to his ear, and disappears through the glass doors.

Yikes, we both say with our eyes.

We finish the rest of our food in silence, our friends still nowhere to be found.

After throwing our trash away and grabbing our stuff, we head towards the convention center. As we turn the corner by the entrance, I crash into someone.

The man is knocked just enough off balance that he has to steady himself by grabbing my elbows. It takes me a few seconds to register that it's Damien. Our eyes meet and a small jolt vibrates through my body at his touch.

He laughs. "You okay there, Els?"

Ethan eyes us curiously, standing off to the side.

"Yeah, I'm good. Why haven't you all been answering your phones?" I ask as I slowly extract myself from his arms.

"Oh sorry, I left mine up in the room, and then I got separated from Jade about a half hour ago. So she's not with you?"

"No, we were looking for you. How was the mission? You learn anything?"

Damien is missing the blue tulle portion of his costume. If I had to guess, it's probably stuffed in his satchel, along with the fake beard and mustache. I can't imagine it was all that comfortable to begin with.

"Yeah, Jade might have a lead. You?"

Ethan steps closer and whispers, "We found the hat Tamara was wearing when she was taken. It was tossed in a gross alleyway a few blocks from here. Andy's bringing it to the cops right now, and we're going back over to the hotel to talk with them."

"Holy shit! They'll have to investigate now. Which means we can all get back to enjoying the con!" Damien pumps his fists in the air. "I'm gonna grab some food real quick, and I'll meet you back over there, cool?"

I give a quick nod and Ethan answers, "Yep! See ya, brother."

Ethan lowers his sunglasses in place and smiles as we step outside. I kind of want to smack him.

Both of them are way too happy right now. We basically confirmed that Tamara was taken — *abducted* — and they are perfectly content to just move on with their lives and go have some fun. How is this not affecting them?

Maybe I'm overreacting, but I can't stop thinking about her and what she might be going through.

If they don't want to help find Tamara Jenkins, then I'll just have to do it myself.

10

As Ethan and I cross the street to the hotel, I notice the sky changing colors ever so slightly as the sun begins its descent towards the horizon. I haven't even been paying attention to the time today, but I guess it is starting to get late.

This day is going way too fast.

We walk through the sliding glass doors of the hotel and spot Andy over on a plush sofa on the far side of the lobby, talking with a broad-shouldered man dressed in a nicely tailored navy blue suit, no tie, who is sitting in a high-back leather chair. This must be the detective.

That was fast.

Andy spots us and waves us over.

"Here we go," I mutter to Ethan.

I let the calming lavender aroma and soft piano music wash through me as I rub my sweaty palms together and take a deep breath.

"Hey! I want you both to meet Detective Michael Hawthorn." We shake his hand while Andy continues, "He's actually an old buddy of mine, and he's going to be helping us out."

We give awkward smiles and nods as Ethan and I scoot in next to Andy on the sofa.

"Good to meet y'all. Nice costumes, by the way. I just have a few questions before we can start the investigation. I, uh, understand you found this hat…" He holds up the green baseball cap we gave Andy earlier, now residing in a large plastic evidence bag. "Yeah? Can you tell me more about where y'all found it?"

This guy reminds me of a quirky TV show detective, like he studied every famous detective character and practices in front of a mirror each night. He's even chewing gum in an exaggerated manner.

"Yes, my brother Ethan and I—" I gesture over to him, "—went a few blocks over to Melvin's to see if we could find anything that might help. When we were walking back to the convention center, I noticed the hat in an alleyway just one or two blocks that way." I point to my right, towards the back of the hotel.

"And then what did y'all do with it?"

"Well," I start a little nervously, "I picked it up and then we came back over here to find Andy. We figured since it had only been a few hours, and there was no official investigation or anything, it made sense to bring it to Andy to confirm it was hers."

Ethan adds, "You know, in the moment, we really just wanted to get out of that piss-filled alley, but later we thought this might actually be evidence of foul play. I mean, just being thrown in an alley like that? What do you think?"

Detective Hawthorn nods, his expression borderline bored, and continues writing his notes, smacking his gum. "Well, we really won't know until we look into it, yeah?"

I look at Andy, slumped on the arm of the sofa, hand resting in his hair, staring off into space. The picture of exhaustion. It's only been a few hours, but he looks like he's been through every emotion today.

"So neither of you knew the victim personally, correct?"

I flinch slightly. It's the first time I've heard Tamara described as a victim. The look in Andy's eyes tells me he doesn't like that term either.

Ethan answers. "No, we've never met her. Just fans of her show, I guess."

Well that's an understatement, but Detective Hawthorn certainly doesn't need to hear about my fandom status, or that I know her middle name is Dana.

He writes in his notebook for another few seconds and then shuts it, looking back up at us. "So, how do y'all know our boy Andrew here?" He gives him a goofy smile and a playful smack on the knee with his notebook.

I'm suddenly fascinated with their relationship and learning more about how *they* know each other.

Though they're sitting, I can tell the detective is shorter and stockier. He's certainly odd, but charming. I could definitely see the two of them getting into trouble together when they were younger.

"Oh, we met Andy at Comic Con a few years back," Ethan replies.

"What about you guys? You said you're old buddies?" God, I'm so nosy, but I don't care. I must know more.

Andy gives a quirk of his mouth, and his eyes soften a bit, endearment shining through. "Yeah, Hawthorn and I go way back. We went to grade school together, then we were college room-mates. He even let me stay with him when I was building my house out here. He's a good friend, who's always been there for me."

Hawthorn. He says it with such fondness, such familiarity. Andy gives a slap on his friend's knee, and for a moment, I get a glimpse of the man I know and remember. I'm glad he has a friend out here to help him through all this.

"Aww, thanks, man." He turns to us and continues, "I used

to see this guy all the time, but Mr. Bigshot here has been so busy lately, flying out to LA every chance he gets, I hardly see him anymore!" He chuckles.

"Part of the job, you know?" Andy shrugs.

Now I have even more questions. "So, wait, you have a house here in Glenville, but work in LA? Why don't you move out there?"

"I actually used to live there for a while, but it was just so damn expensive. Plus, I missed my hometown and wanted to be closer to my parents as they get older and need more help."

I nod. I never knew that about him.

"I ran the numbers, and it was way cheaper to build a house out here and just fly into LA as needed to meet with my team. Most of my work I can do from home anyway."

"Big city boy must be working on something big then. I'm happy for you, man. I can't wait to hear all about it," Detective Hawthorn says with an elbow jab.

If he's been flying to LA a lot lately, I wonder if that means the rumors are true that they're moving forward with turning The Quantum Protector into the next big superhero movie. That would be so amazing for him. If anyone deserves success for his talents and hard work, it's Andy.

Damien walks in through the sliding glass doors and sees us right away. He approaches our group, finishing the last bite of a burger with a big smile on his face. Like this is just any other day.

"Damien, this is Detective Hawthorn." Ethan motions between them.

They exchange a firm handshake before Damien takes the leather chair to my right.

Andy's face slowly falls. Like he let himself forget for just a moment what was going on and why his friend Hawthorn is really here. Reality crashing down on him.

More than ever, I'm determined to help find her. But how? We have nothing to go on.

Maybe we need to approach this another way. Like a party embarking on an epic journey. I can see it now: The Quest to Find the Lost Princess.

"So what happens now?" Ethan asks.

Damien hasn't taken his eyes off Andy since the moment he got here. I think he's still a little starstruck around him. I know he's a big fan of The Quantum Protector, and I'm sure in his wildest dreams he never imagined having this much face time with him.

Though, nothing about this weekend has gone the way we thought it would.

"Well…" Detective Hawthorn chews his gum and takes a deep breath. "We filed the missing person's report earlier today, and we were able to keep her name out of public record, but… well, unfortunately, once this investigation gets going, and considering the victim is a public figure, everyone here in attendance knowing that her events were suddenly and mysteriously canceled…?" He pauses and scratches the side of his face, looking at Andy before continuing. "I'm afraid people are going to put two and two together here real soon, and word is going to get out that she may have been taken. We should be prepared, as we may have a real media frenzy on our hands."

11

The three of us say our goodbyes and leave Andy to catch up with his buddy. Crossing the street back over to the convention center, I'm anxious to find Jade. I know she can handle herself, but it would just make me feel a whole lot better to know she's okay and to be with her right now, since we haven't heard from her in hours.

I pull out my phone to call her again, pausing only to marvel up at the sky painted in brilliant oranges and pinks, along a wall of fluffy clouds. The beauty of it takes my breath away, and I decide to take a picture of it. How long has it been since I've stopped to appreciate the beauty around me?

Jade finally picks up on the fourth ring.

"Hey, babe!" she yells.

I can barely hear her over the insane noise coming from her end. I stop walking before we reach the convention center doors. I'll never be able to hear her if we walk inside. "Hey! Where are you?"

"*What?*" she yells even louder.

"*Where…are…you?*"

The guys shake their heads chuckling, and I give them the finger.

"Dance party in Ballroom One!"

"Copy that!"

I hang up, relieved that she's safe and sound. Not that she wouldn't be, but this whole situation has me on edge. It's hard not to worry.

"Dance party, Ballroom One. Let's go." I point towards the doors, and we step inside, nearly getting knocked over by the crowd noise.

Damien seems to be extra happy, walking with a little more pep in his step. Clearly, he is relieved at the idea of not having to indulge me in any more of this investigating nonsense. I guess I can't really blame him, though it still just rubs me the wrong way for some reason.

I'm not sure why I care so much about finding Tamara Jenkins. Maybe it's because I see so much of myself in her portrayal of Serafina. This character means so much to me and helped me discover a part of myself during some tough times. I feel strangely connected to her, even though I obviously know that Serafina and Tamara are not the same person.

We reach the ballroom and head into the dance party, music blaring so loud it hurts my ears. The last time we were in this room, we had come to see Tamara, before everything changed. Now the space is dark, with colored lights flashing and swinging all around. People are waving glow sticks and dancing to the beat as I try to ignore the faint musk of hundreds of sweaty bodies.

We all start looking around for Jade, but knowing her, she's already grabbed the attention of her next hookup. Men and women find her irresistible and can't help but be drawn to her. Sometimes it's like she's put a spell on them.

I admire that she's so confident and unapologetically herself all the time. Something I used to be, once upon a time.

I wonder if I can ever be like that again.

Jade sneaks up behind us and hands me some red drink, immediately tapping my cup in a cheers. "Hey, babe!"

Ethan and Damien give her a quick nod of acknowledgment before heading over to the bar along the side wall to get their own drinks. I lean back into her for a hug and can't help but smile from her infectious energy.

She's out of costume, which I now realize was a really smart move. We've been so busy all day, I haven't had a chance to head back upstairs to change. With all her orange body paint taken off, she must have found time to shower as well, changing into a tight-fitting ripped top and leather miniskirt.

I definitely need to go shed this armor soon, 'cause it is hot as hell in here, and my muscles are aching. It's been way too long since I've been in costume all day, and somehow I forgot how tiring it can be.

"How long have you been here?" I yell.

She motions for me to follow her over to the far end of the room away from the speakers, where it's slightly quieter. The crowd is gathered in the middle of the room, closer to the stage where a DJ is set up. She is seamlessly mixing popular club songs with movie and video game soundtracks, the likes of John Williams and Nobuo Uematsu.

"Sorry, my phone died earlier, so it was charging up in the room the past few hours."

"No worries. Where'd you go?"

"The DJ was working at the bar next to Melvin's earlier today, so I've been busy getting on her good side to find out more before she started her set tonight." She looks back towards the DJ on stage and smiles, giving a flirty wave of her fingers.

"Good thinking! She tell you anything? Damien didn't seem to know any details."

"Yeah, we decided to split up when I found out she was

working there earlier, so I could get closer to her. We ordered takeout from the hotel restaurant and talked for a while."

Damn she's good.

She leans in a little closer. "All I've been able to glean so far is that word got out about Tamara being next door at the diner, so a lot of eyes were on her. Fans were being respectful though and leaving her alone."

I nod, taking a sip of my drink.

"She was with Andy, like he said, but there was nothing out of the ordinary. She confirmed his story, that Tamara got into a blue car around two o'clock, and he didn't go with her. But she couldn't really see much outside the bar, so that's all she really knows."

Relief washes over me that Andy was being truthful. Not that he would have any reason not to, but still, it feels like there's something he's not telling us.

"Oh, and the cops already interviewed her, and they asked the owner about seeing any security camera footage from the bar parking lot. But apparently the cameras weren't working, of course."

"It's not so much about what happened at Melvin's or the bar but what happened right after."

"True. Did you find anything?" Jade asks.

I look around to make sure no one is within earshot. "We found her hat in an alley a few blocks away."

She nearly chokes on her drink and puts out a hand. "Wait, *what*? Are you serious?"

"She had to have been taken, right? I mean, it seems pretty sketchy. What other explanation could there be?"

Her eyebrows rise. "Holy shit. So what now?"

"Well, we handed it over as evidence, and now they're investigating..." I notice Damien and Ethan walking towards us, weaving through the crowd, drinks in hand. "Damien thinks we should stay out of it and leave it to the police."

Jade just quietly sips her cocktail and looks off to the side, avoiding my gaze.

I narrow my eyes at her. "Not you too."

"What? Come on, think about it. If she really was taken — as fucked up as that is — it doesn't involve us, and we could end up interfering in the investigation."

My shoulders slump and I finish the rest of my drink.

"Look, I know how much you wanted an adventure, but this is real life. I've seen some fucked-up shit with my job, you have no idea. We don't know what or who is involved in all of this."

I know she's right, but I can't help the disappointment settling in my chest. I wanted to be a part of something bigger and to believe I could make a real difference. Distract myself from how empty I still feel and keep the dark thoughts from consuming me.

Without a mission to focus on, I might be forced to deal with my own issues, and I really can't have that right now.

"Besides," Jade continues, putting an arm around my shoulder as the guys join us, "this weekend is supposed to bring you back to your old self again. Come on, we look forward to this every year! And since you missed it last year, we have to make up for lost time. Let's have some fun!"

Damn. I can't argue with that.

She's right. They're all right.

At least for tonight, maybe I can admit there is nothing more we can do for Tamara Jenkins. Andy is dealing with the police and has his detective friend on the case, and we have no other leads or information.

I look to my best friends and my brother, and I can see in their eyes they're just waiting for me to drop this whole thing. And I certainly don't want to be the reason they can't have fun this weekend.

I owe them better than that.

"*Fine.* You win. Let's do this."

They all cheer and raise their drinks, which pulls a smile from me.

I decide, for tonight, I can let things go.

After another round of drinks, Jade waves goodbye to her DJ friend and we head to the party in the next ballroom, this one being a *Battlestar Galactica*-themed "Frak Party."

It is absolutely decked out. The walls have a metallic shine to them, as if we are suddenly inside an enormous spaceship, with twelve long banners hung all around the walls representing the twelve colonies of Kobol, each bearing the colonial seal.

Several projectors line the spaces in between with images and video of stars and planets, as if looking out the windows of a spacecraft. Red, roaming lights swing back and forth to give the illusion of being surrounded by Cylons.

In the center of the ballroom sits an ice sculpture in the shape of the WyvernFest logo. Con workers dressed in the show's classic double-layered, grey and black tank tops are walking around serving colorful shots for a couple bucks each.

We order our drinks from the bar along the back wall. I ask for a Caprica Twist, Damien and Ethan get a Cylon Chaser, and Jade orders an Adama Colada. Clinking our glasses together, we kick off our night.

Tonight, my friends are most worthy of my focus and atten-tion. We will catch up with Andy in the morning and help out in whatever way he asks.

But right now, it's the first night of WyvernFest, and we are going to party like there's no tomorrow.

12

By nine o'clock, the party is in full swing, and I have to take off this costume. Damien offers to come up to the rooms with me to change as well, carrying Ethan's Doc Ock machinery and trench coat to stow away for the night. I'm not sure how any of us lasted this long in costume.

"Did you have a good day today?" I ask awkwardly. I still haven't quite found my groove with him again yet. We used to be able to talk so easily, about anything and everything.

"Yeah, it was…interesting," he says with a quirk of his lips. "What about you?"

"Aside from the whole celebrity kidnapping thing, it was pretty good."

"Hate when that happens."

"So inconvenient."

We share a quick glance and fall back into silence. I can't stand this energy between us. Just before Tamara's events were canceled, Damien all but forgave me and said we were good. But it still feels like he's holding back.

I would like to cast Detect Thoughts, please.

As Damien and I cross the skybridge, I turn my head to him and ask, "Are we good?"

He tenses for a split second before leveling me with a curious look. "What do you mean?" He shifts the load in his hands to the other side but doesn't say anything more.

"You and I. Are we okay?"

"Of course we are. Why do you ask?"

I scoff. "You know why."

He looks around and pulls me off to the side by my elbow. "Hey. What's up? Where is all this coming from?"

"I just…it's nothing. Like you said, we're good."

His eyes narrow, but a small smile plays on his lips. "You can't fool me. What's going on up here?" he says, gently tapping my forehead. He used to do that when he knew I was getting too deep in my own head.

"Nothing! Let's just go." I turn back towards the elevators.

"Okay…?" he says as he follows behind.

When the doors open, I jab the button for the fifth floor before he can and cross my arms.

The doors close, leaving us in tense silence. Damien is the one to speak first. "What's going on? I thought we were having a good night."

The sweet look on his face nearly breaks me. But I can't help it. I can't keep wondering, waiting for the other shoe to drop.

"I need you to be honest with me. I want us to be okay and to go back to how things used to be. But…" I fumble for the right words.

Shit. I should not have started this conversation without thinking it through. And definitely not after a few drinks. My mind is too fuzzy to articulate how I'm feeling, so I just say it.

"Just…tell me that you're pissed at me already and put me out of my misery!"

The elevator doors open on our floor to a crowd of people waiting to get on. I manage to work my way around a Vault

Dweller from *Fallout* and a group of various *One Piece* characters until we are past them, suddenly met again with awkward silence as we continue down the hallway towards our rooms.

I start to unbuckle the pauldrons at my shoulders, which have been getting in my way all night, ready to throw them down the hallway like a child.

Damien grabs my arm to stop me and spins me towards him, his eyes pinning me in place as the armor pieces drop to the floor. He chews on his lower lip, the way he does whenever he's trying to come up with the right words to say.

"Damien, please. I know you're still mad."

He slowly drops his hand from my arm and tosses Ethan's machinery and clothes to the floor. Pressing his palms to his temples and squeezing his eyes shut, he finally yells, *"Fine,* you want me to say it? I am mad. I'm *pissed,* okay?" His hands fall to his hips as he turns away from me.

All the air gets sucked out of the space we're in, and my heart sinks. At least he's finally being honest. At least I'm finally getting what I deserve. So I just nod, letting him continue at his own pace. I'll bear it as long as I have to.

After a moment, he turns back to me with glossy eyes. "I'm pissed, but—" he rakes a hand through his hair, normally raven black but still partially white from all the color spray, "—but not...not at you. At *him.* At myself. But not at you. Never."

I try to let his words sink in, but I don't understand. "Why would you be pissed at yourself?"

"Because I should have tried harder? I don't know. I should've told you..." He shakes his head. "I just...I should've tried. You always made it sound like everything was fine, and you really had us all convinced that you were happy. I should've known..." He squeezes his eyes shut.

When he opens them again, he continues slowly. "I never wanted to be that guy. The one who told you who you should or shouldn't be with. That was your choice to make. If I took that away from you, I would be no better than him. So...I had to let you go." He shrugs, and it's anything but casual or light.

I look off to the side, unable to meet his gaze with tears clouding my vision. "Damien...I don't know what to say to that. I'm..." I take a deep breath. "I'm so, so sorry for everything that happened. I'm sorry for cutting you out like that. That was so shitty of me, and you didn't deserve that, at all. I'm sorry."

We used to have such a natural, easygoing relationship, where we could tell each other anything. There was mutual trust and fondness in everything we did together. That all went away once Jared made me choose between them.

I cradle my arms, but I keep going, despite not being able to look at him just yet. "I'm sorry that I let Jared get between us. I was just so focused on trying to avoid all the arguments and fights and..." I start to scratch at my throat. "I don't know, and I thought maybe he would change his mind once you started... dating someone else?"

I finally look up at him, but his expression is unreadable. Like he still wants to say something, but I won't push him any more.

"But that's not an excuse. That should have been the moment I left. I was weak and couldn't see the truth about who he was, and I should never have done that to you, and I'm so, so sorry. I just...I want things to go back to how they used to be with us."

His shoulders drop slightly, and he studies me for a moment before pulling me in for a hug that instantly warms me up. "I never blamed you for any of that. I always knew it was him." He pulls back and looks at me, squeezing my shoulders. "And you are not weak."

I finally let it all go and sob into his robes, the side of my face pressed into his neck. We stand there embracing for several minutes, no more words needed.

After the tears subside, I whisper, "Your wild cherry and cypress scent is drifting through my senses."

His chest rumbles with soft laughter. "And you smell of... cardamon dewdrops and honeysuckle and...another scent I can't quite name."

We pull away from each other smiling as he wipes a stray tear from my face. It feels like something has shifted between us, and I catch a glimmer of hope in his eyes that he's thinking the same thing.

We grab our stuff off the floor and walk the remaining steps to our rooms.

I stop at my door as Damien continues to his. "Hey," I say before he can open his door. "Pull yourself together, will you? You're making a scene."

He purses his lips but can't stop the smile from overtaking his face at the memory, creating those dimples I love so much.

"Elsie, Jade...this is Damien Amoruso," Ethan declared with his hand on the shoulder of some random, tall dude dressed as Samwise Gamgee. "We just met over in the Dealers Hall looking at some new tabletop games, and it turns out he lives just ten minutes from us. Damien, this is Jade, and my sister, Elsie."

A flush crept up my neck as I extended a gloved hand out to shake his. He was bigger than Ethan — than all of us really — and incredibly good-looking. One might describe him as husky, but more than anything, he was just...adorable. Like a big teddy bear.

I wanted to curl up in his arms and watch movies and play video games with him all day, despite the gross-looking hobbit feet I just now noticed he was wearing. His wavy strawberry blond hair was clearly a wig, and I had the sudden urge to take it off him to see what he looked like underneath.

Get a grip, Ethan glared at me.

I ignored him and cleared my throat.

Ethan and I were cosplaying as Team Rocket's Jessie and James from *Pokémon*, and Jade was Ruby Rose from the popular anime *RWBY*. This was our sixth WyvernFest together, and one of the few times I could ever convince Ethan to do a dual cosplay with me.

"Aren't you a little tall for a hobbit?" I asked, barely able to contain a creeping smile. To my absolute dismay, his returning grin was utterly gorgeous, producing dimples on each side, which threatened to take out my knees.

I needed to get a handle on whatever it was I was suddenly feeling for this towering stranger I just met, whose striking brown eyes were searing straight into me. But I was instantly attracted, and desperately wanted to know more about him.

Before he got a chance to respond, an equally tall, gorgeous woman with a curtain of silky, chocolate brown hair and a perfect heart-shaped face, wearing a tight-fitting top and jean shorts, sidled up to him and linked her arm in his.

"There you are!" she said before giving him a quick peck on the cheek.

My stomach dropped to the floor. Never mind, I guess. Always attracted to the unavailable men. Could I be more predictable?

Jade seemed to notice my shift and linked her hand in mine, a silent affirmation that she knew exactly what had just transpired inside my crazy head. She always saw everything.

I told myself I couldn't be jealous. I didn't even know these people.

Damien stiffened slightly before returning a tight smile to her. "Hey, you. This is Ethan, Jade, and Elsie. Everyone, this is Callie."

She gave us a quick, warm smile and wave, and turned back to Damien with a pout. "You ready to go soon? We've got those reservations tonight, and I want to start getting ready."

Jade and I exchanged a knowing glance. She was beautiful and seemed very sweet, but there was some obvious tension between them. I was surprised she wanted to leave already, considering the events just started.

Damien glanced at us uncomfortably and chewed his lip. "Callie, we just got here," he said with a nervous chuckle. "Don't you want to hang out for a bit?"

Jade, Ethan, and I all sensed the awkwardness brewing and immediately needed to extract ourselves from it.

"It was nice to meet you!" I offered with a small wave, as we all turned back towards each other.

Damien got the hint and gently took Callie by the elbow, walking them a few feet away, just out of earshot. Sadly, I couldn't hear their conversation, but based on body language and hand gestures, this was going to get ugly.

"Yikes, that's awkward," Ethan said to break the silence, no doubt also trying to eavesdrop and decipher the drama unfolding behind us.

After a few minutes of arguing, the girl — Callie — stomped away in a huff, leaving Damien, the enormous hobbit, standing there all alone with a look of defeat written all over his face.

He let out a long breath and removed his shaggy Sam wig, revealing shoulder-length, wavy, raven black hair. So silky that it begged to be touched. Hair that perfectly complemented his olive brown skin.

I quickly turned back to the group with wide eyes after realizing I was staring. A moment later, he approached us and raked a hand through his hair, drawing my attention up there once again.

We made room for him in our standing group and gave him a hesitant glance.

"Hey, so I really just came over here to tell you all that you should really pull yourselves together. You were making quite a scene back there," he deadpanned.

We all burst out laughing.

Cute *and* funny. Great.

I nudge him playfully with my elbow. "You know you'd make a decent Frodo with that hair?"

He puts a hand to his chest. "Ah yes, but what of his heart? There's no one else with a heart like Sam's." He flashes that warm smile again.

I couldn't agree more.

In that moment, it felt like something clicked, and Damien suddenly became the fourth and final piece of our group we didn't even know was missing.

Our party was now complete.

13

I open the door to my room, and before I even step foot inside, I notice a ripped piece of paper about the size of my hand, lying on the ground. I know our room was messy when we left, but that definitely wasn't there before. It must have been slipped under the door.

When I pick it up, my stomach bottoms out.

MIND YOUR OWN BUSINESS OR YOU'LL END UP LIKE PRINCESS HOLLYWOOD

What the hell? Is this real?

My heart is pounding in my ears.

I'm frozen in place, unsure of what to do.

Whoever took Tamara Jenkins was *here*. They know where I'm staying, and they know I'm trying to help find her.

I'm still not moving, and possibly not even breathing.

Am I breathing?

I feel nauseous.

I don't even know when I started scratching at my throat again.

I snap myself out of my spiraling thoughts and realize I haven't even closed the door to my room yet. I just got a threatening note from Tamara's abductor, and I'm just standing here, holding my door wide open for all to see.

God, I'm an idiot.

Letting the door swing shut behind me, I fold up the note and stuff it in the back side of my con badge for safekeeping. I remove all my costume pieces and change into my black leggings and an oversized, grey *Katamari Damacy* t-shirt that says "This is how I roll!" paired with my trusty sneakers.

Swapping my green-colored contacts for glasses, I sag a little at the relief of my poor dry eyes.

Once I'm all changed and ready, I peek my head out into the hallway, looking in all directions to make sure no one is watching me, before going to knock on Damien's door. I considered for a moment not telling him about the note, so he doesn't worry, but I don't have it in me to keep on pretending that everything is fine. I've never been able to lie to him anyway.

He'll know something is up the moment he sees me.

I try to plaster on my best smile when he answers the door, but his expression is hardened, eyebrows drawn together and jaw clenched. I'm not sure I've ever seen him like this, and for a moment I think maybe he has more to say to me and wants to continue our fight from earlier.

"Hey, what is it?" I ask gently.

He holds out a ripped piece of paper, and I hesitate before reaching out with shaky hands.

You should all go home before it's too late

I look up at him with wide eyes and reach into my badge to pull out my own note. I give it to him without breaking eye contact, and I can feel the anger rolling off him as he reads it.

"Maybe you were right," I whisper. "Maybe...we should stay out of this. This is getting out of hand."

Damien looks up from the note and raises an eyebrow. "Is that what you want?"

"I don't know!" I drop my hands to my sides. "I mean, it's my fault you got roped into this in the first place. I never meant for this to happen, and I don't want you all in danger because of me."

"Hey, none of this is your fault, okay? You have to stop taking the blame for everything."

I look away and nod, unconvincingly.

"Look, I want nothing more than to be able to keep bad things from happening to you, and to keep you safe, but come on, that's not who you are. That's not what you want, is it?"

What I want? I don't even know what that is anymore.

I didn't used to be like this. Scared, apologizing for everything.

The old me would have crumpled up that paper and spit on it, letting it fuel my determination to keep going. Proof that I was on to something. But now I'm not so sure.

He places his hands on my shoulders. "I have never doubted how capable you are, and the Elsie I know would never back down from a threat."

"I'm not sure that's who I am anymore." I shake my head. "Or if I ever will be again."

"Fuck that!"

I startle a little. He hardly ever gets riled up like this, aside from when he's losing to me in *Smash Bros*.

"Okay, well, what should we do?" I ask.

"What do *you* want to do?" His eyes pin me in place yet again, and his stare is so intense I have to remind myself to breathe. He drops his hands to his sides. "Do you want to pack it all up and go home? Or do you want to say 'fuck you' to whoever wrote this? Find whoever just threatened us, who took Tamara Jenkins, and be the one to help put them away."

I think for a moment, a little stunned by this sudden role reversal. Damien is a protector, who has always looked out for me and everyone in our group. Now he's the one suggesting we don't back down, that we keep going.

But deep down, I know he's right. It's exactly what I would've done.

What kind of person would it make me if we actually got close to solving this thing, and the moment it got tough I ran away to where it's safe? What if I stayed quiet and just went on with my life, but there was a chance I could have helped her?

I think to myself, *What would Princess Serafina do?* But I already know the answer. She would find the courage to do what's right. To draw strength from herself and from those around her, no matter what. To do what had to be done.

"Well..." I look back up into those striking brown eyes, unable to stop the smile forming on my lips. "I did say I wanted some excitement in my life..."

Damien returns the smile and slowly nods. "There she is."

I look back down at the note and notice something strange. I snatch the one from Damien's hand and flip them both over, and for the first time, realize they are two halves of the same page.

A page that's been ripped out of the WyvernFest guidebook.

The side that the note was written on was blank, but the backside is the map of the convention center and surrounding buildings. In blue ink, there is a star marked on top of Exhibit Hall C, with numbers written on the side that I can't make sense of.

5
12
10

I line up the notes and flip them towards Damien and ask, "What do we have here?"

"What are those numbers?"

"I don't know. I'm not sure this person meant for us to see this. I wonder what it means."

"Let's take a picture of it. Once we show the detective, he'll want to confiscate the notes as evidence."

"Good call," I say as I lay the notes on the floor and pull out my phone. I take one photo of the map with writing on it, and another of the handwritten messages. "We should see if the detective is still here. Hopefully he hasn't left yet. I'll message Andy."

Damien's right.

This is not the time to back down.

14

We spot them casually sitting across from each other at a table, engrossed in conversation. You can tell by the way they interact that they know each other well. There's real familiarity there.

Detective Hawthorn stands up from his chair when he sees us — Andy following suit — and motions for us to join them at their table. "Hey! What did y'all need to show me? Is everything alright?"

I place the notes on the table facing the detective as we all sit down. He leans over the table and reads them with furrowed brows. After a beat, he leans back and runs his hand through his short, wheat-colored hair, letting out a sharp breath. "Where did y'all find these?"

Andy snatches them up, cupping his forehead in his hand as he reads them. When he looks back up at me, his eyes are wide in shock. "Oh God. Elsie, are you okay?"

"I'm fine. They were slipped under our doors."

"When was the last time you were up in your rooms before now? So we might get a timeframe." He puts on a glove and gently slides each note into its own plastic evidence bag.

I think for a moment. "Not since around noon? Well before Tamara even went missing. We've been in costume all day and hadn't gone upstairs to change until just now."

Damien puts up a hand. "Actually, Jade went up there to change before the party tonight."

"Shit, that's right." My stomach tightens at the thought of her being there when this person came up to our rooms. What *could've* happened if she'd caught them and they did something to her.

"Last I saw her was around six maybe? And she was still in costume then," Damien adds.

The detective pulls out his notepad and writes something down. "So the timeframe for these notes is around…six p.m. to —" he checks his watch, "—ten p.m."

Okay, that's not too bad. It should help narrow things down a little, but there are still thousands of people here this weekend, it could be anyone. There are too many potential suspects.

Andy looks at me with concern. "Elsie, I'm so sorry you all got dragged into this. We're not going to let anything happen to you, I promise."

I give him a polite nod, knowing he can't possibly promise me that, but appreciate him saying it all the same. We're in this too far now to stop.

I realize in all the chaos of finding the note and notifying Andy and the detective, that we never told Ethan and Jade what happened. I pull out my phone to shoot off a quick text in the group chat so they can meet us over here.

BROWNCOATS

ME (10:02 P.M.)

hotel restaurant NOW!

"Detective Hawthorn—" I start but am cut off.

"Please, just call me Hawthorn." He waves a hand. "Detective Hawthorn sounds so formal, and any friend of Andrew's is a friend of mine."

"Okay…Hawthorn." I open my palm towards him. "Can you get any information from these notes? Like handwriting or fingerprints or something?"

"Handwriting, possibly, but we don't have anything else to compare it to yet. And as for prints, we've now had—" he motions around the table, "—a few people here put their hands on them, so…maybe, but I wouldn't get my hopes up."

I curse under my breath. I didn't even think about the fact that this was evidence and just let my fingers roam all over it like an idiot. Just like I did with Tamara's hat. Veronica Mars would be so disappointed.

"But I'll certainly hold on to these in case we can cross reference any more handwriting later on."

"More handwriting? Like if there are more notes?"

I feel that pit opening in my stomach again. Luckily, the sight of Jade and Ethan pulls me out of my thoughts as they approach our table with worried expressions.

"What happened? Your text was annoyingly vague," Ethan whines. He sways a little, and I realize they're both drunk. I did just pull them out of the epic Frak Party for this.

Finding these notes sobered me up real fast.

I look to Andy and then Detective Hawthorn, who hands them each a note in their plastic bag.

"These were put under our doors sometime tonight," I say as I stand to pull two more chairs up to the table. They're going to want to sit for this.

They both go pale as they read them, sinking into their seats.

"Oh shit." Ethan looks at us. "Els, you okay?"

"Yeah yeah, I'm great. Just a little uneasy. I'm not thrilled that they know where we're staying."

"Do you want to move rooms?" Ethan suggests.

"First off, you know all the rooms here have been booked since last year's con. And second, if this person found our room once, they'll find it again. It's fine, we just have to watch our backs and stick together. I'm not going to let this asshole scare me. If anything, I'm more determined than ever to find them."

I look to Jade who has been fairly quiet this whole time. Which usually means she's thinking things through and putting all the pieces together.

"Jade? Whatcha thinking over there?" I ask, and everyone turns toward her.

"Andy, can you think of anyone who would want to take Tamara? Has she had any problems with stalkers or anything?" Jade asks.

He scratches the back of his neck. "Not that I know of. I mean, she said she gets some weird fan mail from time to time…but her team would flag any serious threats."

Am I crazy or did Andy just look at me when he said "weird fan mail?" I only sent the five letters, and she wrote me back the sweetest response.

"I just can't figure out the motive here," Jade continues. "We haven't seen any type of ransom or demands, they just…took her. Right? So what does this person — I'm assuming it's a *he*, but we can't be sure just yet — what do they want from all this?

What is the end game here, and how are *we* getting in the way of that?"

We all nod, even Andy, who is clearly uncomfortable talking about this. She certainly sounds sobered up too. I push my glasses back up my nose as I think it over.

Detective Hawthorn cocks his head and looks at Jade with curiosity. "Well now, I don't believe we've had the pleasure of meeting yet. What is it you do for a living, if you don't mind me asking? You're not a detective, are you?"

She gives a small quirk of the lips. "Lawyer."

He winces dramatically and smiles back. "Ah. That explains it."

"Yeah yeah, cue the lawyer jokes," she says with a chuckle. "My next question is, can you get access to the hotel's security footage? It's possible they could be seen on there when they left the note."

"Way ahead of you, ma'am—"

Jade cuts him off with a raised hand. "Please, call me Jade."

"Only if you call me Hawthorn."

"Deal," she says with a wink.

Are they seriously flirting? Right now? I try to keep my expression neutral, but my eyes find Ethan's. *Are you seeing this?*

He returns, *I dunno, I'm kind of into it.*

"As I was saying, *Jade,*" he says with a playful grin, "I've already got a request in with the front desk for footage before and around the time of Tamara Jenkins's disappearance. They said they can go over it with me here shortly, so I can have them pull the footage from tonight as well. Can you confirm when you were last up in your room today, so we can get a good timeframe?"

She pinches her chin, thinking. "Umm...it was right after I split with Damien—" she motions towards him, "—so like...just after six? Six thirty maybe?"

"Thank you, that's helpful. But it may take some time for

them to pull up all the footage. I'll let y'all know if we find anything."

I sigh. I suppose it's too much to hope we just happen to catch this person on camera. I doubt the hotel footage will give us any real answers about Tamara either, but we're really in this now.

This is far from over.

<h1 style="text-align:center">15</h1>

I'm awoken with a piercing headache when Jade pulls back the curtains to reveal blinding sunlight spilling into our hotel room.

"Good morning, sunshine!" she says in a sing-songy tone.

"Ewww, what are you doing? Are you a maniac?"

"Babe, it's nine thirty. We gotta go eat breakfast and then come back up and get changed. We're not sleeping the day away."

I curl up tighter in my sheets, covering my head and willing this throbbing pain to leave me and never return. "You're lying. There's no way it's nine thirty," I yell through the sheets. Starting to get my bearings, I add, "Wait, did you even sleep here last night?"

Though I can't see it, I know she's smiling when she happily replies, "Nooope!"

I flip down the comforter away from my face and peer through one squinty eye. "The DJ?"

She winks and walks away without saying a word.

The memories of last night slowly come back to me. I remember us all going back to the Frak Party after handing over the notes to Hawthorn. I was determined not to let some asshole ruin con weekend with my friends, right as I was starting to feel good about myself again and believing everything was going to be okay for me.

I may have been a little too determined though, as I lost count of exactly how many drinks I consumed. In fact, I'm not even sure how I got back up to my room or what time that was.

"If you were with the DJ, how did I get back up here?" I yell to Jade as I unplug my phone from the charger and put on my glasses.

"The guys of course! They said to check your phone." She chuckles.

Texts from Damien and Ethan confirm they were, in fact, the ones who brought me back up here. Including a photo attached of me passed out in this bed...with the word "PENIS" written on my forehead.

I'm going to kill them.

I jump up to look in the mirror and immediately start scrubbing the word off my face. Luckily, it starts to come off fairly easily, so it wasn't done in Sharpie. Real mature, guys.

Thank goodness we always have several packs of makeup wipes on hand for these weekends.

I don't even bother changing out of the leggings and oversized shirt I passed out in. We'll be back up here to change into costume soon enough.

The moment we enter the food hall to meet up with the guys, the distinct aroma of bacon and coffee instantly makes my mouth water.

Three of the restaurants in here serve breakfast food, but Budgie's is by far our favorite. Their food is always delicious, but for breakfast they have an incredible buffet and a made-to-order omelet station that just can't be beat.

We aim for a large table with our plates piled high and stomachs growling. This coffee is the size of my head, but it won't be nearly enough to cure this hangover.

We take our time enjoying our greasy eggs, savory bacon, and perfectly crispy hash browns. I suddenly find myself wondering where all this food would fall on the mouthfeel scale, but I don't dare start that conversation again.

"So, did everyone have a fun night?" Ethan asks the group, staring pointedly at my forehead.

I narrow my eyes at him and give him the finger. I had to use extra foundation to cover up the redness and lingering smudges from his and Damien's prank.

"You know, you should be a whole lot nicer to people who could easily slip something into your drink," I say with a saccharine smile, shifting my eyes down to his coffee.

"Jade, where did you end up last night?" Damien asks, steering the conversation in a new direction.

A sly smile crosses her lips. "None of your business."

"Oooh, okay!" Damien rubs his hands together.

"You were getting pretty cozy with that DJ. Did you go to her room and…you know, blend your tracks together?" Ethan jokes.

Damien adds, "Put a little backspin on that—"

"Okay thank you," she interrupts as we all erupt in laughter. "You are both insufferable."

I shoot her a quick wink. She looks happy, and that's all I ever want for her.

Letting the coffee seep into my soul, I think about everything that happened yesterday and suddenly feel that pit in my stomach again. The reminder that while Tamara is still missing and possibly in real danger, we were just out partying like nothing was wrong, all to prove that we weren't going to be intimidated.

The guilt washes over me, and I suddenly want nothing to do with these eggs anymore.

It's time to get back down to business.

"So!" I clasp my hands together. "What do we think about the notes from last night? Any ideas?" I pull up the photos on my phone, placing it in the center of the table for everyone to see. "In case you didn't notice, the notes were actually two pieces of the same page, ripped from the con guide. And on the map, there are some random numbers scribbled on the side next to Exhibit Hall C."

They all lean forward to get another look.

5

12

10

"Any idea what these numbers could mean?" I ask with a glance around the table.

Jade scrolls back and forth between the pictures of the map side and the handwritten notes. "It's written in different ink. Not sure what that means though."

"Yeah, I noticed that too, like the numbers were already on the other side when the notes were written and ripped out."

We all continue staring at it in silence, like the answers are just going to fly out of my phone. But there's nothing else to see.

Ethan sets down his coffee and scratches the side of his face. "I'm not sure this is much to go on."

"Okay, what else do we know? What are we missing?" Damien asks.

"If we're trying to figure out who took Tamara, then we need to think back to the moment she was taken." Jade steeples her fingers under her chin. Total boss move. "The handler."

"Keep going," I urge. When she gets like this, it's best to let her talk it out. She's always been good at looking at every angle.

"Andy said there was confusion amongst the handlers, and

who was supposed to be assigned to her." She sits up a little straighter. "Her original handler said he was reassigned to someone else at the last minute."

"Right, and the guy in charge said that he *didn't* actually reassign him," I add.

"Exactly. So the person we're looking for had to have inside knowledge of the con handlers and how they get assigned to guests. If they were able to infiltrate the department and reassign an employee elsewhere, they could easily pick up Tamara without raising any alarms."

"Maybe someone with the technical skills to hack into the employee database?" Ethan suggests. "Access the files of workers and volunteers?"

We all look to one another, nodding.

"So, how are we supposed to look into that?" Damien asks. It's a fair question, but simply highlights how little we still have to go on.

"No idea. We also don't know why the exhibit hall had a star on it." Ethan points to the map on my phone. "Maybe there's something else there that we're missing."

"Let's finish up so we can get dressed and start walking the con," I say.

"Wait, Andy has a signing at noon." Ethan checks the time on my phone. "Let's meet back over there. We'll check on him and keep an eye out for anything strange in the exhibit hall."

"Jesus, do you think that's still happening?" Damien asks, looking around the table. "I figured he would've canceled all his events with how upset he's been. Have you talked to him today?"

"Not yet. He's had enough going on, I didn't want to bother him," Ethan says. "Also, there's the *Serafina* panel at three we should check out."

"Oh, that's right. Without Tamara, it's just going to be Mitchell and the showrunners though." I shrug. "That sounds slightly terrible…but could also be very interesting. Especially since we haven't ruled him out as a suspect yet."

We finish the last of our breakfast and stand up to throw our trash away. I get a refill of my enormous coffee, because lord knows I'm going to need it to get through today.

16

"Who's on deck today?" Jade yells from the bathroom.

I ponder for a moment. I brought four costumes for the weekend, and already wore one — my favorite, obviously. The remaining three aren't as epic or as time-consuming to put on, so I could probably get away with doing two today, changing mid-afternoon.

But the one I'm itching to wear is already bringing up old memories.

"I think it's a Daenerys kind of day, don't you?" I try to keep the tremble from my voice, convincing myself I've moved on and that this is just any other costume.

It fit perfectly. After all this time and effort, it fit and it was perfect.

This Daenerys Targaryen outfit was from the beginning of season seven of *Game of Thrones*, when she first arrived at Dragonstone.

Nothing earth-shattering, but it was intricate and beautiful, and I was so proud of it. The class I took to learn how to sew leather —

which ended up taking me forever to get just right — was all worth it.

With a huge grin, I ran out of our bedroom to find Jared in the living room watching Thursday Night Football.

"Ta-da!" I proudly exclaimed with my chin held high and my hands on my hips like a superhero. "What do you think?"

After a moment, he pried his eyes from the TV screen and raised an eyebrow. "Wow, Elspeth. Is this the one you've been working on for two months?" he asked, disappointment hidden cleverly in his words.

My gut clenched, but I forced myself to keep the smile plastered on my face, knowing immediately what he thought about it. "Yeah, don't you like it? I mean, I know it's not much, but I think it turned out pretty good." I twisted the hem between my fingers.

With a shrug, he turned his attention back to the TV. "I was kinda hoping it would be one of the sexy outfits from earlier in the series, you know before the show turned all feminist." He paused and then turned his head towards me. "I know I've seen some of those at the Halloween store. You could've just bought one and saved yourself all that time and money."

And there it was.

As if all my efforts could be reduced to a silly little Halloween costume. As if a Halloween costume could even come close to the level of detail and care something like this required.

He would never understand my passion for this, but maybe that was okay. He didn't have to be involved in every part of my life for me to know that he cared about me. Still, it would've been nice to share this with him, even if he had to fake enthusiasm.

But that was not who he was.

I nodded as I turned back to my room to FaceTime Jade so I could show it off to someone who would actually appreciate it.

That was the last costume I made.

He always found ways to belittle the things I cared about, and for some reason, I let him. I would always ignore or make excuses for his behavior. I couldn't see it at the time, but all those little comments slowly chipped away at my entire being until there was nothing left but this scared, lonely little girl, desperately seeking validation. Seeking the love and affection he showed so much of in the beginning.

Without me even realizing, he had let the mask slip. Slowly, he transformed back into his true self: an absolute dickweed, who never really loved me.

I find myself scratching at my throat again.

I think about the following year when I read the entire *Throne of Glass* series and loved it so much I immediately wanted to start working on a Celaena Sardothien cosplay for the next convention right away. Since they were books, I only had the covers as a reference, so it would require a bit more creativity and work to create, but I was so pumped.

I sketched it out beautifully and fell in love with the design. But as I started coming up with a list of materials and a plan to actually make it happen, I remembered how Jared made me feel about making these "silly Halloween costumes," and I stopped myself. Never following through with actually making it.

Looking in the mirror, I clench my fists at my sides and fight back the tears threatening to fall.

I never want to be that person again.

Jared knew my weaknesses and exploited them to turn me into an "acceptable" person that he could control, knowing the underlying threat that he could leave me and do better would keep me in line.

Jade peeks her head around the corner when I don't answer, pulling me out of my spiraling thoughts. "Babe? Did you hear me?"

I shake my head to clear out the lingering emotions. "What? Did you say something?"

"I said, I think you're right. The Mother of Dragons needs her time in the spotlight."

I shoot her an appreciative smile and nod.

She gets it. She remembers how Jared viewed cosplay and how it made me feel. She knows just how much this one means to me.

As I pull out the pieces for this costume, I fight the anxiety rising to the surface. Pushing through, I'm determined to redefine what this one means to me.

I swap out my worn, black leggings for the nicer pair to start. The next layer, the biggest piece, was the most time-consuming to make: a long sleeve, dark leather dress with two slits down the front starting at the waist. I run my hands along the shallow dragon scales I added to the arms and chest and appreciate the beauty of it.

Over top, I place the final layer, my favorite: a shoulder piece made out of foam in the shape of a V coming to a point between the breasts. More subtle dragon scale texture runs along the outer edges, nearly fading into the dress. Hanging from the shoulders on either side, draping the arms and back, is a flowing cape made of thick, dark brown cotton, that falls all the way down to the floor.

After slipping my feet into the matching dark leather boots, I look in the mirror and take myself in. It's beautiful. Stunning. I can't believe I ever let him convince me otherwise, that this isn't worth appreciation.

I finally see through all the bullshit and admire my work for what it really is, and for the first time in a long time, feel a swell of pride in what I've made.

I top it all off with a long platinum wig braided down the back with strands of loose curls framing my face.

After just a bit of face makeup, I am ready.

Jade is cosplaying as Aegwynn from *World of Warcraft*: the most powerful — and only female — protector of the land of Tirisfal. Her long, blonde wig frames her sharp, beautiful face perfectly. White, flowing, layered robes edged in shining gold lay underneath a periwinkle scaled breastplate, also lined with gold. Around her waist is a deep purple belt, matching the cuffs of her long, flowing sleeves. It's topped off with tall matching shoulder plates that connect at the back and stand up behind her head, holding a white and gold cape, the insides a contrasting emerald green. In her hands is a tall golden staff named Aluneth, that she has rigged to glow a bright purple at the touch of a button.

You don't have to be familiar with the character to appreciate the amount of effort she put into creating it. It's breathtaking.

"Gods, you look incredible," I say, looking her up and down as she gives a courtesy spin.

"As do you." She gives me a wink and turns to assess herself in the mirror one last time, taking a deep breath and smoothing out the fabric down her sides.

"You good?" I ask when I see a flash of hesitation in her eyes.

"I'm good. Promise."

I nod. I've known Jade long enough to guess what she might be thinking right now. She has a few costumes in her arsenal that have garnered some unwanted attention.

Any time she cosplays as a character that is originally drawn or portrayed as fair-skinned, Jade has to deal with the possibility of people saying hurtful things about the color of her skin. Saying she shouldn't be *allowed* to cosplay as certain characters.

She once showed me the type of comments she gets on her social media posts, and it absolutely broke my heart. I'll never be able to fully understand her experiences, but I do my best to be aware and informed of what she deals with so I can support her and take as much of the burden off her as I can.

Jade is one of my favorite people and I will always be protective of her.

So today, I will be by her side, ready to fight off any assholes who dare come at her with anything less than complete and total respect.

I may not always have my own shit together, but you can bet I'll always be ready to stand up for my friends.

17

The convention center is already buzzing, and I wonder how many other people here are in the same boat as us, trying to push through the hangovers so we can do it all over again.

Approaching the exhibit halls, I can't help but laugh when I see Ethan in his Iron Man costume — another con favorite — knowing he's dressed impeccably as Tony Stark underneath, which he will reveal later in the day. He built all the pieces with his 3D printer, rigging it to be removed dramatically at will. He loves to show off the transition into Tony when he's got enough eyes on him.

Ever the show-off, he'll do anything to be like his hero, Tony Stark.

Damien is in a simple Gandalf the Grey getup. Out of our friend group, he is definitely the least obsessed with the whole cosplay aspect of it all, and is here more for the camaraderie part of WyvernFest.

He works long hours at the hospital back home, which does not allow for much free time to build and design intricate costumes. In fact, after a long day, you can usually find him playing video games with Ethan.

Nevertheless, he looks fantastic in his long, dark grey robes, bushy beard and grey wig, topped with a raggedy wizard hat.

When he sees me, his smile is genuine.

He gives me a high five and pulls me in for a side hug. "Looking incredible, as always m'lady. But where are your dragons?"

"Never got around to making them," I say as evenly as possible. "Let's just pretend they're flying around here somewhere."

Damien shoots me a curious look but doesn't push.

As we walk into the exhibit hall, I notice the line for "Comic Book Author Andrew Locke" is pretty decent, with about ten minutes left until his signing officially starts. He rose to fame with The Quantum Protector, which first started blowing up about eight years ago and has only gotten more popular since.

The story follows a goofy, yet brilliant, scientist whose experiment in a cutting-edge quantum physics laboratory goes awry, exposing him to a surge of quantum energy that leaves him with the ability to manipulate quantum particles. Throughout the series, he discovers and perfects his new abilities, including time and space manipulation, as well as creating Quantum Constructs by solidifying quantum particles into tools and weapons on command. Not to mention he has a kick-ass mech suit that allows him to become invisible.

With the recent talk of it being adapted into the next round of Hollywood superhero movies, it seems a lot of people are eager to meet him.

The four of us get in line as Ethan raises the visor on his helmet and pulls out his phone to text Andy and let him know we're here, adding me into a group chat.

ETHAN & ANDY

ETHAN (11:55 A.M.)

hey man we're in line for your signing

see you in a bit

ANDY (11:56 A.M.)

Thanks. See you soon

Andy comes out from behind a black cloth partition a few minutes later to roaring applause. Right away, I notice he looks even worse than yesterday, like he spent the night crawling through the dumpsters.

I feel awful for him. These signings are a big deal for him; it's his time to greet fans and interact with everyone who came out here to support him, especially while the comic is rising in popularity.

In years past, he always looked so happy to be meeting his fans and geeking out during con weekends. Now it looks like this is the last place he wants to be.

"Yikes, do you think he slept at all?" I ask our group.

"Doesn't look like it," Damien answers. "He's going to burn out soon if he doesn't get some rest."

A group of four young men — not in costume — start walking in our direction, and I immediately put up my guard as they stare at Jade and whisper to each other. I take a step forward, ready to go *dracarys* on their asses, when one of them finally yells, "Jade! It's really you! You look amazing!"

All four of them start clapping and fawning over her, asking for pictures, which she, of course, obliges. Sometimes I forget she has so many fans on social media. I don't know how she deals with that level of attention, but she thrives on it.

When she steps back in line with us a few minutes later, I shoot her a quick wink.

The four of us finally get up to the front of the line.

Andy's face softens a little, and he gives us a half-smile that doesn't quite meet his eyes. "Hey, you all look great. Thanks for coming out."

"Hi, Andy. Any updates? You doing okay?" I ask gently.

He takes a few headshots from the stack next to him to sign for us. Not that we are actually here for an autograph, but likely, it's more to keep his hands busy while we talk.

He pauses, scratching the top of his head. "No updates, but…there's a video going around on social media. Have you all seen it yet? I can't bring myself to look at it." He moves on to the next sheet to sign.

Holy shit. I haven't even been online since last night.

"What kind of video?" Ethan whispers.

"Can't really talk about it right now. There's already a lot of people coming around, asking me what I know, and about what happened yesterday. People know we were together before she disappeared, and they think I had something to do with it. Fucking vultures just looking for gossip." He rakes a hand through his shaggy hair and squeezes his eyes shut.

After a moment he adds, "Sorry. I've got to get through this signing. You guys want to meet up later?" He finishes signing the other sheets and hands them to us with shaky hands.

I take the signed sheets. "You got it, Andy, whatever you need."

"We'll be around all day. Just text us," Ethan adds.

Jade gives Andy an assessing look as he shakes hands with Ethan, then we all walk away.

"Wow, I think I need a drink after that," Jade says once we're all out of earshot.

"He looks terrible," Damien says.

I tuck the signed headshots into my bag and pull out my phone as we approach the doors leading into the atrium. I motion everyone to stop at the side of the doors where it's less crowded, desperate to see the video Andy was talking about.

I barely have to search for it though. It's everywhere.

From the video thumbnail staring at me, I already know what this is. It's cell phone footage of the moment she was taken just outside of Melvin's yesterday.

Shit.

My stomach drops, and I question whether I even want to see this. But I already know I will, of course.

"Hey guys?" I call out to get their attention. "You're gonna want to see this."

They gather around me, and I press play.

We all watch in stunned silence as we witness Tamara in a green baseball cap walking out of the diner with Andy, who looks all around before opening the car door for her. He says something to her as she gets in, he closes the door, he waves at her, and the car drives away.

Nothing crazy happens, and it's all over in the span of eight seconds. This was the last moment anyone else saw her, before everything changed.

The thought sends a shiver down my spine.

I play it back and look closely for any moment where the driver is visible. If we can figure out who this person is, we might have a chance at finding her. Unfortunately, there's not much to see.

The video title is "LAST MOMENTS TAMARA JENKINS SEEN AT WYVERNFEST!" with plenty of comments speculating about all the awful things that could have happened to her, and how Andy might be involved. Someone else mentions a missing person's report filed yesterday.

Word is getting out then.

People are piecing it all together, and it won't be long before everyone knows Tamara really has been kidnapped, or abducted, if there's even a difference. If people were suspicious after the cancellations and with the police detectives hanging around, this all but confirms it.

I watch it again and notice their faces as she gets into the car.

I wonder…

That look on Andy's face. The way he gazes at her. I know that look.

Longing.

He said they're friends, but what if he actually has feelings for her? What if he wants to be more than just friends?

"Damn, so everyone knows Andy was with her right before she disappeared," Ethan says, adjusting a piece of his Iron Man suit.

"And if he canceled his signings that would make him look even more suspicious," Damien adds as he runs a hand through his long, grey beard.

I look around the con and feel a weird energy in the air. It's always buzzing, but it's slightly different today, and I'm pretty sure it has everything to do with Tamara Jenkins and this video circulating online.

Cons are notorious for drama and gossip, and now one of the headlining guests is the victim of a mysterious kidnapping.

People here must be eating this up.

In truth, it is the most extraordinary thing to ever happen at WyvernFest, surpassing the year we found out Henry Cavill was in attendance but was in full costume and a mask the whole time, so no one knew it was him until he left and posted his con photos online. It's not uncommon for celebrities to attend conventions dressed in disguise so they can just enjoy the con as a fan, without being recognized and mobbed everywhere they go.

But this is miles beyond that.

People love a true crime story. And if I'm being honest, if it weren't for Andy, and us having that personal connection to Tamara during this whole ordeal, we would probably be guilty of treating it that way too.

But this isn't entertainment, it's real life.

18

"We hanging out in here or what?" Damien asks, looking around the exhibit hall.

From where we're standing, I can see four or five sectioned-off areas to the left, where guests have tables and partitions set up with their names and photos of their work. Next to Andy's area there are a few voice actors with a decent number of people waiting for autographs.

On the other side of the hall there are a few more areas for signings, and in the back corner is a huge backdrop for taking professional photos with the guests. There's no one there right now, but I imagine there are several scheduled for later in the day.

"Let's split off and look around," Ethan says. "I'm with D-man this time."

"Elsie and I will take the other end of the con, maybe check out the events in the room blocks." Jade links her arm with mine.

"Copy that." Ethan gives a mock salute, lowering his visor back into place, and Damien flashes a bright smile before turning away.

Jade and I head through the crowd towards the room blocks, stopping every once in a while to chat with familiar faces or to take photos. We make it all the way to the far end of the convention center when I spot a con worker — I think it might be one of the men I saw yesterday in the ballroom, freaking out about Tamara — walking through a plain-looking door along the wall.

I nudge Jade and whisper, "Hey, I think that's the same guy from yesterday who first said Tamara was missing."

Her eyes are already trained on the door as it closes behind him. She looks back at me with a raised eyebrow, and I nod in return. We casually approach the door, looking around to make sure no one is watching us as I try the handle. But the door is locked.

Shit.

Too bad it's a keypad entry and not an actual key lock, otherwise I could have this thing open in no time. A skill I can thank Ethan for. Since we were left alone a lot as kids, Ethan naturally gravitated towards activities that one might call troublesome. It's not his fault though. Without a strong role model in his life day in and day out, he wasn't really shown how to behave properly.

Honestly, it's a wonder he turned out as well as he did after all the shit we went through.

He got into trouble a few times with the law, but eventually, he got really good at getting away with things. Each time he got smarter and smarter about it, learning the best ways to not get caught. Petty theft from the drug store here and there, breaking into houses he knew were empty just to prove he could. Nothing too harmful.

Once he mastered lock-picking, he taught me and assured me it was a valuable life skill. I actually loved it because it was like solving a puzzle. Learning which tools you needed to open a particular lock, getting just the right angles.

And I love a good puzzle.

I never took to breaking into houses or anything like that, but Ethan and I would play games in our own house and make up elaborate scenarios where we had to break into a bank vault or pick the lock of a serial killer's lair where he was hiding the bodies before he killed his next victim.

Super normal childhood things.

I study the keypad and am struck with an idea.

The numbers that were written down on the other side of the notes.

I punch them in as my stomach flips.

5-1-2-1-0

Beep-beep. Red light.

Dammit! I guess it's too much to ask that it be that easy.

"We really need to get near some of those workers and maybe find out more about the handlers. Let's see if there's another way around." I start to walk away, but Jade puts her hand on my elbow to stop me.

"Hold up. Before we go back, I wanted to ask you something."

"Okay sure, what's up?" I ask curiously.

But she doesn't talk right away. Instead, she pins me with those sharp purple eyes so intense I can barely move.

All around us the hallway is busy and loud, but the silence between us is deafening. My instinct is to crack a joke to break the tension, but the look in her eye stops me. Like I'm under a spell.

She still has her hand on my arm when she asks, "What are we really doing?"

"What do you mean?"

"I think you know," she says evenly. "Look, I've been playing along here, but I'm growing a little tired of this, to be honest."

Heat creeps up my neck under her scrutiny. The truth beneath her words I'm scared to hear.

"Tired of me?" I ask softly.

"Not you, *this*. What is going on? Why are we really doing this?"

When I don't answer, she doesn't back down.

"What aren't you telling me?"

"Nothing!" I shout. "I'm fine!"

"Don't give me that shit." She drops her hands to her sides. "You keep saying *'I'm fine, I'm fine,'* but you're not. I know you. Why won't you talk to me?"

I jerk my head to the side, unable to look at her. Not when the back of my eyes are starting to burn with the threat of tears. I fiddle with the hem of my costume and bounce my leg. Trying to push the rising emotions back down where they belong.

"Elsie—"

"I don't...want to talk about this. Not here." There are too many people around, and I'm not prepared for this conversation. I'm just going to end up ruining her weekend.

We were supposed to be having fun, not thinking about Jared and everything he put me through. Although, I've managed to pull them all into an even worse situation, but still. The last thing I want is to continue to be a burden to my friends.

She pulls me through a nearby set of doors leading out to the convention center courtyard. The blast of humidity slaps me in the face as she leads us to a secluded stone bench next to rows of shrubs with fragrant, purple flowers.

Sitting us down and laying her golden staff on the ground in front of her, she looks me in the eye, unwavering. "So we're just going to keep on investigating clues for a missing person, putting ourselves in harm's way after being threatened, like it's just some everyday thing we do? Really?"

Dammit, she sees everything.

"Why is this so important to you?"

"I just...I need to do this, okay? I need to see this through." I feel my heart beating faster, my hand raising to scratch my throat. She sees that too.

"Why?" she presses.

"Please," I beg, wiping my sweaty palms on my legs. "Please, just stop." I squeeze my eyes shut, knowing she won't let this go. I feel like I'm spinning.

She grabs my hand. "*Why?*"

Something inside me snaps.

"Because every time I stop for too long and think about what he did to me..." I choke on a sob. I can't say it.

This is what I've been trying to avoid.

I don't want to bring her down. I don't want to put this on anyone else.

But Jade is looking at me with understanding and compassion, waiting for me to say whatever it is I need to say. She won't give up until I tell her the truth.

I take a moment to compose myself, forcing a deep breath. Reminding myself I'm safe with her.

"Because," I continue, slowly, "the thoughts I have when I stop for too long...when I'm alone, and I really sit and think about everything...those thoughts scare the shit out of me." I clasp a hand over my mouth to try and stop the sobs, but it's no use. The floodgates are opening and there's no stopping it now.

"Did he lay a hand on you? I swear to God I will 100 percent risk jail time to go find him and put him in the dirt."

I huff a small chuckle. She would, too. She's that ride or die friend who would do anything for me, just like I would for her.

"No, it's not that. He didn't touch me." I pause, trying to control my breaths. "It was like...mind games, you know? He was so deep inside my head, I don't even know how it happened, but I became so dependent on him, so focused on keeping him happy so he would stay."

I squeeze my eyes shut, willing myself to keep going. "So when it ended...it felt like it was all my fault. That it was because of me, that I wasn't enough...and..." I pause, wondering if there's any way out of saying what comes next, but come up empty. "And I started thinking maybe everyone would just be better off without me."

There, I said it.

I finally look up at her, and her eyes are swimming with tears. I've known Jade most of my life and can count on one hand the number of times I've ever seen her cry, and each time is like a knife to my heart.

Jade pulls me in tightly for a hug while I sob on her shoulder. I know she's hurt that I didn't open up to her about this sooner, but I never really let *anyone* know just how dark my thoughts had become.

Not even Ethan.

Not even my therapist, really. Putting those theater classes to good use, I knew exactly how to act and what to say to her to avoid setting off any alarms. Though it was likely the fact that I downplayed everything so much that she was hesitant to prescribe any kind of medication.

I feel like I've come a long way and have made progress since those darker moments, but ever since I got to WyvernFest, I've been terrified of those thoughts returning. Every time that wave of guilt washes over me for being a burden, for feeling like I'm ruining their weekend, it brings me back to that dark place.

Selfishly, once everything happened with Tamara, it actually seemed like the perfect thing to keep my mind busy and to have a goal to focus on.

"Why wouldn't you tell me?" she asks softly in my ear. "Why wouldn't you let me know how bad it was?"

"I didn't want to bother you with my...drama." I sniff. "That didn't seem fair to you."

"What the hell are you talking about?" She pulls away but keeps her hands on my shoulders. "This isn't *drama*, this is your life. It's your well-being. Shit, I wouldn't have said half the things I did if I knew it wasn't just heartbreak. After all this time, how could you possibly think you would be bothering me?

I could've helped you, I could've been there for you. I just... wanted you to talk to me."

"But—"

"No. No buts. You are not a burden to me. You are my best friend."

I wipe my face with the back of my hand.

I don't deserve to have a friend like her, but she makes me want to try.

"Okay. You're right."

She takes my hands in hers. "None of it was your fault. You know that, right?"

I just nod. I know it in the logical sense, but I still can't seem to shake the guilt of it all. That I wasn't strong enough to recognize his manipulation. That I knew something was wrong with us but couldn't bring myself to walk away from it, because the idea of being alone felt worse to me than anything else.

That even towards the end I still thought he would change if I just tried a little harder.

"Elsie. I see you nodding, but I'm going to say it again. None of that...was your fault. Any guilt you feel about what he put you through, and how you dealt with it, you need to let that shit go. And that includes how you think you treated us."

I know she means Damien especially but doesn't say it. She doesn't have to.

Dammit, she knows me so well.

I look into her eyes and see nothing but love. In this moment, it's as if I can feel a physical weight lifting off my shoulders, and I let out a long breath.

I should've known she wouldn't let me dance around the real issue. And I love her so much for it.

So I choose to believe her.

Even if I don't fully believe in myself just yet, I do believe in her.

So the dam inside me bursts open yet again, but these tears

hold something else in them. Love for my best friend, and hope that one day I will be okay. That I can believe I'm worthy of love and that my presence and my needs are not a burden to those around me after all.

I cover my face and lay my head on her shoulder until the tears run dry.

19

I'm trying to compose myself enough to stand again when my phone buzzes, and I slip it out of my back pocket. I assume it's the guys asking where we are to meet back up.

Instead, the text on my screen stops me dead in my tracks.

JARED (12:47 P.M.)

Can we talk?

My heart hammers in my chest.

What the actual fuck?

As if talking about him out loud summoned his very presence.

Like a curse.

Jade senses my shift and says, "Hey, you okay? What is it?"

I'm still staring at my screen. Unable to form any coherent thoughts.

Another text.

JARED (12:48 P.M.)

Something happened and I want you to hear it
from me. You're at the convention, right?

Can I come see you?

What is he doing?

He wouldn't actually come here, would he?

I've only spoken to him a handful of times since our wedding day. Mostly with him just trying to convince me that the cheating was a one-time thing brought on by too much stress, and that I was overreacting. Or playing the victim to make me feel guilty for "leaving him at the altar" and embarrassing him in front of all his friends and family. In front of his father's rich friends.

He also made a few grand gestures, hoping that, with enough persistence, I would cave and come back to him, playing on my fears of being alone.

It was too late though. I finally saw through all his bullshit and stopped lying to myself about the kind of man he was. But you can't just walk away from years of being with someone you thought you'd spend the rest of your life with and be completely unaffected. At least I can't.

I should've blocked his number, but after about three weeks of nonstop calls and messages, he finally gave up, and I haven't heard from him since.

Until now.

My blood is boiling, and I suddenly want to hit something. But then I realize…rage is a far cry from anxiety or fear. It's not quite indifference yet, but it's progress.

I remind myself that he can't hurt me anymore. And that I'm not obligated to respond to him.

I let loose another long breath, and with it, I feel like I'm releasing *him*. Like I'm giving myself permission to truly start moving on.

"Els?" Jade nudges me after I don't respond.

I open my eyes, click off my phone screen and shove it back in my pocket with a smile. "It's nobody."

"Oh, you're going out tonight?" I asked before I thought better of it. That familiar dread seeped into my stomach when I saw a muscle in his jaw tick. "It's fine, I just…I didn't know."

"Are you being serious right now? I just took you out for a nice dinner, and now you're trying to make me feel bad?" He scoffed and turned to look out the windshield, rain droplets gently pelting the glass.

I closed my eyes and prepared myself for what would come next, and how I could limit the damage.

"It's not enough that I took you to an expensive restaurant, and got you that damn book you've been whining about for months? Do you know how long it took me to find that? I swear nothing is ever good enough, no matter how hard I try. I must be a terrible fiancé," he said, throwing his hands in the air.

I squeezed the book in my lap. "I'm sorry, I didn't mean to seem ungrateful. I had a wonderful night, and really, I love the book. Thank you, honey." I leaned in for a kiss, and when he refused to turn his head, I got his cheek.

I sat back in my seat to unbuckle and heard the clear click of the doors unlocking, but he didn't move to get out or turn off the car.

Oh, so he's not even coming in.

I opened the car door and started to step out. "I'll see you when you get back. I love you."

I closed the door, and he sped off without another word.

Walking the remaining steps towards our enormous, empty house, with only the cool raindrops to keep me company, I held tight to the gift he'd given me. The one I had to write down several times over the past few months, because you couldn't be subtle with him.

As soon as I stepped inside and flicked on the lights, my phone rang with Jade's ringtone. "Hey!" I plastered on a fake smile so she wouldn't hear the sadness in my voice.

"Hey, babe. Happy birthday!" she yelled into the phone. "I know I texted you earlier but wanted to call as soon as I got done with work. Sorry it's been so crazy today!"

"Thanks! Just got back home from dinner." *Alone.*

"Nice! Well I'll leave you both to it. Just wanted to call and officially wish you a happy 2-5 and make sure you were still up for our girl's weekend? I need to take you out and spoil you. Unless you're too busy with wedding stuff."

I smiled, wishing so badly I could ask her to come over right now, but that would've required explaining that Jared was out with his buddies instead of home with me. On my birthday. "It's still on, I wouldn't miss it."

"Awesome. Love you. Bye, Elsie."

"I love you too. Bye."

With the wedding only a few months away, I convinced myself that he was just stressed and needed to relax. We did have a wonderful date tonight, and while we were out in public, it almost felt like it did in the beginning. He was doting and affectionate. The way he looked at me, held my hand, and kissed me deeply reminded me just how much I loved him. It sparked hope in me that he really did love me just as much, and that things would get better after the wedding.

He was just…stressed.

I would work harder at not setting him off, and things would be good again. I just had to remind myself that our love was enough, and that I had everything I ever wanted, and should be grateful to be so lucky.

I pulled out my phone, ready to text Ethan per our birthday tradition of messaging each other at our exact birth times.

The Con

ETHAN (9:32 P.M.)

happy birthday big sis!

ME (9:38 P.M.)

happy birthday little bro!

ETHAN (9:38 P.M.)

ME (9:39 P.M.)

thanks for brunch this morning, it was the highlight of my day!

and thanks again for the necklace. It's perfect

ETHAN (9:40 P.M.)

nothing but the best for my second favorite pisces

Love you Els

ME (9:41 P.M.)

Love you E ♥

Jade and I walk back through the gallery towards the exhibit halls where we last left the guys. Passing by the open door to the Alpha room, I notice it's hosting a workshop of some kind. Tables are set up all around the room with about thirty people filling the space. On the tables are supplies and materials ready for building some kind of handheld contraption, the prototype displayed in the center of the room. Damn that looks cool. I want one.

I walk up to the schedule posted just outside the door to see what it is.

```
10a – 12p : Improv Workshop
1p – 3p : Building a Worlogog
4p – 6p : Writing for Comics 101
6p – 7p : Nerd-Central Podcast Live
8p – 11p : Coloring (18+)
```

"Oh man, we're missing out on building a Worlogog!" I whine, looking back at Jade, who is smiling and shaking her head. I'm second-guessing this decision to investigate rather than taking advantage of all the fun WyvernFest has to offer. Maybe next year.

Focus.

Up ahead, we spot the guys. Gandalf Damien's eyebrows draw together the moment he sees me, no doubt noticing my red, puffy eyes. I knew I should've gone back upstairs to reapply my makeup.

"Okay, what's the word? Find anything?" I ask once we join them outside the exhibit halls, pretending like nothing just happened.

"Not much, except we're missing the massive *Mario Kart* tournament going on in B right now." Ethan jabs a metal finger behind him.

Damien rolls his eyes. "The other guests signing in C had no connection to Andy or Tamara. We did a quick lap around the vendor booths in A, but nothing out of the ordinary there, either. What about you?" he adds with a grin under that ridiculous mustache and beard, his brown eyes meeting mine.

I tuck a strand of platinum Targaryen hair behind my ear. "We followed a con worker, thinking maybe he could lead us to some clue about the handlers, but the door was locked."

"Never stopped you before, sis." Ethan chuckles.

"I'm not sure what else we're supposed to be doing," I admit.

Everyone just shrugs.

Great. Another dead end.

"We can only do so much, right, babe?" Jade shoots me a wink. "We've got some time to kill before the *Serafina* panel. What do you all want to do in the meantime?"

"Let's see, there's a Pokémon meetup in one of the ballrooms. Or..." Damien snaps his fingers. "I just remembered. That guy from *Sailor Moon* is hosting an event in Gamma soon, if anyone is interested."

"Maybe," I reply. "I kinda want to hit up the vendor booths though. See what they're selling."

Ethan nods. "I actually saw some stuff in there I want to go back for. I'll come with you."

"Jade, do you want to join me?" Damien asks.

Of our various friend group dynamics, Damien and Jade are the least likely to hang out just the two of them. Not that they haven't, of course. They paired up yesterday when we were looking for evidence, but it was at Ethan's urging due to their Star Wars costumes. They just seem to have the least in common out of all of us.

But one thing they do share is a love for anime.

"Hell yeah, let's go!"

"Are you changing costumes later?" I ask Jade.

She quirks her mouth to the side. "Nah, I'll probably go post up in a bit and get some more photos taken of Aegwynn."

Photos.

That's right, there are photographers all over this place. I tuck the idea away for later.

Jade adds, "And remember Kat's party is tonight, and we'll need to dress up for that too."

"True! Sexy themed, right?"

"You know it!"

I look to both of them. "Meet back here for the panel at three o'clock then?"

They both nod and excitedly head off towards the meeting

rooms with a quick wave in our direction. I can't help but smile as I watch them walk away. I would love for the two of them to become closer.

Friend groups can definitely get tricky. Jade and Ethan have their own unique dynamic from being platonic friends for two decades — and over the years, have expressed many times that they would never hook up because they're too much like siblings at this point, and it would be too weird. I agree.

Damien and Ethan are about as close as two dude bros can be. They are supportive of each other and lift each other up like family. I've even caught them on a few occasions casually and tenderly ending their gaming sessions with, "I love you, man."

It's pretty adorable, especially considering Ethan didn't have any good friends of his own growing up.

Then there's Damien and...me. I'm not quite sure what the hell we are anymore. We've never crossed that line into being romantic, and with how I treated him this past year I wouldn't be surprised if it's completely off the table for him.

Which is fair.

Even if he insists he doesn't harbor any ill feelings towards me.

I wouldn't trade our friendship for anything, but I'd be lying if I said I never thought about being more. They say sometimes best friends make the best couples, but what if that wasn't true for us, and in the process of changing our relationship we ended up ruining it? I'm not sure how he feels about me now, but I wouldn't want to risk what we have.

Not to mention that I'm not even his type.

I'm not the one people choose.

20

Once we're done here at the vendor booths, I want to find a photographer and see if they might have any photos from yesterday at the time of the abduction. I'm not even sure what we'd be looking for, but it couldn't hurt to try.

If anyone from the hotel or the con was involved in Tamara's disappearance, then maybe someone was acting suspicious around that time yesterday.

At least it's an idea, and we're kind of running out of options.

Off to the side of the hall I see someone cosplaying at Din Djarin, a.k.a. the Mandalorian, posing for photos with other attendees.

I nudge Ethan's side to make sure he sees him.

His costume has unbelievable attention to detail and top-notch craftsmanship. Shining armor plates cover his shoulders, chest, thighs, and forearms. The pieces sit upon a black cloth bodysuit, topped with a matching billowing cape. The helmet is pristine and looks like it could be the real Hollywood prop from the show. Leather holsters adorn his waist and cross in front of his chest. In his arms, is an extremely lifelike Grogu.

I can't help myself and *must* have a picture.

We move up closer to him and wait for an opening.

When he's free, I blurt out, "Hey, man, you look amazing! Mind if we get a photo with you? Is now a good time?"

He nods and I hand off my phone to Ethan. He poses with me for a few pictures, then Ethan wants a turn.

Mando and Iron Man together make quite the peculiar pair, but I'm here for it. They're the same height and everything, so they almost look like they could go together with their shining metal armor.

When I'm done snapping their photos, Ethan presses the button that lifts up the visor of his helmet, turning to Mando. "Did you make all this yourself?"

"Yeah, all the armor plates are 3D printed," Mando says, and I notice his voice is going through some sort of modulator to sound more mechanical and projected, like it is in the show.

"Hell yeah," Ethan replies. "This is all 3D printed too." He motions down at himself. "What paint did you use to make it shine like that?"

"Glossed black spray paint, then brushed with graphite powder."

"Shit, that's incredible. You made the mask too, I assume?" Ethan asks, completely fanboying over him right now.

"Yeah, the mask is a hybrid of foam and plastic. Took forever though."

"I bet."

"It's fantastic, I love it!" I say. "Hey, thanks so much for the photos, we'll see you around!"

I always try to be respectful of other people's time and not hold them up too long. Some people love to stay and chat and become fast friends, while others would rather just take a few pics and be on their way. Either way is totally fine, and I try to give everyone the choice of hanging around or exiting the interaction without letting it become awkward. Since I have plenty of experience in that department.

There are a lot of unofficial etiquette rules for cosplayers, and it takes some practice to be able to read others and how they want to interact. The most important rule though, is a popular mantra you'll hear a lot: "Cosplay is not consent." Some people believe that if you're dressed a certain way it gives them permission to touch you or act however they want. Mostly creeps looking to fulfill some gross fantasy, believing they're entitled to take advantage under the guise of *hey, we're all just having fun here*. Those people are the worst, and word will get around fast about people like that.

There are also things that should just be common sense, like not taking pictures of someone in the bathroom or bothering them while they're eating or trying to take a break.

"Aren't you getting a little tired of being in that thing?" I ask Ethan. I know the whole Iron Man getup is pretty heavy, and he's probably sweating bullets under there.

"Yeah, I'll probably change in a little bit. You know the drill. I've got to have my transformation first."

"Yeah yeah, you big show-off."

"Hey, you know how long it took me to make this thing. I'm not wasting an opportunity."

I grab him by the elbow and lead him back towards the vendor booths. "Speaking of wasting an opportunity, are you going to tell me what's going on with you and Kat?"

He levels me with a bored expression. "Are you going to tell me what's going on with you and Damien?"

I avert my gaze and purse my lips.

"That's what I thought," he replies with an arrogant smirk before lowering his visor.

"Jackass," I mutter under my breath, and squeeze his arm a little tighter.

As we near the back of the hall, I spot a photographer I recognize.

I drop Ethan's arm. "I'll catch up in a bit, okay?"

He nods in return.

"Hey, Greg!" I say as I approach the photographer.

"Oh hey there, Elsie. Long time no see!"

"I know, right? How have you been?"

"Can't complain. Keeping busy with the usual cons."

"That's awesome, I've missed seeing you around! Hey, I have a quick question for you. Were you here taking photos yesterday, earlier in the day?" I cross my arms, hoping I sound casual enough.

"Yeah, I was out on the floor all day. Why, what's up?" he asks curiously.

I wave a hand. "Nothing really. Just wondering if...you saw anything unusual?" I raise an eyebrow, hoping I don't have to spill too much about what we're actually doing.

"Ha! Unusual you say? You're going to have to be a little more specific than that. Yesterday I saw a Deadpool-Minion crossover, a person dressed as a giant magical tree, and a group of muscled men dressed in skimpy *My Little Pony* costumes, all before I had lunch."

I snort. "Okay, fair enough. I guess I mean, unusual for the con? If that makes any sense?"

He narrows his eyes. "What exactly are you looking for?"

"You know what, never mind, I shouldn't have asked—"

"Does it have to do with Tamara?" His voice is low as he looks around.

"Yes. Did you see anything? We were hoping maybe we could catch someone doing something suspicious. Not that we're looking for gossip or anything. We legit want to help if we can."

"I'm sorry, I don't remember seeing anything like that. I was scheduled to take photos of her with fans yesterday at the signing before…" He shakes his head.

"Yeah. Okay. Thanks anyway."

"But hey, I'll tell you what, when I unload my photos tonight, I'll take a good look back at yesterday's stuff and let you know if I see anything of interest. I want to help too, if I can." He looks away for a second and takes a breath. "She's one of the good ones, you know?"

"Thanks, Greg. You still have my number?" I ask.

"Yep, I'll let you know if I find anything."

"It was good to see you, Greg."

"You too. Take care."

I find Ethan perusing a booth showcasing a new tabletop game with intricate, painted miniatures.

"Hey, I'm going to head upstairs to change, I'll meet you all at the panel?"

"Do you want me to come with you?"

"Nah, I'm fine. I'll be quick."

"Okay. Try to stay out of trouble," he says playfully with a jab to my arm.

"You too."

Taking the nearby escalator up to the skybridge to avoid having to walk outside, I nervously look over my shoulder to make sure I'm not being followed or watched.

Once I'm on the hotel side, I step into the elevator and press five repeatedly, as if that will make the doors close any faster. I can't help my foot tapping as I watch the numbers rise alongside my anxiety. Once the doors open again, I sprint to my room and quickly rush inside, closing the latch to lock myself in, so I can finally let out a breath.

In the deafening silence, I realize I haven't actually had a moment alone since I got here — minus being passed out in my bed last night.

I'm grateful that Jade made me open up to her about everything I've been going through. I thought unloading all that would be a burden, when I should've known she would want me to be honest and confide in her.

That's the thing about true friends: they would gladly shoulder any burden if it means you can feel lighter. If it can ease your pain, even a little, even for a moment.

My friends are more of a family to me than my own parents ever could be.

I start to change out of my Daenerys costume and get the pieces ready for my second one of the day, Yennefer of Vengerberg from *The Witcher*.

Some of my favorite costumes have ended up being the simpler ones. For me personally, it means I can hyperfocus on details and get every piece just right. The big, flashy, elaborate costumes are badass, but they can take forever, and I feel like I have to sacrifice a little quality when the scale gets too big. Those are the ones I prefer to draw, but not actually make.

I love portraying characters I really connect with, and those characters tend to be the more relatable, ordinary people, who face extraordinary odds to become the best version of themselves they can be.

I take off my pants, along with the last of the costume pieces and wig, allowing myself a moment to rest and reset. Lying back on the plush hotel bed, I close my eyes and take deep breaths, reminding myself that my thoughts are just that. Thoughts I can observe and acknowledge, then let go. They don't control me.

After a few blissful moments, I start to get a little too comfortable and force myself to get back up before I fall asleep. It's time to face the rest of this day.

I start by stepping into the tight leather pants. Next is the white button-down shirt, covered by a corseted, black leather top with fur covering the shoulders and pearl buttons running down the front. A thin brown belt cinches my waist.

I put on the leather arm bands and gauntlets, matching thigh-high boots, and adorn my neck with a glowing blue star hanging from a black choker necklace. A wavy, black wig parted down the middle flows down my shoulders and face, partially obscuring my bright purple eyes. Having several different color prescription contacts gets pretty expensive. I really should get LASIK one of these days. Of course, that would require actual money and a steady job.

I first made this outfit based off the video game, before it was made into a show. I hadn't learned how to sew leather at this point either, so I exchanged services with Kat that year. She sewed my leather pieces together, and I created a full-color illustration for her upcoming project. It was a win-win partnership.

I really should see if she wants to work on something again soon.

With that thought, hope blooms within me about my future. Like a seed planted in my soul, begging to be nurtured. Making plans with friends, planning out future costumes and conventions is all I want right now.

I can't believe I ever denied this part of myself.

Never again.

21

We all meet back up outside the ballroom for the *Serafina* panel just before three. Jade is the only one still in the same costume she was wearing this morning.

While I was getting dressed, Ethan flawlessly pulled off his transformation into Tony Stark in a fitted tuxedo, and is now sipping a glass of whiskey. At some point, Damien must have gone upstairs to stash the Iron Man gear and to change into a suit as well, ditching the Gandalf attire.

Complete with aviator sunglasses and an earpiece, he is now acting as Tony Stark's bodyguard. They love this bit, and people eat it up year after year.

"Better?" I motion to Ethan's tuxedo as he takes a sip of his drink.

"So much better. That thing feels like it gets heavier every year." He turns to Jade. "You know, J, it's not too late to go change into something skimpy and be my arm candy."

"In your dreams," Jade replies with a laugh.

Ethan clutches his chest. "How'd you know?"

A large group of Stormtroopers approaches, presumably

members of the 501st Legion. People step back and make way for them to march through the hallway. Off to the side is a man holding the hand of a happy little girl, likely his daughter, who is dressed as Princess Leia in a flowing white robe and cinnamon bun pigtails.

My heart squeezes at the sight of them smiling and waving at the Stormtroopers.

***

"Graham Crackers! Come on, the movie is starting!" he yelled across the house as Ethan and I barreled down the stairs in our matching pajamas.

Dad had *The Empire Strikes Back* all queued up and ready for part two of our movie night. We were only six years old, and we had just finished *A New Hope* about ten minutes earlier. Being so young, most of the actual story went right over our heads, but we were already in love with the characters, the creatures, and all the cool action scenes.

Plus, Dad was letting us stay up super late because he claimed *Empire* was the best — he wasn't wrong — and we had to keep the night going. After brushing our teeth, of course.

Mom would be furious that he let us stay up so late, but he didn't seem to care.

Star Wars ended up having such an effect on us that Ethan and I wanted to dress up for Halloween as Luke and Leia that year. Mom and Dad bought us basic costume sets from the store, which were perfectly fine, but we decided to make some modifications to make them even better.

It was the first time we worked on any type of costumes, and we quickly became obsessed. Several other costumes down the road would also be the product of those special nights with Dad.

We looked forward to movie night every single week. It was the one time it felt like we could really bond with him. He loved to share his love of movies and video games with us, and we loved to be included in something he was so passionate about.

For the next two years, no matter what happened at school or with friends that week, we had Friday nights with Dad to look forward to. The movies we watched and the games we played would ultimately shape who I grew up to be.

And so, too, would the fact that he had been having an affair that entire time, and once he finally left us, Friday nights became a whole lot quieter.

"Alright, we ready?" Ethan asks, bringing me back to the present.

I rub my chest to clear out the lingering ache from the memory. "Let's go watch this train wreck," I say as we head into the ballroom.

Damien gently nudges a few people out of Ethan's way. "Excuse me, ma'am, excuse me. Make way, please." He turns to Ethan with a finger on his earpiece. "Sir, right this way."

Shaking my head, I try not to focus too much on how good Damien looks in that suit.

But then something stops me.

Bodyguard.

Ethan and I had talked about it yesterday, wondering why Tamara didn't have a bodyguard or any security with her this weekend. Something about that still bothers me. We need to remember to ask Andy about it.

For now, I have my sights set on someone else: Mitchell Brantley.

The panel is going on as planned, but without Tamara, leaving just Mitchell — the lesser-beloved costar of *Serafina* — and the two showrunners, to discuss the show and answer fan questions. Even without Tamara, I don't want to miss this.

I will consume all things related to Princess Serafina for as long as I'm living and breathing.

Afterward, Mitchell will be heading over to do his signing, and that's where we're going to have a little chat.

An average-looking man steps out on the stage and takes the microphone. "Hey, friends, how we doing today?"

He's greeted with applause, and I suddenly pray we don't have to suffer through another half hour of riffing like yesterday.

"Thank you all for coming to the *Serafina* panel. I have a few quick announcements before we kick this thing off. First and foremost, we are all, of course, shocked at the news of Tamara Jenkins's disappearance, and we are praying for her safe and speedy return. On that note, however, our guests today will not be answering any questions about the incident, or about anything related to Tamara Jenkins outside of her character in the show."

The crowd mumbles a little, but no one outright protests. I would hope not. It would be in very bad taste to discuss it in this setting with everything going on.

"Now that that's all out of the way, let's welcome our guest today. You know him as Hardy, please give a warm welcome to Mitchell Brantley!"

Mitchell walks out on the stage towards the furthest seat at a table adorned with his nameplate, to appreciable applause and cheers. His greased-back, dark brown hair matches his expensive, shiny shoes, and his wave and smile are so fake and performative that it borders on creepy.

On camera, he seems fairly normal, but in real life, he kinda sucks.

"Do we really think he's involved with Tamara's disappearance?" I ask Jade beside me as the crowd claps for him, and they continue to introduce the showrunners.

"Meh...it's possible. Just because he's slimy doesn't mean

he's guilty of anything though. Remember it all comes down to motive, means, and opportunity."

"True," I reply.

I think through possible motives. It could be that he's jealous of her fame and attention from the show, which he does not get nearly as much of. Or maybe the rumors are true, and they *were* dating and she broke it off with him and his fragile ego couldn't handle it, so he lashed out. It could be any number of reasons.

What we need right now is more information, and I'm really looking forward to making Mitchell squirm.

It starts out as a fairly uninspiring and boring panel. Not surprising since Mitchell has about as much personality and charisma as a Sarlacc. As if to prove my point, he says, "...as the old saying goes, the *'Hardy'* wants what it wants, am I right?"

He flashes his too-white teeth, as most of the audience chuckles politely.

After about twenty minutes of PR bullshit, and Mitchell trying to convince everyone he's actually more important than he really is, they open the floor to questions.

The first fan approaches the microphone, an older woman with curly blonde hair. "Hi, this question is for Mitchell. What's your favorite episode of *Serafina*, and why?"

Ah yes, your standard "favorite episode" question. This should be good. No doubt it's whichever one featured him the most.

Mitchell leans forward. "What's your name, sweetheart?"

"Jessica," she answers with a beaming smile.

"Pleasure to meet you, Jessica. Let's see, my favorite episode? That's a tough question, there are so many good ones. I guess I'd have to say the one where Hardy and Serafina meet up in Lorg to find the Obsidian Conjuring Stone."

Called it. Granted, it was a great episode, but that was definitely one of the more Hardy-centric episodes. He goes on to talk more about himself while I look over at Ethan and Damien, who are not paying much attention either and just talking about lord knows what.

Jade leans over and whispers, "Yeah, this dude definitely sucks."

"Agreed."

After Mitchell finishes talking about how great he was in that episode, a young woman, probably around twenty years old, steps up to the mic with a look of concern on her face.

"Hi, my name is Amanda. My question is about…the rumors that Tamara's character is being written out, or at least going to be written in a way that would let Mitchell's character play a more equal role. Is there any truth to that?"

Excellent question, Amanda.

I would be pissed to no end if they minimized Princess Serafina's role *in her own show* and elevated Mitchell's character, Hardy, to be as much of a major character as she is. The whole story is supposed to revolve around her own journey of self-discovery and personal triumph, and not tying her self-worth to some man she is romantically involved with.

Mitchell squirms a little in his chair, no doubt trying to figure out how to spin this to make himself look good, but graciously, one of the showrunners speaks up first.

"There is no truth to that rumor. Tamara Jenkins is, and will always be, the heartbeat of *Serafina*. Without her, there would be no show, and we're not about to change that now."

Without her, there would be no show.

Ouch. The flash of anger in Mitchell's face is only evident for a split second though, before he flips the switch back to his slimy public persona, with a huge flashy grin and soft chuckle. He nods, as if he actually agrees with that sentiment, but I see right through it.

It's clear he hates being in Tamara's shadow, and it makes

me wonder just how far a person like that would go to change his circumstances.

They go on to talk about storylines of the show and how the next season should line up more with the third book, which makes me happy. Maybe they are finally listening to fans and remember why it became so popular in the first place. I've always said, do not piss off the fans that helped make something a success.

The panel wraps up just before four o'clock, and Mitchell is ushered away towards the signing booths in Exhibit Hall C.

Showtime.

22

The four of us stand in Mitchell's line, looking at his booth display featuring action photos of him starring in *Serafina*, as well as a few of his previous, unsuccessful TV shows.

I silently practice what I want to say to him once I get up there. We'll need to be quick and efficient, because if he catches wind of what we're trying to do, he could alert his handlers and make us leave. Asking him where he was at the time of Tamara's disappearance will be too obvious, but I have a feeling Mitchell is the type of guy that will talk about himself all day if you let him.

I make it to the front of the line and step up to his table. Up close, his smarmy smile is even worse, and I have the sudden urge to slap him across his stupid face. Instead, I plaster on my own fake smile and step into the role of "Mitchell Brantley's Biggest Fan."

Worst cosplay ever, by the way.

"Omigosh! It's really you!" I stick out my hand.

"Hey hey. Always nice to meet a fan." He shakes my hand quickly and takes a headshot off the stack in front of him, a Sharpie in his other hand. "What's your name, sweetheart?"

I try to do my best impression of a swooning fangirl and put my hand over my heart as if trying to calm myself down. "It's Elsie. E-L-S-I-E. Can I just say how excited I am to meet you?" I hear a snort from behind me and try to ignore my friends as I act my ass off.

"Pleasure is all mine, Elsie."

"Have you been having a good weekend so far? Been to any other events?" I twirl Yennefer's black hair in my fingers.

"Oh, it's been great. Met some great people and ate some great food."

Great. Is that all this guy knows how to say? That's all I get?

"Hey, thanks for coming out, Elsie." He hands me his signed headshot and essentially dismisses me with that slimy grin.

Shit.

I blew it.

Maybe Jade will have better luck. Who am I kidding, of course she will. She could charm a man on his deathbed with her powers of seduction.

I stand off to the side, pretending to look at my phone while I try to listen in on their conversation. After a moment, I peek up and find Jade leaning over his table, whispering something in his ear while he laughs...her cleavage mere inches from his face.

My wide eyes snap to Ethan and Damien, still in line, who are equally as impressed as I am.

What the fuck? I think towards Ethan.

He simply shrugs.

Damn she's good.

Mitchell pulls a small piece of paper from his jacket pocket and writes something down, but from here, I can't quite tell what it is. Jade takes the paper and her signed headshot and gives him a flirtatious wave before turning and walking away, majestic cape billowing behind her. Mitchell watches her leave and shakes his head, smiling.

She links my arm in hers and walks me towards the entrance of the hall.

"What the hell was that?" I ask with a laugh.

She flips the paper between her index and middle finger to reveal a phone number and the words "Call Me" scribbled on it. "Just a little harmless seduction. In case we still need more information later."

"Gross. Did Mitchell say anything? Did you find out where he was yesterday?"

"I tried to ask, but he wouldn't stop staring at my tits, so I decided to play that card instead," she says, stuffing the paper inside her breastplate for safekeeping.

"Okay, not bad. They are nice tits. Hopefully the guys can find something out. Mitchell really didn't seem interested in chatting with me." What else is new? I'm just the frumpy, boring sidekick. Jade is clearly the one with main character energy.

Jade pretends to gag. "He's a slimeball. Whether or not he's involved in any way, he'll be out of our lives very soon."

While we wait for Ethan and Damien, a few people politely stop us to take photos — mostly Jade, who, after five hours in costume, still looks flawless as Aegwynn. We gladly indulge them. Some people want to be in the picture, others want us to pose on our own.

This is definitely one of the most fun parts of con weekend. Normally, I'm fairly introverted, but putting on a costume and being in character gives me so much more confidence.

We wave goodbye to our new friends, still waiting for Ethan and Damien, when I have a thought. "Hey, let me see his phone number again."

"Why, you want to call him?" she asks with a raised eyebrow as she digs the paper out of her cleavage.

"No, no, the numbers. Look at the fives." I point to the paper. "What if the handwriting matches the notes?"

I start to pull out my phone, my heart thumping wildly. Could this be it? Could we nail Mitchell Brantley to the wall right here, right now? I pull up my photo of the numbers written on the back of the note to compare, as Jade looks curiously over my shoulder.

I deflate just as quickly when I see it.

The numbers are completely different. I flip it over to see if any part of *Call Me* matches the writing.

Not even close.

"Dammit!" I crumple up the paper, shoving it back at her.

"It was a good thought, babe. But yeah, that definitely doesn't match. Maybe he's working with someone? Someone else who might want to see her off the show too?" Jade offers with a shrug.

Without her, there would be no show.

Without Tamara, there would be no *Serafina*.

Mitchell may not want to be overshadowed by his costar, but if the show was canceled, he'd be out of a job too. The likelihood of Mitchell being involved in any of this dwindles by the second.

I see the guys approaching, and they point over to the hallway for us to meet them out there.

Once we are far enough away from the crowd I ask, "Any luck?"

Ethan takes a sip of his whiskey. "Little Mitch is gross as hell, but I don't think he's our guy."

"Why do you say that?" Jade asks.

"Because he's only here for the day. He landed this morning and is leaving in a few hours."

"Wait, he only just arrived today? So he really couldn't have been involved with Tamara's disappearance. At least not directly," I say, even more defeated.

There goes the Mitchell theory.

"Yeah, this dude sucks, but he doesn't seem capable of kidnapping," Damien says.

"Never underestimate someone. You do not know what they are capable of," I say quietly, reciting Princess Serafina's most famous line.

Ethan nods. "Rule number one."

"In any case, if he wasn't here yesterday, I'm afraid that rules him out," Jade says.

Back to work.

We do a lap around the con, taking more photos and talking with acquaintances we haven't seen in a while. I chat with the folks at the costume repair station, who say they haven't seen anything strange, but I'm glad to get a chance to catch up.

It all feels so good, just relaxing and reconnecting with fellow con friends, I almost forget we're on a mission to solve Tamara's disappearance.

Before I can suggest more side quests — like checking out some of the rooms and events — a loud, piercing alarm shrieks, causing all of us to jump and cover our ears.

What the hell is that? I look around the space and notice white lights flashing on the walls atop bright red boxes.

Fire alarm.

Seriously?

This should be interesting, evacuating several thousand people out into the streets and sidewalks. At least it's overcast right now, so maybe it won't be as blazing hot outside.

Too quickly, I'm surrounded by a swarm of people headed towards the same doors as us. My head begins to pound, and I feel a bead of sweat trickling down my spine as too many bodies close in on me, suffocating me.

The sheer volume of the alarm overloads my senses.

I force myself to breathe, but I can't get enough air.

Fuck.

Jade must sense something is wrong, as she instantly takes my arm and helps steady me through the crowd. In the massive sea of cosplayers, we've lost sight of Damien and Ethan, but my focus right now is just getting outside.

Because I can't breathe.

After finally getting through the doors and turning off to the left, further away from the crowd of people, Jade sits me down on a wooden bench and takes a seat next to me. She rubs slow circles on my back until I gather myself and the panic subsides. She doesn't need to say anything, and I'm grateful when she doesn't ask if I'm okay. She already knows.

We spot Damien in his fine black suit approaching, but he's alone.

"Where's Ethan?" I ask, looking up at him, trying to keep my voice steady.

"He was right behind me, but we got separated by the crowd. I've never seen such a turnout for WyvernFest. This has got to be a record." Noticing the growing alarm in my eyes, he kneels down in front of me, putting a hand on my knee. "Hey, I'm sure he'll be right out. He's fine."

"Some bodyguard you are, D," Jade says with a smirk.

I'm sure he's right, but I still feel like we need to be on alert and watch each other's backs.

It's easy to make yourself believe you're perfectly safe, and that no one would try to hurt you or do anything around so many other people, but in actuality, wouldn't that be the best time? When there's chaos and commotion and no one is really paying attention?

My breathing picks back up as I start to look around nervously at the gathered crowd. Pulling out my phone to text Ethan, my fingers tremble so much I can barely type.

ME (4:31 P.M.)

hey where are you?

He doesn't respond right away, causing my heart to continue pounding in my ears.

Come on, come on.

He should be out here by now.

I continue to stare at my phone for another few minutes, until I notice Jade and Damien exchanging glances. When I finally see the little bubble pop up signaling that Ethan is typing, I exhale a sharp breath.

ETHAN (4:34 P.M.)

I'm fine. see you in a sec

What does that mean? What is he doing? At least he's okay, but he's definitely up to something.

Jade opened the front door of her house, her face going stricken when she notices the tears staining my pale cheeks. I tried to speak, but only sobs broke through. Without a word, she hooked her arm through mine and pulled me inside, shutting the front door and leading me upstairs to her room. She placed me on her bed, nudging me forward ever so slightly, then rubbed slow circles over my back.

About ten minutes passed before I was able to compose myself enough to talk. "I saw my dad today."

She nodded, her brows furrowed. "Tell me what happened."

I explained that I ran into him at the grocery store, and that he was with his wife — the woman he left us for — and their kid.

I hadn't seen my dad since that day he walked out on us five years ago. We had heard rumors that, at some point, they started a family together, but…I wasn't expecting the kid to be so big. He had to be right about five years old.

I did the math, and it all hit me at once. I looked at his sweet face — a face that reminded me of a little Ethan — knowing that Dad got her pregnant, and that's why he left Mom. Left us.

"I just…froze, you know?" I wiped my dripping nose with my sleeve.

"Did he see you? Did you talk to him?"

"Are you kidding? I hid around the corner by the freezer and watched them until they left…like a coward." I played with the rip in my jeans. "She's pregnant again."

Jade wrapped an arm around my shoulders and leaned her head against mine. "You don't need him. You have us."

Her and Ethan. They were my true family.

I placed my hand over hers and squeezed. "What would I do without you?"

"You'll never have to know."

After a few moments passed, she released my shoulders. "Okay. You ready for some good news?"

I nodded and wiped away a tear. The last tear I would ever shed for him.

She ran over to her desk drawer and pulled out a piece of paper, holding it up proudly. "Ta-da!"

"What's that?" I stood up and moved closer to see.

"WyvernFest, babe. Mom's taking us. You, me, and Ethan."

I gasped and clapped a hand over my mouth. "*Are you serious?*"

She nodded with a grin, and we both broke out into squeals, jumping into each other's arms and laughing until there were only tears of joy.

23

We continue to look around for any sign of Ethan in the crowds. Some people are walking across the street to the hotel, others heading towards the food hall. Looking off to my left, I spot a black sedan poking out behind the corner of the convention center. I squint, but I definitely see Mitchell Brantley in the back seat just before the car peels away.

His signing *just* ended and he's leaving already?

He must have been anxious to get far away from here. Not that I blame him after that disaster of a panel. No sense in hanging around when everyone around you is disappointed that *you're* here instead of your more famous costar.

Poor Mitch.

"Hey, did you see that?" I ask Jade and Damien. "Mitchell just left in quite a hurry."

They both look around. "Where?"

I point to where I'd seen him leave down the block. "He came out of that alley over there. Must be the VIP exit where all the celebrities can avoid the crowds."

My head snaps back to them. The three of us stare at each other, eyes wide with understanding. Without saying a word we nod, stand up, and start making our way casually, slowly, towards the side of the building, where maybe we can find some more answers.

Or at least one clue?

If Tamara was supposed to be brought here after lunch with Andy yesterday, then maybe we can get a better understanding of what that situation would have looked like. Or maybe it will lead us to some information about the con handlers.

We turn the corner and disappear into the alleyway without a second glance at the crowd still gathered out front. The alley is long and narrow, just wide enough for one car to drive through.

Reaching the backside of the building, I peek around the corner to make sure no one else is out here, when I spot a set of plain, unmarked metal doors.

The coast is clear, and I wave them over.

Reaching for the handle to see if it's even unlocked, the doors suddenly burst open, sending us all flying backwards in a fit of panic. I can't help the shriek that escapes me before Ethan is in my face, covering my mouth with his free hand.

"*Shhhhh!* Jesus, do you want to get caught?"

He lets go of my face, looking around as I struggle to catch my breath. "What the hell are you doing back here? Where have you been?"

He opens the door wider and motions for us to follow him in, pressing a single finger to his lips. At least the fire alarms have finally stopped.

He leads us down a bare hallway with a few closed doors along the wall. The fluorescent lights create stark shadows around every corner, clearly an area we are not supposed to be in.

When we reach a set of double doors, Ethan stops and turns to us. "Remember the guy in the Mandalorian costume we took pictures with earlier?" he asks me as he takes a sip of his whiskey. When did he get a refill?

I look around the space. "Yeah, what about him?"

"When the fire alarms went off and everyone headed towards the front doors, I saw him looking around all suspicious, and then he started walking in the opposite direction. So I followed him."

"Seriously?" Jade chides. "With everything going on — people going missing and us getting threatening notes — you decide to follow a *stranger* into the dark corners of the convention center *alone*?"

Ethan looks around at us with a mischievous grin. He's enjoying this. "Well when you put it *that* way it sounds like a bad idea, but look where it led us! This is where Tamara was supposed to be dropped off by the handler. I thought maybe we could look for some clues while everyone else was distracted."

"And did you find anything?" I ask. "What happened to Mando?"

"Eh, I eventually lost sight of him. He was busy typing stuff on his phone though, so I don't think he saw me following him. Once I got to this back hallway, he was gone."

Damien looks around. "What do you think are behind some of these doors?"

"No clue," Ethan says with a shrug. "Probably electrical stuff, maybe a server room, but they're all locked, and you need a keycard to get in."

I pinch the bridge of my nose. "And you didn't see his face or anything?"

"No, he kept his mask on the entire time. He's committed to the character, I guess."

That's disappointing.

But he's right, it certainly seems suspicious. What would someone be doing back here if the fire alarms were going off? Did he pull it himself to create a diversion? If so, why come back here?

"So, what do you think we're even looking for here?" Jade asks, as if she can read my thoughts.

"No idea. These doors lead back out between the exhibit halls and the ballrooms. It's where I followed Mando from."

"I'm not sure what we're going to find if Tamara never even made it here," Damien offers.

"I don't know, okay!" Ethan brings his free hand up and drops it dramatically. "We have nothing else to go on. We're stuck. But you're supposed to follow the clues until you can't anymore. Right, Els?"

I nod. "Okay."

"Unless you just want to pack it up now and go about our weekend. I'll happily drop all this and enjoy the rest of my day as Tony Stark, just say the word."

"No, no, you did good. Let's look around. We keep going."

The moment the words come out of my mouth, a door to one of the unmarked rooms opens, revealing a con worker, eyes wide in shock when he spots us.

We all freeze.

It seems to take him a moment to gather his wits, then he shouts, "Hey, you're not supposed to be back here!"

The four of us look to each other, and without a word, we bolt through the door leading back to the con floor.

People are already returning to the halls, allowing us to hide among the growing crowd.

"That was close," I say, panting.

"It's fine," Ethan says, waving his hand. "Dude looked like he was going to shit his pants. He probably doesn't have any real authority around here."

We hang out for a few minutes, catching our breath and making sure we're not being followed.

"I think we're in the clear." Damien puts his finger on his earpiece and nudges Ethan, as Tony Stark, back into the crowd.

While the guys stop and talk to some friends, Jade and I spot Kat among the crowd, dressed as Eris Morn from *Destiny*. We only know it's her because it's one of her most popular costumes.

A black mask covers the top half of her face, with three glowing green dots underneath, making her nearly unrecognizable. Various facial markings drip down her cheeks, and she is clad in brown leather from head to toe, with spiky shoulder plates and a cloth head covering.

When she sees us, she extends her hand, holding a bright green glowing orb.

Jade runs toward her, and they embrace as a small crowd gathers around them. I forgot that Jade wasn't with us yesterday when we first caught up with Kat. Both of them have huge followings on social media, and together they are a cosplay powerhouse. After a few seconds of talking quietly together and laughing, they turn around and start posing.

Fans in the crowd have already pulled out their phones to take pictures of the two of them together. Eris Morn and Aegwynn. Hunter and guardian from two completely different games, but together they look absolutely incredible.

You'd think they were full-on celebrities with how much attention they're getting.

After a while, they wave to the crowd and thank them, respectfully dismissing them from their presence, like queens to their royal subjects.

Damien approaches, and I look around for Ethan...again. What the hell?

Damien notices my confusion. "He said he was going to go grab something from the room."

Before I can respond, Kat sidles up to me and elbows my side playfully. "You must be relieved, huh?"

I tilt my head to the side and ask, "What do you mean?"

"About Tamara."

Huh?

The video that was posted this morning didn't prove anything, except now everyone is convinced that it points to foul play. I've watched it several times and it really gives me the creeps. She and Andy both look happy when she's getting in the car. The moment he closes that car door is the moment he's lost her, but he doesn't know it yet. It's devastating.

Especially now that I'm convinced he's harboring feelings for her.

She sees the confusion written all over my face. "Didn't you see her post?"

"*What?* No?" I'm completely thrown. "Are you saying she posted something? Where? What does it say?"

Kat pulls out her phone and scrolls for a moment, handing it to me with Tamara's social media profile pulled up, where a single post was written just twenty minutes ago at 4:45 p.m.

@TamaraJenkins ✔

Apologies to all my fans for canceling the panels and signings at WyvernFest this weekend! I am currently recovering from the flu. Hope to see you next time!

Well that's…interesting.

I suppose it could've been her assistant or her PR team trying to contain the story and control the narrative. But this doesn't feel right at all.

Whenever it's really Tamara herself posting updates, she always signs it with "-T." I've been following Tamara online for a while now, and this sounds nothing like her or her team.

And the *flu?* Andy sure as shit would've known if she left because she was sick. He said he hasn't been able to get ahold of her, and that they know each other well enough that she wouldn't just leave without saying goodbye.

Plus, who would write us threatening notes if this was all just as simple as her canceling for the flu?

"Huh," I say after rereading it about five times and handing the phone back to her. "That's crazy."

Kat seems unfazed, like she's totally fine with this explanation and can't be bothered to speculate any further. "You all coming to the party tonight?"

I'm still looking off in the distance, unable to shake this odd feeling, when she elbows me again. I look up at her and blink a few times, trying to bring myself back to the present. "What? Oh yeah, we wouldn't miss it!"

"Great, see you there!" Kat walks away, ever the entertainer and social butterfly.

But I can't move.

This is all wrong.

Whoever took Tamara must have posted this to throw everyone off track and try to stop the investigation. Could it really be that simple? Would the police just end their investigation if they believed she actually wrote this?

We need to find Andy.

24

I'm hoping Andy has some insights into what the police are planning to do next. He'll know the post is complete bullshit, but will the police?

"Hey, where's Andy been today anyway?" I ask Ethan when he finally returns. "Where did he go after his signing?"

"I texted him a while ago, but he said he had to go deal with something, and that he would be back here later."

I look around the con and see more and more people with drinks in their hands. The excitement in the air is palpable, and the vibe is definitely shifting. It's getting to that point in the day where everyone is ready to let loose again.

Distracted, I nearly knock over an R2-D2 roaming around as we stroll through the atrium lobby. I can't stop thinking about that post.

If the kidnapper posted that to throw everyone off the trail, then he may not be done with whatever else he has planned. If someone went through the trouble of posting that, does it mean we're getting closer? By continuing to investigate and ignore the threats, are we getting in over our heads?

I can't shake the feeling that something else is about to

happen, and that we might be kidding ourselves about how much danger we're actually in.

Guilt washes over me. What was I thinking getting us involved in this? So desperate to distract myself from my own problems that I jump in to try and solve someone else's? Classic me.

"Andy!" Ethan yells, waving over the crowd behind me.

I turn and see Andy walking through the crowd towards us, still looking awful as ever.

"Hey, Andy," I say with a sympathetic smile. I'm sure he's like me in that he doesn't want pity from anyone. But I can't help it. I still want to ask him about the whole bodyguard thing, but from the looks of it, now is not the right time.

"I'm sure you all saw the post?" He looks around at us as we nod. "It's bullshit."

"Right. It doesn't make any sense," I say. "What do the police think about it? Have you talked with Hawthorn?"

"Yeah, we're going to meet up later tonight. He agrees that it's strange, but they still have to look into it."

"Is there anything else we can do?" Ethan asks.

I can tell it pains him to see his friend and mentor like this. Someone he's looked up to for years and has been such a positive influence in his life, falling apart before his very eyes.

"I don't think so. You've already been such a huge help, truly. I don't want you all putting yourselves in further danger." He rakes a hand through his toffee brown hair. "Do you have any plans for tonight?"

Ethan looks around at our group. "I think we might be headed to Kat's party tonight up in the suites, right?"

I level him with a slow feline grin.

Stop, he thinks at me.

"I don't know." I look around the group. "Is it weird to party and just act like nothing is wrong right now?"

Surprisingly, it's Andy who says, "You should go. I know

how much you all look forward to this weekend. Hawthorn is on it, and you guys have done more than enough through all this. Plus, it'll be good for you to be around all your friends and keeping an eye on each other right now."

Because the kidnapper who threatened us could still be watching us is what he doesn't say, but doesn't have to.

"What about you?" I ask. "Do you want to come? Take your mind off things for a while?"

"Nah, I'm fine. I think I'm just going to head home and try to rest. I haven't slept much. But text me the room number, in case something comes up and I need to find you all later tonight." His eyes shift to Ethan. "I don't live far from here if you need me for anything."

My instinct is to keep working on this for him and try to make him feel better. But I know there's nothing more I can do.

It's hard to trust people these days, but Andy has always been one of the good guys, and it kills me to see him like this. But he's right.

"Okay." I look to the rest of the group. "Food first?"

They all murmur their agreement, except for Andy, who shakes his head and points a thumb towards the exit. "I'm gonna head out. Thank you all so much for everything. Seriously."

I reach up to give him a quick hug, his tall frame swallowing me whole. "Get some rest. Let us know if anything comes up, and we'll do the same."

"Stay safe, Elsie," he says as we separate. "I'll text you both Hawthorn's number so you can stay in touch with him too." He gives Ethan a firm handshake and turns to walk away.

We all watch him go through the main doors, running his hands through his hair once again before shoving them into his pockets, defeated.

.   .   .

As soon as we enter the food hall, my senses are assaulted with the aromas of several different cuisines all at once. I've only had a small granola bar since breakfast, and now it's definitely catching up to me.

The Thai and sushi place sounds heavenly. I need all the panang chicken curry and egg rolls they have.

Damien comes with me, and Jade and Ethan both go off in different directions. We don't say much as we order our food. I think we're both too hungry to even hold a conversation right now.

The tangy scent of my curry and Damien's pad thai is enough to make my mouth water and my stomach grumble.

We all meet back in the common space in the middle of the hall, setting our food down and settling into our chairs, more than a bit relieved to be off our feet again.

I look around at everyone's food. "What did you all get?"

"Burger," Ethan replies before taking a huge bite, eyes rolling in the back of his head.

"Chicken parm from Nonna's," Jade says with a grin.

"Ooh, I love Nonna's!"

We all dig into our food in silence and barely come up for air until we've finished our entire plates. Rookie mistake not bringing more snacks to keep our energy up throughout the day.

"God, that was so good." Damien groans and slumps back in his seat, covering his face with his hands.

"I know." I wipe my mouth with my napkin. "I thought about grabbing a spiked donut shake from Shaky Dough, but I can't possibly eat another bite."

"Oh my God, Shaky Dough." Damien looks at me and grabs my arm. "Let's come back for those tomorrow, okay?"

I can't help the smile overtaking my face. "Deal." When he drops his hand, I instantly miss the warmth.

"Okay, time to go get changed. I'm so pumped for this party," Ethan says, practically jumping out of his seat.

"When are you going to tell us what's going on with you and Kat?" I wiggle my eyebrows at him.

"Probably around never. But thanks anyway! I've got something special I want to give to her tonight."

"Yeah, I bet you do." I shoot him a wink.

"Hey, honey! I've got something special for you!" I closed the front door behind me and plopped down beside him on the couch, shoving a small gift bag in his face.

"What's the occasion?" he said stiffly, like I was trying to catch him forgetting our anniversary or something.

"No occasion. I just saw this and thought of you." I leaned in and gave him a quick peck on the cheek.

When I was out shopping earlier, I found a Funko Pop of Batman and bought it immediately. Just last night we were watching *The Dark Knight* — one of Jared's favorite movies — while snuggled up on the couch. Seeing it out today made me smile, and it just felt like such a coincidence that I had to get it.

He opened the bag and peered inside. Silence ensued.

"I don't get it," he said as he looked up at me with a raised eyebrow.

"It's a Batman Funko! You love *The Dark Knight*."

"Well…yeah, as a film."

My heart sank. "Oh. I just…I thought it was so crazy that I saw that out today after we just watched it last night."

"Yeah, no, I get it. I'm just…not really into toys, you know? That's more your thing."

"Oh. Yeah…Okay, sorry."

He handed the bag back to me, and pulled me in for a passionate kiss, like nothing ever happened. Like he didn't just completely reject my gift and hurt my feelings.

The Con

I guess it was silly.
Maybe it was time for me to grow up.

<h1 style="text-align:center">25</h1>

After getting changed for the party, we all take the elevator together up to the top floor. Kat's party is sexy themed, so everyone is encouraged to wear a sexy version of one of their costumes. Most people just take one of their existing outfits and keep the makeup, hair, and accessories and then don lingerie along with it.

Walking down the hallway alongside Jade, she towers over me even more than usual in her sultry version of Raven from *Teen Titans*. A long purple cape with a hood covers a bobbed purple wig, and a red glowing gem adorns the space between her eyebrows. She has on a black leather bikini set under a sheer nylon top with a red belt, fishnet stockings, and tall black leather boots.

Insanely sexy. Gorgeous. Radiant.

How does she do it?

No matter what she is wearing or doing, she always manages to carry herself with unwavering confidence and magnetism that pulls the energy of the entire room right into the palm of her hand.

I'm in half of my Serafina costume: golden twisting crown on top of my hair pulled up into a simple bun, with the pauldrons and armored skirt layer, a bright red lacy bra, and nothing covering my midriff.

The boldness of it contrasts how I actually feel on the inside right now, but I'm determined to fake it 'til I make it, as they say.

There was a time when I used to wear much, much less to these types of parties. Of course, once I was dating Jared I toned it down a bit, but he still threw a fit once he found out. Not long after the last lingerie party, the backhanded comments about my weight started. Comments meant to make me feel grateful that he still found me attractive *at my weight*. Which was *average*. But it was just enough to make me self-conscious, so I wouldn't bare my body in front of anyone else.

Fucking Jared.

Walking down the hall, I fight the urge to cover my exposed skin, feeling that familiar dread seep in, as if everyone was staring at me and judging. It's hard to break old habits.

Ethan and Damien are behind us, debating about which superheroes would win in a fight against the other if their powers were taken away.

"But Batman's only power is wealth," Ethan states. "So are you saying he's fighting without using anything he bought or made with his own money?"

"Yeah, he'd have to, or else he'd have an unfair advantage."

"Well, what about Iron Man? Tony Stark used his money to build his suit too."

"Okay fine, only superheroes who have actual abilities in this scenario. No weapons, gadgets, or suits," Damien says.

"I'm gonna need more time to think this through, then."

Ethan had been waiting for an excuse to dress up as Walter White from *Breaking Bad*. Unfortunately for all of us, it's the Walter White from scene one of episode one, where he's in tighty-whitey underwear, a green button-down shirt, tan loafers with argyle socks, glasses, and a gross, stringy mustache.

He thinks he's hilarious.

Damien, on the other hand, is wearing his sexy Gandalf costume. No long beard or wig, but he is wearing his ratty wizard hat. The only thing under his open grey robes is a tight pair of black boxer briefs below his olive brown chest and bare torso.

As we approach the room, I turn back to them at the same moment Damien raises an arm to scratch his head, causing his robe to slide open further, exposing the soft love handles at his side. I look away a moment too late, and he catches me staring.

Dammit.

Just inside Kat's suite is a stocky man dressed in a navy pinstripe suit guarding a large metal box. There's a no-phone rule at these parties to avoid inappropriate photos being taken and uploaded, protecting the attendees — some of whom are semi-famous around these parts — so people can actually unwind and relax.

If you're caught with a phone or any type of camera you'll be kicked out and banned from all future gatherings. Kat's parties are epic, and there's no telling what could happen.

We purposely left our phones in our rooms so we didn't have to deal with giving them up at the door, making sure to let Andy know first where we'd be in case he needed us.

About thirty people are mingling in the elegant double suite, some sitting, some standing around. Kat has hired handsome, muscled men to carry trays of drinks, dressed in skimpy spandex shorts, no shirts, and various colorful capes.

Sexy superheroes, then.

We all grab a flute of champagne off the sexy Superman sauntering by.

Jade tracks him and asks us, "Okay, so where did we land on

how Superman would fare in a fight? 'Cause I'd go a few rounds with *him*."

"I forgot how amazing Kat's parties are," I say, ignoring her. "This is just what I need."

"How could you forget?" Ethan says excitedly as he looks around, probably for Kat.

I swear I'm going to get to the bottom of their situation, so I keep pressing. "So did you bang last year or what?"

Ethan practically spits out his drink and levels me with a warning glare.

You shut your mouth, sister, his eyes scream at me.

I answer with a smirk. *You could not be more obvious, brother.*

He shakes his head and walks away from me. He seems to be getting agitated, and not in the funny, teasing sort of way, but in a way that suggests that I should mind my own business.

Jade comes up next to me and whispers, "What was that about?"

"I've been giving him a hard time about him and Kat, 'cause he won't tell me what's going on with them."

"Well, maybe you should...back off a little," she says, then takes a sip of her drink.

"Why, do you know something?"

She looks at me and twists her mouth to the side. "I mean, I think it's pretty obvious he has feelings for her...but..." She pauses.

"But what?"

"I don't know, maybe he's...trying to figure out how he feels about everything. You know?"

The look on her face tells me I should be putting two and two together already. "Wait, you mean because she's trans?"

She shrugs. "All I'm saying is, I know you like to tease him 'cause he's your brother, but maybe give him a little space to work things out on his own. Ethan has only ever been with cis women, so this is kind of new to him, right?"

"Fuck. Of course." I cup my hand over my eyes. "I didn't even think about it like that. I feel like such an asshole."

"You're not an asshole. We don't know the whole story, if there even is one." Jade glances at Damien, who looks busy scanning the room, and taps him on the arm. "He hasn't said anything to you, has he?"

Damien, being completely oblivious to the entire situation, answers, "About what?"

I shake my head. "Never mind."

Sometimes I wonder about Damien and what's going through his head at any given moment. He's one of the smartest dudes I know, but there are times when I swear he's off in another world. Other times, I catch him watching me so intensely it's like he can see straight into my mind and soul.

Currently, it seems like he's off somewhere else.

Or...maybe he's looking for someone to hook up with tonight.

The thought sends a strange feeling through me, almost like jealousy, but I squash it right away. I have no claim to him. Still, the idea of him being with someone else makes my stomach churn, and I realize that this is the first time in years that both of us are actually single at the same time, and there would be nothing stopping us from crossing that line if we wanted to.

If *he* wanted to.

I shake my head to clear the intrusive thoughts.

I can't go there.

Three months ago, I was ready to commit the rest of my life to someone. If it was ever going to happen with Damien, or anyone really, I should be on more solid ground first. I have a long way to go before I'll feel secure enough in myself to be with anyone romantically.

To trust someone with my heart again.

Especially someone as important to me as Damien.

Our timing has always been terrible, so I can't fault him for dating or hooking up with someone else. He deserves to be happy.

Maybe the universe has kept us apart all this time for a reason. What if we're meant to be just friends?

I decide to do us both a favor and give him some space tonight. He doesn't need me around killing his vibe while he's trying to have fun with some smart, gorgeous woman. I take Jade by the arm and wave quickly at Damien without a word before we walk to the other side of the suite. Hurt and confusion flash across his face, but I try not to dwell on it.

This is for the best.

I don't need to be developing any feelings for him right now. I'll nip this in the bud, and we can go back to being just friends.

After about an hour, the party is in full swing. I'm grateful Jade never questioned why we moved away from Damien, since I'm not really sure how to answer that. I've felt uneasy about it ever since. To my surprise, he didn't start chatting up any of the beautiful women here. Instead, he went straight to Ethan, sparing me a glance every so often.

"...originally did the voice of Jar Jar Binks in the prequels, he ended up being the Jedi who saved Grogu from the temple!" I hear Jade explaining to a friend dressed as a sexy Darth Maul, who was, no doubt, in full costume earlier today. His face makeup is insanely well done.

"That's awesome," Sexy Darth Maul replies. He continues talking but that feeling of unease pulls my focus yet again.

Suddenly, I feel a prickle along the back of my neck, like someone is staring at me. Turning my head quickly, I scan the room, but don't see anyone looking. Nothing out of the ordinary.

I must be imagining it.

I realize I haven't even thought much about the whole

Tamara situation tonight, or the fact that we received threatening notes from some dangerous kidnapper just last night.

But I convince myself I'm safe here, surrounded by friends.

Besides, we're technically staying out of it like the note asked us to. There shouldn't be any reason to believe we're still in any kind of danger.

Except for that nagging feeling that I'm being watched.

26

As the party goes on, I try my best to stay alert in case the kidnapper does show up. Though it's hard when you have no idea what you're even looking for. Con weekends are chaotic and otherworldly, so there is no real semblance of normalcy here.

Maybe that's what's throwing me off so much. I've become untethered to reality and have no compass to bring me back to the very real danger I've managed to put us all in.

The suite is dark, the music thumping so loudly I can barely think, but I try to convince myself we're okay. What happened to Tamara has nothing to do with us, and in this moment, surrounded by friends, we are safe.

But are we, really?

It's my fault we're in this mess in the first place. Maybe inserting ourselves into this whole thing was crazy, but if we didn't, who would be looking out for Tamara...or for Andy?

While I still can't quite put my finger on what's going on with the two of them, I still care deeply for Andy and have a natural urge to protect him. He reminds me a lot of myself in some ways.

And Tamara, while I don't know her personally, she is still a human being, and she's clearly important to him. I also have great fondness for her through her portrayal of Princess Sera-fina. I feel a connection to her, and something inside me calls out to help.

So as much as I would like to "mind my own business" and keep myself safe and stay out of the whole thing, I think it might be a little late for that now.

And if I'm being honest, I selfishly really, really want to be the one who saves Tamara Jenkins's life…and then we become besties.

I look around for my friends. Nothing seems to be amiss, and everyone looks to be having a great time.

Then why am I so uncomfortable?

I feel it in my gut, that something is wrong here. Not just in general, but specifically here in this room, right now.

Someone is watching me, I can feel it.

Why are there so many people here right now, anyway?

Suddenly, the room is closing in on me, and I'm struggling to catch my breath. Panic begins to set in as the room spins, and I have to lean against the wall, letting my golden crown tumble to the floor. My entire body flashes with heat.

My stomach roils as I force air into my lungs, but it's not enough.

The next moment, Damien is in front of me with his hands cupping my face. "Els? What's wrong? You okay?" His voice sounds far away.

I squeeze my eyes shut, barely able to stay upright. "I don't know," I say between sharp breaths. "I just…I think I need to get out of here. Need some air."

"Come on, let's go. I've got you."

Without hesitation, he leads me out of the room, holding me up by the arms, acting as a protective barrier between me and the swelling crowd of people.

How many people are in here now? Fifty? Sixty?

A thousand?

I still can't breathe.

The noise and laughter around me is muffled, but I distinctly hear someone yell, "Shots!"

Damien wraps an arm around my shoulders and is no longer politely scooting around empty spaces in the crowd. Instead, he is actively pushing his way through. My people-pleasing sensibilities are aghast, but I squash them down, because right now, more than anything, I really just need to get the fuck out of here.

We get out into the hallway and Damien continues to lead me around a corner, towards an unmarked door.

"Come on, I know a place."

I let him take me by the hand and lead me through a super suspicious entryway, not unlike the secret hallways of the convention center we discovered just a few hours earlier.

He leads me carefully up a flight of sketchy stairs, until we reach the top and he opens a door that leads us to the roof, propping it open with a large red brick. His Gandalf hat lands next to it.

When I step through the door, the cool blast of fresh air hits my lungs like I'm taking my first breath. My hands interlace over the top of my head, and I close my eyes, gasping to take it all in.

It's not quite fall yet, but the weather is mild, and the evening breeze is a magical caress on my bare skin.

The fear and anxiety of being in that overbearing crowd, and even the idea of being watched, all melts away. I take a few more cleansing breaths, clearing out the negative energy from my body and ground myself to the present moment.

When I finally open my eyes, I find Damien gazing at me with those beautiful chestnut brown eyes, standing a few feet away at the parapet overlooking the city. I've never seen

Glenville from this vantage point, and it's stunning. From here, the tiny city shines, so charming and full of life.

I try not to focus too much on the fact that Damien is practically naked as I approach the edge and stand next to him. Those thoughts can't lead us anywhere good tonight.

He reaches around my back and rests a hand below my shoulder armor, and I lean into his warmth, snaking an arm around his soft torso.

"Better?" he asks, rubbing his thumb back and forth along my arm.

"Better," I reply with a smile. "Thank you for bringing me up here."

After a moment, he removes his hand and rubs the back of his neck. "I discovered this access to the roof last year. I was stumbling drunk, actually. I'm lucky I didn't fall over the side," he says with a smile that doesn't quite meet his eyes, looking back over the city.

I almost ask why he didn't bring me up here as soon as he discovered it. Then I remember...I didn't come here last year.

Jared had just proposed and surprised me with a trip that just so happened to coincide with WyvernFest weekend. It's so obvious now that he planned it that way.

"You were drinking up here...alone?" I ask gently as I tuck a strand of hair behind my ear. He doesn't move.

I had to let you go.

A weight settles on my heart as I remember those words from last night.

As if he sensed my shift, he quickly shakes his head and tries to deflect. "Crazy right? You never know what's going to happen at one of Kat's parties."

I can tell he didn't mean for that bit of information to slip, so I tuck it away for later. Tonight, I won't push it.

"I actually ended up passing out up here when I couldn't

figure out the door handle to get back down," he continues. "Such a cliché getting locked up on the roof, am I right?"

I chuckle, but I can't help looking back nervously at the door, propped open with a single brick. "We can't get locked out now though, can we?"

"Nah, we're good. That brick isn't going anywhere. Just enjoy the view. And remember to breathe."

I do as he says and allow myself to slow down, to lean back into his warmth. He has an incredibly calming presence, and you can't help but feel at ease around him.

It's no wonder he's so good at his job. To be a critical care nurse, you have to stay calm under pressure and be able to help others amidst constant chaos. He saves lives and helps people feel better every day.

I'm so lucky to have such a caring friend who's always looking out for me.

"How's the family?" I ask, trying to change the subject. "You talk to them lately?"

His relationship with his family was a little shaky after he changed his professional course from doctor to nurse. His parents have extremely high expectations and worked him so hard in school. Always expecting him to bring home an A in every subject, on every test. It took a toll, having that much pressure put on him.

They had a falling-out last year but have since reconciled and are working on their relationship.

"They're good. I spoke to my parents last week. Not sure if you heard, but things were pretty rocky there for a while."

"Yeah, Ethan told me."

A heavy pause hangs in the air.

"I'm sorry I wasn't around for you during all of that."

"Els, you don't have to keep apologizing. I already told you, I don't blame you…for any of it. You know that, right?" He turns to me and takes my hands in his. "Hey. I'm serious. You're one of my best friends, and I need you to believe me when I say you have nothing to be sorry for. Okay? You're here now, and that's all that matters."

I nod my head. Both of my best friends keep begging me to stop apologizing for what happened with Jared. For the things he was responsible for.

It's time I finally believe them both.

"Okay. You're right."

"Yeah, I know," he says with a smug grin. He drops my hands and leans his hip against the wall, crossing his arms and looking off in the distance. "But really, I should be thanking you."

"Thanking *me*?" I rear back. "For what?"

He glances back over at me with a mischievous look. "I never told you why I pursued nursing instead of the doctor track like my parents wanted."

I think for a moment. "No, we never really talked about it, but I assume you just realized that was what you wanted and went for it."

His smile fades a bit. He uncrosses his arms, shoving his hands in his pockets. "Sort of. I was all set to go down that path, knowing it would make them proud, knowing I could be good at it, and just hoping that, eventually, I would find some joy in it."

"So what changed?"

"Well, that year I started classes, I was dating a nice girl, and everything was going...fine, I guess. On a whim, I decided to take her to a nearby cosplay convention dressed as Samwise Gamgee. Where I met you three."

I smile, letting him continue.

"Something clicked when we all met, at least for me. I had been coasting along on other people's expectations, trying to make everyone around me happy, I had forgotten what it was like to feel my *own* joy. And you..." He trails off, looking at his feet, and my heart picks up.

Kicking a stray rock, he continues, "you were just so… unapologetically yourself. You did what made you happy, and didn't care about other people's expectations, and I thought to myself, *wow*, I want to be like that." He looks back up at me.

"You wanted to be…like me?" I say with pinched eyebrows.

"Meeting you all changed everything. For the first time, I felt the courage to go after what I truly wanted. Like I finally had people in my life who understood me and just wanted me to be happy." He swats me playfully on the shoulder. "So…thank you."

"I had no idea." I don't know what else to say to that. "Why didn't you ever tell us that before?"

He shrugs. "I dunno…it's crazy to think I'd still training to be a doctor, probably married to what's-her-name by now."

"Come on, Callie wasn't so bad, was she?"

He huffs a laugh. "She was fine, she just wasn't…my type."

I'm not really sure what he means by that. All the other girls he dated after Callie were just like her.

I turn away, thinking about what else he just admitted. About him thanking me.

It's weird to hear someone say that I inspired them to be brave. That I was so happy and living my best life that they wanted to be like me. I haven't been that person in a while. But maybe I can try to draw that same inspiration too.

I cross my arms over the parapet, needing to steer the conversation before I get all emotional again. "What about Sasha, how's she doing?" He's always gotten along well with his little sister. I'm grateful he had her while things with their parents were rough.

"She's great. Still getting used to campus life and all that. I just hope she doesn't overdo it with all the partying. Mom and Dad weren't as tough on her as they were on me, but still pretty strict. I worry she won't know how to handle all this newfound freedom."

"She'll be fine. We've all got to go through it at some point. She's a good kid."

"Well, she's a little more wild than I was at her age though. If you remember, the four of us were too busy coming up with shit like chicken nugget tournaments to get into too much trouble."

"Those rankings were skewed." I slap my hand down on the ledge. "Most of the nuggets were cold by the time we went to all *eight* restaurants and brought them home to judge!"

"We needed eight for an even bracket! But you're right, reheating them did affect the categories."

"Oh shit…we never judged on mouthfeel."

"So we truly have no champion," he says wistfully.

I shake my head, laughing. "Good times."

"The best." He smiles, turning back to the city.

We stand there, just enjoying the view and each other's company. It's been so long since we could just exist together in the same space and talk and laugh like we used to.

I've missed this so much.

I hear a strange thumping sound, almost like footsteps, and whip my head around. "Did you hear that?"

He follows my gaze to the open door. "No, what?"

It's probably just random mechanical sounds. I have no idea what kind of equipment they have up on these roofs. I was certainly never smart enough to be an architect or engineer or anything like that.

"Never mind." I shake my head and look back at him with a smile. "Thanks again for bringing me up here."

His returning smile, those dimples, make my knees wobble. "You're welcome."

"How is it that you always seem to know what I need, even before I do?" The question hangs in the air, and I suddenly wish I could take it back. I meant for it to sound casual and cute, but between us right now it feels like so much more than that.

He seems to contemplate it though, as he tilts his head. "Elsie, actually I—"

Bang!

We both startle and look to the access door — which has been slammed shut — then back at each other with wide eyes.

We sprint back towards the stairwell. I turn the handle to find it locked.

"No...no. No, no, no!" I bang on the metal door. *"Dammit!"*

I glance back at Damien, who looks like he's seen a ghost.

He simply asks, "Where's the brick?"

27

There has to be some explanation for this.

A brick doesn't just disappear.

My mind is searching for an answer, not wanting to come to terms with what I already know in my soul: Someone else was up here.

Someone followed us to the roof and closed this door on purpose to lock us out. They also had a chance to hurt us and didn't. So perhaps their motivation is to just scare us?

I instinctively reach for my phone— "Fuck!"

It's not there. We all left them in our rooms before going up to Kat's party.

"How did you get back inside last year?" I ask.

He chews on his lower lip before responding. "I banged on the door until some employee opened it and let me back in."

My shoulders slump. "I was afraid you were going to say that." I raise my hand, about to slam it against the metal door, but I stop. "Wait. What if they're still in there?"

"If they were going to hurt us, he — or she — could've done it when our backs were turned. Probably just took the brick and bolted."

"Yeah maybe. We've got to get in there and call the police."

"Then we better get pounding," he says before thinking better of it, closing his eyes.

I laugh way too hard at that. "I'm not even going there, that was too easy."

After ten minutes of banging on the door and yelling, still no one has come to rescue us from the roof.

"What are we gonna do? Whoever locked us up here will be long gone by now. They'll never catch him." I slam my fist against the door one more time.

"Hey, we don't know for sure this was our guy. Maybe there's some other explanation. Maybe the brick wasn't heavy enough and it's sitting just inside the doorway."

I turn and lean my head back against the wall, covering my face with my hands and trying to quell the rising panic.

Damien pries my hands from my face, forcing me to look at him. "Hey. It's okay. We're going to be okay."

"I know, it's just...I—I'm scared."

He pulls me in for a hug.

He doesn't say anything. He doesn't need to.

He just stands there holding me, stroking my hair. Knowing what I need from him is just his steady, calming presence. That's all I've ever needed.

Suddenly, the metal door swings open in a rush, nearly knocking us over.

"What the hell?" the hotel employee says when he sees us. "What are you two doing up here?"

Damien takes my hands and pulls me inside towards the stairs, screaming, *"Run!"*

I take off with a squeal and try to focus on my steps, making sure I don't fall and break my neck. But I can't help laughing as we make our way to the base of the stairs.

"We'll keep going down to five so we can get our phones," Damien says, still leading me by the hand.

We come to the stairwell door to the fifth floor and walk briskly down the hallway towards our rooms. Only when we reach our doors does he let go of my hand.

"Bet I'm faster," he says with a wink, before quickly unlocking his door with his key card and bolting inside.

"What? Wait! *Fuck!*" I was not ready for that.

I fumble to slide my key card out of my badge and open my own door. I run in and grab my phone off the nightstand as fast as I can, hurrying back to the hallway, but of course, Damien is already there smiling, leaning casually against the wall admiring his nails.

"Dick," I say with a smirk.

Trying to catch my breath, we head down the hall towards the elevators, and I pull up Hawthorn's contact info that Andy gave us earlier, in case we needed to text him.

ME (10:27 P.M.)

> Hi this is Elsie, Andy's friend at the convention. You around?

Hawthorn replies back immediately.

HAWTHORN (10:28 P.M.)

> Hi Elsie, unfortunately I'm about an hour away right now, but I can send some of my guys over if you need. Are you ok?

ME (10:29 P.M.)

> I think the person we're looking for might be here

> They may have been following us, I'm not sure

HAWTHORN (10:30 P.M.)

Get somewhere safe, I'll send my guys out
soon.

And no-go on the security footage from earlier.

Widespread outage.

I stop Damien with a hand on his arm. "Look at this," I say, handing him my phone.

He cocks his head to the side. "What the fuck?"

"That's weird, right? I mean, what are the chances that both the diner and this hotel just happen to have their security systems down during a high-profile kidnapping?" I ask as I take my phone out of his hands. "There's no way that's a coincidence."

Damien crosses his arms. "This guy must know how to tamper with the security systems then. Or he had help?"

"I guess that also dashes the hopes of having any footage from tonight up on the roof."

I keep coming back to what the motivation behind all this could be. Why Tamara? There are other high-profile people here this weekend, so why her? Is it a money thing? Or are we dealing with a stalker?

I lean against the wall, pinching the bridge of my nose.

Where do we even go from here?

There is no trail, no evidence to lead us to her. No security camera footage, just the video posted online that confirms what Andy already told us. The kidnapper, as far as we know, has made no demands.

So how are we supposed to find her?

But also, why are they still hanging around here? What do they want with *us*?

If they already have Tamara then why continue to come around here and follow us, and leave us threatening notes? And lock us up on the roof?

Unless we're getting close. Or they think we found something.

"Come on." Damien reaches out his hand again, knowing I'm getting too deep into my own head. "You look like you could use another drink."

I take his hand. Walking towards the elevators, we turn the corner and are suddenly face to face with…Andy?

"Hey, Andy," I say with furrowed brows and a tilt of my head. "What are you doing here? I thought you left for the night."

His eyes are wide and bloodshot. "Oh. Hey, guys. Yeah. I did, but…I couldn't stay there. I kept getting this nagging feeling that I'm missing something. So I came back to…look around, I guess."

I nod. "We think the kidnapper might still be around here. We were followed up to the roof and locked out. And I think you're right, I think we're close to figuring it out, but we're missing something. Something big."

His eyes narrow. "Wait, they followed you? When?"

"Just now. Whoever it was could still be around here. But Hawthorn texted and said the security systems have been down. So it looks like we're at another dead end, unless we can lock this place down."

"I'll call him," Andy says as he pulls out his phone. He doesn't wait for a response before turning around and heading into the main stairwell. The one guests are *actually* supposed to use.

"Okay…" I say to him, but he's already gone.

What was Andy doing here, on *this* floor?

I shake away the invading thoughts. This is Andy we're talking about. We can trust him. My faith in people really is shaken these days.

Damien turns to me. "Ready to go back upstairs for that drink? We are still dressed for the occasion after all, and it's a terrible waste to be anywhere else looking this good." He grabs the top of his head and yells, "Oh shit, I left my hat on the roof!"

I look down at myself, realizing I'm still basically just wearing lingerie and fake battle armor.

Jesus, what am I doing?

Playing detective while running around in my underwear? Why did I think I could do this? Why did I think I could have any real impact or make any kind of difference here?

Maybe I do need to grow up. I look like a damn fool.

"Hey, what's going on up here?" he asks with a smile, gently tapping my head.

"Sorry. I'm just...you know, thinking maybe I'm out of my league here. I never should've gotten us involved in all this."

When he doesn't say anything, I continue, "I thought it would be fun and just like...an adventure for all of us to do together, but...maybe we should just stay out of this from now on, for real this time. We should lay low."

He considers my words. "Is that even possible at this point? After all this?" He waves his hands around. "I mean, we were 'laying low' after we got that note, and we were just minding our own business at Kat's party, yet this person still followed us and locked us on the roof. I hate to say it, but we're in this. I don't think it's going to be that easy to walk away. Unless you're saying you actually want to leave and go back home?"

Is that what I want?

I hadn't really considered that as an option, but maybe we should. I hate that we would be cutting short this one weekend we look forward to all year, but this is bigger than us.

We're in over our heads here.

"I don't know. What do you think?"

He just shrugs. I know he will do whatever I ask, support whatever decision I make.

After a moment, I say, "Let's go back upstairs and talk it over with Jade and E. We should probably go check on them anyway, since they don't have their phones on them."

"Okay," he says, but doesn't look away from me, doesn't move. "You good?"

"Yeah. I'm good," I say with a smile. And for the first time in a long time, I actually mean it.

I link my arm with his, and we head up in the elevator in comfortable silence. I let his positive energy seep into me, warming me from the inside out.

We get off on the top floor and look around, both of us tensing immediately.

Something feels…off. It's too quiet.

The top floor is usually party central, with music thumping, people dancing in the halls, and yet right now…nothing.

We take off towards Kat's suite. My heart picks up speed with each hurried step. The moment I cross the threshold of room 721, my entire world collapses around me.

Lying lifeless on the floor…is Ethan.

28

"*E*than!" I scream.

There's nothing in my head except him.

Our entire lives together flash before my eyes in a single agonizing heartbeat.

I scramble to get to him, falling to my knees at his side. "Oh my God! Is he okay? What happened?"

He's not moving.

This can't be happening.

Damien drops to Ethan's other side and begins assessing him. "He's alive," he says to me, "but his breathing is slow. Too slow. What did he take? What happened?" Those questions are directed at Kat, who is dressed as Harley Quinn, sitting on her knees by Ethan's head.

"Paramedics are on the way. I don't know what happened!" Tears continue sliding down her face, smearing her makeup. "I don't know, he just...we were talking, and he suddenly started acting kind of weird and loopy. Slurring his speech and stumbling, and then he just crumpled to the floor."

Damien continues checking Ethan, but I'm barely cognizant

of what's going on around me. I can't really understand what he's saying.

Of course this would happen when he's not wearing any pants, dressed as Walter White during a mental breakdown.

Fucking hell, Ethan.

A small crowd has gathered nearby, but most people have left Kat's party completely. Words are muffled and time has slowed down.

"His pulse is weak. Did anyone see him take anything?" Damien asks from miles away as he checks Ethan's eyes.

It takes me a moment to process what he just asked, but I manage to say, "Take anything? Like drugs?" I blink a few times, trying to focus on what's in front of me. "You know he doesn't go near that stuff."

"We all took shots earlier, but we've just been drinking," Kat says. "Nothing else."

"What was he drinking? What shots?"

"Umm…we did a few shots of tequila, but he's mostly been sipping on rum and Coke all night as far as I know."

"Elsie," Damien says sternly as I gently wipe a strand of copper hair away from Ethan's forehead.

He knows I'm teetering on the edge, ready to spiral down into a dark place.

"I need you to focus. Does he have any medical conditions I don't know about? Any heart stuff?"

"No," I manage to croak. "Just like…some asthma, but it only flares up when he's working out."

"Any medications?"

"No, nothing! Damien, what is it? What's wrong with him?"

"I…I can't say for sure. If he took something *and* was drinking alcohol…" He looks at his watch, not finishing that thought. "Where the *fuck* is that ambulance?"

I don't understand. He didn't take anything, he wouldn't.

Watching our mom turn to pills after Dad left, and seeing what it did to her, really messed him up. We've talked about it before, and I know him. I know he stays away from that stuff for a reason.

But that can only mean one thing.

Someone must have put something in his drink.

Fuck.

I look around the room but realize something...no...*someone* is missing. "Where's Jade?" I ask unsteadily to no one in particular.

Kat looks to me and Damien with raised eyebrows. "You mean she wasn't with you?"

"No, when we left, she was still here with Ethan." My heart hammers in my chest. "When did anyone last see her?"

Kat puts a shaking hand to her forehead. "Umm, I don't know, not long. Maybe...half hour ago? It was after we took shots, but right before he collapsed. She was asking if we had seen you all, so I figured she went looking for you."

God. What if something happened to her too?

This is all my fault.

I can't think.

Nothing is making sense right now.

It's like I'm inside a snow globe and someone just grabbed it and shook the hell out of it.

Ethan is unconscious.

Jade is missing.

Somebody followed us and locked us up on the roof.

In a sudden flurry of motion, the paramedics finally arrive and surround Ethan's nearly lifeless body.

Damien quickly tells them everything he did and what he suspects happened, but I can barely hear them. I can barely breathe. I can't even move.

They take some quick vitals, but in the next instant, he's strapped to a gurney being rolled away from me, snapping me out of my stupor. I stumble to my feet and run to his side, grabbing his hand.

"He's my brother, I'm not leaving him," I say to the EMTs as we enter the hallway.

Everything is happening so fast.

"I'll meet you there!" I hear Damien shout as we reach the elevator that's being held open.

I can't process anything around me as I squeeze Ethan's hand. The next moments are a complete blur of climbing into an ambulance, squeezing his arm against me and whispering in his ear that he's going to be okay, the EMTs asking me questions I can't answer, and then finally arriving at the hospital.

My wrist is throbbing after someone has to pry his hand from mine.

Strong arms hold me back as they push him away from me, taking him behind more doors where I cannot follow.

My throat is sore. I must have been screaming.

Then I'm just...standing there. My heart ripped from my chest.

People scramble around me in a flurry of motion, but I'm no longer in control of my own body.

I have no idea how much time passes before someone — a nurse, probably — gently guides me into the waiting room and lowers me into a chair.

And suddenly, I am alone.

Completely and utterly alone.

I look down at myself and realize I'm *still* in bright red lingerie and gold armor. But I don't care. Can't bring myself to care about anything right now. Not until I know that Ethan is okay.

He has to be, because I won't accept any other outcome from this.

I can't.

Numbness overtakes me.

At some point, the sliding glass doors of the emergency room open, and in walks Damien, and behind him…Jade.

I practically fall out of my chair at the sight of her. She's really okay.

In an instant, they are both at my side, gathering me in their arms. We just stand there embracing each other, them holding me up more than anything, but no words are needed between us.

When we all separate, I slide back down in my seat, unable to hold myself up any longer, as they each take a seat on either side of me.

"Any updates?" Jade eventually asks, lacing her fingers with mine.

I look down at my lap and shake my head.

It takes me a moment, but I suddenly realize they're both out of costume. Jade looks cozy in her indigo velvet tracksuit, and Damien is wearing worn blue jeans and a plain white tee, holding something in his lap.

I look closer…

Clothes.

He brought me clothes.

In the rush and chaos of everything that happened with Ethan, Damien had the forethought to go get me actual clothes, so I wouldn't have to look like a cosplaying lunatic while my brother fought for his life.

My chest tightens.

"Are those for me?" I barely get out, my throat like sandpaper.

"Oh, yeah yeah. I, uh…thought you might want to change out of that Sexy Serafina costume. You look…really inappropriate," he says with a lift of his lips as he hands the clothes to me.

I elbow him in response and chuckle softly. "Thank you." I

look down at the clothes. *My* clothes. "Wait, these are *mine*. How did you get me my own clothes?" I look up at him curiously.

"Ah, you see, that's where I found this lovely lady," he says, jabbing a thumb in Jade's direction. "I was going to just grab you something of mine, but I heard some noises coming from your room next door, so I knocked, and there she was, flushed face and all. She helped me pick something out for you."

Jade leans over and swats him on the shoulder. "I did no such thing; it was all you." She gives me a sly wink.

"So, you weren't kidnapped or murdered? You were just hanging out in our room? Doing what?" I snap my head in Damien's direction. "And what kind of noises did you hear?"

As soon as I say the words, I instantly regret it.

Jade looks off to the side and says, "Umm…definitely something completely innocent that Damien *did not* interrupt, like…a study group? Is that a thing?"

Damien lowers his eyebrows. "Oh yeah, your study partners looked *super smart.*"

"Hey look, a vending machine!" she shouts as she runs — literally *runs* — away from us.

I chuckle again as I excuse myself to the restroom. Damien settles deeper into his chair, clasping his hands and resting them over the top of his head.

I open the restroom door and assess the clothes Damien brought me: soft, navy blue leggings and an oversized grey hoodie sweatshirt adorned with a stack of books over the words "Just One More Chapter." My favorite sweatshirt. One of the few things Mom ever bought me, during a short period a few years ago when she was trying to get clean and reconcile with us. It didn't last long.

As I get dressed, I can't help but think about her and Dad. Would they even want to know what happened to Ethan? We've barely spoken to either of them since Dad left, but I really can't risk having them show up here. I suppose I can just wait until we get an update on his condition, and then have the hospital make calls to them if we have to. But he's going to be fine, and we'll be out of here soon. So it won't even matter.

Lord knows we don't need Mom and Dad in the same room during a crisis.

The thought spikes my anxiety, and I have to remind myself to breathe. I lean on the sink and squeeze my eyes shut while taking deep, steadying breaths as I count to four. Inhale, hold, exhale, hold.

Once I compose myself, I open my eyes and study my face in the mirror. I barely recognize the girl staring back at me. My eyes are red and puffy. The blues that normally remind me of the ocean are now dull and empty. My hair has escaped its bun, the hair tie nearly undone.

I pull it all back up into a top knot, the movements reminding me of how this whole weekend started just yesterday morning in my car.

I exit the restroom and take my seat between my best friends. Jade has since returned from her fake adventure to the vending machine and is mindlessly crunching on some Cheetos. After stashing my costume pieces under my seat, I hug my knees to my chest and sink down low in the chair.

Silence surrounds us as we all just sit there, forced to think about Ethan.

What the hell even happened? Was this just a freak medical thing? Or did someone actually do this to him?

The EMTs on the way here kept asking about his drug use, and I insisted that he didn't take anything, but they wouldn't believe me or take me seriously. I suppose being drunk and partying in your underwear is not a convincing position to be in.

But none of this makes any sense.

The longer I sit with it, the harder it is to believe that this was just an accident. But I'm also not ready to sort through what that really means. I can't bring myself to face the reality of all this just yet, not when Ethan is still fighting.

He has to be okay.

There's no other alternative.

29

My leg bounces uncontrollably, and I'm only vaguely aware that I'm chewing on my thumbnail. I shift nervously in my chair, the worn maroon fabric scratching the backs of my arms.

"Did someone do this to him?" I ask no one in particular.

Damien and Jade exchange glances.

"We don't know yet, babe."

"Okay, but you *think* you know." I look up at Damien. "Right?"

He puts a hand over mine and says, "Let's not jump to conclusions."

But I yank my hand away. "Damien, please don't do that. Please."

He looks at me, and to his credit does not back down. "Okay. No, I don't think this was an accident."

I squeeze my eyes shut, feeling the guilt coursing through me, as if it lives in my veins, constantly reminding me that all of this is my fault. It's always my fault.

"But hey." He grabs my hand again, this time squeezing it so

I don't pull away from him. "We're going to get through this. Whatever happens, we'll deal with it. Together…okay?"

I just nod while my leg continues to bounce.

"Why don't I go see if I can get an update," Damien says wearily, getting up out of his chair and walking towards a nurse at the reception desk.

I pull out my phone, needing a distraction from my own thoughts.

There's a missed call from Andy. I'm not really in the mood to talk right now, but I should let him know about Ethan. One more thing to pile on him.

I pull up our text thread, my fingers hovering over the screen. Is this really something I can text him? I should probably call, but I'm not sure I can actually say the words out loud.

ME (1:04 A.M.)

> hey I'm sorry to do this over text but I wanted to let you know that Ethan is in the hospital… he collapsed

I pause, forcing a deep breath.

ME (1:04 A.M.)

> we're not really sure what happened

I look around the waiting room. Only a few strangers sit nearby, looking just as hollowed out as me. The surrounding drab brown, beige, and maroon motif is doing nothing to lighten the mood around here.

ANDY (1:06 A.M.)

> Oh my god.

> Do you need me to come over there?

> Do you need anything?

Do I need anything? Yes, I need answers. I need him to be okay.

ME (1:08 A.M.)

no we're okay here, just waiting

ANDY (1:10 A.M.)

I'm with Hawthorn right now, he just picked me up.

If you do need anything, we can be there right away.

St. Mary's Hospital?

ME (1:11 A.M.)

yes. and I'll let you know… thanks

ANDY (1:12 A.M.)

Doesn't matter what time it is, please keep me updated if you can.

ME (1:13 A.M.)

I will

Thank you

Even while he's going through his own crisis, he's still so willing to be there for me and Ethan. No wonder Ethan has looked up to him so much these past few years. All the more reason to continue our search for Tamara.

Damien returns to his seat, and before I can even ask, he shakes his head. "No updates yet. I'm sorry."

My eyes drop back down to my phone. I pull up my social media and start mindlessly scrolling, trying to keep my mind thoroughly busy and distracted. I hate feeling this way. Completely helpless. Restless.

Reading through various celebrity updates, I think about Tamara's mystery post from earlier. She clearly didn't write that, but who did? And why? It was posted around the same time we were searching those back hallways of the convention center.

Wait…

I sit up a little straighter in my chair, willing my brain to focus and think this through.

Ethan brought us around those secret hallways because he was following that person in the Mandalorian costume when the fire alarm went off. He said the guy was too busy on his phone to notice Ethan.

"No way," I whisper.

Both Damien and Jade turn to me.

"What's that?" Jade asks.

"I think…what if it *is* the Mandalorian?"

Damien's eyebrow shoots up. "What do you mean?"

"Ethan was following someone dressed as the Mandalorian, right? He went into those secret hallways when the fire alarm went off, and he said the guy was busy typing stuff on his phone, acting all suspicious. I know it might be a stretch, but right around that time was the weird Tamara post on social media."

They both contemplate it for a moment.

"I guess it's possible," Jade offers. "But how do we know for sure? I mean, it could just be a coincidence."

"Hmm…"

My head whips to Damien, whose eyebrows are scrunched together. I know that look.

"What? What are you thinking?" I ask.

"Well, do you know what Tamara's phone looks like? I mean, maybe she's been photographed with it in the tabloids or something?"

"I don't know, maybe," I reply, slowly understanding what he's getting at. "Okay so, if we knew what her phone looked like, we could just ask Ethan if he got a good look at the one Mando had to see if they match!"

As soon as I say the words my heart sinks. *Just ask Ethan.*

If he survives this.

They both seem to realize it too, Jade lacing our fingers together again and Damien putting a warm arm around my shoulders.

Every time the door just past the reception desk opens, my heart stops, wondering if it's someone with news about Ethan. But it never is.

Closing my eyes and leaning my head back in my chair, I try to rest as much as my racing thoughts will allow. My eyes feel so heavy.

I have no idea what time it is when the door finally opens and a tall man in blue scrubs and a long white coat appears. He looks around the waiting room, his gaze landing on us.

I immediately rise from my chair on shaky legs.

"Family of Ethan Graham?" the doctor asks as he approaches us.

"Yes, I'm his sister. Is he okay? Please tell me he's okay."

"Miss Graham, I'm Doctor Hendricks. So, he's stable. We're keeping him in the ICU overnight for observation. But..." He pauses and looks at me, eyebrows pinched together. "Miss Graham, I'd like to get some more information about what happened just before the incident, if you don't mind."

"Umm, yeah okay." I shake my head, trying to clear out my overriding emotions so I can speak clearly and focus on what this man is saying. "Can you just...tell us what happened though? Why he collapsed?"

I need to hear the words. I need him to tell me that this was just some random, freak medical event that has nothing to do with someone trying to hurt him. I need him to tell me that everything is fine.

Instead, he says, "Miss Graham, would you mind coming with me so we can speak privately for a moment?"

The way he keeps saying *Miss Graham, Miss Graham* is grating on my nerves. What isn't he telling me? Why can't he say it out here?

"Umm…sure. Of course." I narrow my eyes before looking to Damien and Jade, who simply nod.

"Go, we'll be right here," Jade says with a reassuring smile.

"We're not going anywhere," Damien adds, the simple words filling something inside me I can't quite name.

I turn back to the doctor — who I already don't like — and he leads me through a set of doors into a smaller, more private waiting room, motioning for me to sit down in yet another scratchy maroon chair.

"What's going on?" I can't hide the quiver in my voice. "What aren't you telling me?"

"Miss Graham…"

Ugh.

He lowers his voice and takes a deep breath. "Your brother is stable now…but he overdosed."

I try to focus on breathing.

The doctor continues, "We found high levels of alprazolam in his bloodstream. More commonly known as Xanax. This type of medication, when mixed with alcohol, can be lethal. He's quite lucky to be alive."

30

My head tilts to the side as if I need to hear him say it again.

Because it doesn't make any sense.

"High levels of…Xanax?" I squint, as if I could force everything around me back into focus. "I…I don't understand. Isn't that like, for anxiety?"

"It is. Now I know this may be hard to talk about, but how long has your brother been taking Xanax, Miss Graham?"

I swear if he says *Miss Graham* like that to me again, I'm going to lose it.

I clench my fists, shaking my head. "He's not *taking Xanax*. I mean…he doesn't take anything. Just like I tried to tell the EMTs."

The look of pity on Dr. Asshole's face has my nails digging into my palms hard enough to draw blood. I squeeze my eyes shut to calm myself down, so I don't punch his stupid face.

"We're not here to judge. We just want to help him." He reaches out, but I pull my hand away as he continues, "It's actually quite easy to develop an addiction to benzodiazepines.

Given the location where the overdose took place...the EMTs described the party—"

"No," I insist. He doesn't understand. He doesn't know Ethan.

"Miss Graham, I understand this is a lot to take in. Many family members are kept in the dark about a person's addiction, and it can be quite upsetting to learn the truth."

"*Stop!* He's not an addict." I'm seething. This guy isn't even listening to me. "Even if he did have a prescription, he wouldn't abuse it or use it recreationally. I'm his sister, I would know!"

I would...right?

Ethan would never keep something like this from me. I know him, and I know how he viewed our mother's addiction. Though, she dabbled in way worse than anti-anxiety medication.

No, this is all wrong.

Of course, if he *didn't* take anything willingly...fuck. I can't go there just yet.

"Okay. We don't have to discuss this right now." He puts up his hands in defense before opening a blue folder, presumably containing Ethan's chart. "Let's talk about your brother's condition. The amount of alcohol and medication in his system was quite alarming, so they administered a drug called flumazenil to help reverse the effects it can have on the receptors in the brain. Unfortunately, this comes with its own set of risks, and he did have a seizure shortly after arriving."

My heart wrenches.

The alarm on my face has him adding quickly, "But we were able to stabilize him, and he's been responding well since."

Jesus. I really did almost lose him. I drop my head into my hands as he continues.

"He is currently on several medications to detox his system and alleviate some of the other side effects. What we're most concerned with right now is his heart and his airways. This type of overdose can severely compromise his cardiovascular system, so we need to monitor him closely."

It takes me a moment to collect my thoughts enough to speak. "Other side effects?" I rasp. "Like what?"

"With the amount he ingested, there are a number of possible neurological issues that can arise, including hallucinations and paranoia. He's been sedated to help his recovery, so we won't know the full extent of any neurological damage until he's awake and we can run some more tests."

I just nod. What else can I say at this point?

He thinks I'm in denial, so I'll probably never be able to convince this guy that this was done *to him*.

Some asshole actually tried to murder my brother.

Honestly, it's kind of genius, using something as simple and common as Xanax. Most people would just assume that he already had a prescription or was taking it recreationally, having been found while also drinking heavily at a party.

No one would ever suspect that it was slipped into his drink.

I shake my head, closing my eyes. "Okay, so what now? Can I see him? Or are drug addicts not afforded the luxury of visitors around here?" I level him with a glare so sharp I hope he feels it.

"He's currently in the ICU, but like I said, he is stable," he says gently. "I can let you come back for a few minutes to see him, but since we are outside of visiting hours, it will have to be quick. He needs to rest."

"Of course."

I stand up from my chair and follow him out. I can see my feet moving with my own eyes, but I don't quite feel in control of them. It's more like I'm simply observing myself from above, walking down this long, bright, halogen-lit hallway.

Why are hospitals like this? It's the exact opposite of cozy.

It fuels my anxiety and puts me more on edge.

The doctor leads me to another corridor marked "Intensive Care Unit," and my entire body begins to shiver uncontrollably.

I rub my arms, but it does nothing. Hospitals have no business being this cold and stark.

He stops at room 156, nodding to the foam hand sanitizer pump mounted on the wall.

I pump a few times and lather my hands as he says, "Miss Graham, I want you to be prepared for what you are about to see. His body has been through a lot, and he's in a fragile state. I'll be around to answer any questions you might have, but for now, I'll give you some privacy."

"You said he's been sedated. Can he hear me?"

His eyes soften. "Probably not, but…you never know, right?"

I nod slowly. "Thank you. I'm…sorry if I was rude earlier, I—"

He holds up a hand to cut me off. "No, it's okay. Believe me, that was nothing. You are more than welcome to take your frustration and anger out on me."

He gives me a sad, half-smile and I have to look away.

I walk through the door into a dimly lit space, the beeping from several machines echoing loudly around the small, bare room. My eyes land on Ethan, illuminated by a few soft lights mounted over his bed.

He may be sleeping, but right now I'm the one living a nightmare.

The doc said he probably can't hear me, but when has that ever stopped me from talking?

I pull up the small blue seat next to his bed and fold my hand over his. Whatever emotions I'd been holding in earlier, to stay composed in front of others, are now pushing their way back to the surface, about to break through.

I'm not strong enough to hold them in any longer.

Before I can even say "hi" to my sweet brother, the floodgates burst open, and I begin sobbing hysterically. I've cried so much these past few months, but that was nothing compared to what is currently happening to me.

I'm hearing animal noises and screams, as if I'm still just a casual observer in this particular encounter. I'm not okay.

I'm worried I may never be okay again.

I almost lost my brother.

My favorite person.

I continue to rub circles over his hand with my thumb as I lean forward and close my eyes, pressing my ear to his chest just to hear the sound of his breathing.

———

Ethan woke up with a fever, but Mom was still passed out in her bedroom down the hall. We knew better than to wake her in this state, knew from plenty of experience.

Children just wanting a small piece of their parent's attention and love, only to be shut out time and time again.

We were going to miss the bus if we didn't leave soon, but Ethan was in no condition to go anywhere, and I was not about to leave him in her care when he was like this.

At ten years old, we shouldn't have had to take care of ourselves, but our mom had certainly shown she was unfit. I tried giving her the benefit of the doubt for so long, but it was increasingly difficult when she was robbing us of a childhood.

I called the school, using my best Linda Graham voice to inform them that "Ethan and Elsie will be home sick today and possibly the rest of the week."

I proceeded to take care of my sweet, sick brother, getting him fever meds, making chicken soup, and rubbing slow circles over his hand while we spent the day lounging in his bed watching *The Lord of the Rings*. Every few hours, I would check his temperature and replace the damp washcloth on his forehead, careful not to get his favorite *TMNT* sheets wet.

Mom eventually emerged from her room, barely spared us a glance, and left for one of her jobs. No questions about why we were home at noon on a Wednesday or how Ethan was even feeling.

Just an observation that we simply existed in her house.

That was all we would see of her for the rest of the day.

———

It didn't used to be like that. I can remember a time when our whole family was actually happy and enjoyed each other's company. Back before Dad left us to start a new family.

Ethan and I wondered if it was because we weren't enough. Would he have stayed if we had just tried a little harder?

As my tears subside, my mind begins to clear. Sharpen.

I didn't lose him. He's right here. I can feel him. I can hear him breathing.

He's going to be okay.

But someone tried to hurt my brother. If they thought we would be scared and tuck our tails between our legs and just go home now, they have made a huge miscalculation.

They fucked with my brother. And I do not forgive that.

Game on, motherfucker.

31

I jolt up in bed, clutching my chest. What the fuck? My pounding heart is thrumming in my ears as I look around sleepily, trying to pull myself into the present moment.

Hotel room.

Jade asleep.

WyvernFest weekend.

My breathing slows down.

But my eyes are so heavy. What time is it?

I look over at the nightstand. 6:45 a.m.

I remember going to sleep around…three.

Because we just got back from the hospital.

Ethan.

It all comes flooding back to me as I rub a hand down my face, trying to clear the last of my sleep haze away. Dread and sadness settling in its place.

The doctors insisted we all go and get some rest, as they didn't expect Ethan's condition to change much overnight. Damien drove me and Jade back here, none of us really speaking all that much, the reality of what happened hanging heavily over our heads.

Someone tried to kill Ethan, and he was almost taken away from me, and we are no closer to finding the person — or people — doing all this.

I reach for my glasses and unplug my phone from the night-stand, settling back against the headboard. My phone died before we left the hospital, and when we got in, I only had enough energy left to take out my contacts, plug in my phone, and curl up in bed.

Apparently, I've missed a few texts from Andy, starting just after three a.m., that I never saw before passing out.

ANDY (3:03 A.M.)

Elsie, any updates?

Are you still at the hospital?

ANDY (3:29 A.M.)

I'll take no updates as a good sign, hopefully you all are getting some rest.

Please call me in the morning.

I hope he wasn't waiting up for an update from me. I wasn't even thinking about him last night, to be honest. I call Andy back, but he doesn't answer. Hopefully he was able to get some sleep too.

Then I notice a missed call and a voicemail from Detective Hawthorn. Lying back under the covers I listen to the message.

Hi Elsie, this is Detective Michael Hawthorn. I wanted you to hear it from me, but Andrew has been detained for questioning...

I jolt upright again.

...I know he is a friend of yours, so I wanted to let you know as a courtesy, because I know he means a great deal to both of us. Please call me back if

you have any questions. We are at the Glenville Police Department on Grady Street. Goodbye.

My head is spinning.

Did I hear that right? Detained for questioning? What the fuck?

Just a few hours ago, he was texting me, asking for updates about Ethan, and now he's being detained? For what?

I need to get Jade up and over to the station. She'll be able to help...somehow.

I throw my pillow at her. "Jade! Jade! We've got to get up!"

She groans as she turns over. "What...what? What's wrong?" She's quiet as her brain gets up to speed. "Is it about Ethan?"

"No, it's Andy. The police have taken him in for questioning. We've got to get down there!"

"Wait...what? Slow down. Has he been arrested or just detained?" she says sleepily, rubbing her eyes.

"Uhh, I don't know, is there a difference? Hawthorn just said detained."

"Okay, that's good. He should be out soon then. They can't detain him for longer than necessary, it's usually just a few hours max."

"So what do we do?"

"Well, so far, there's nothing to do. And if he needs a lawyer, I can't represent him since I'm not licensed to practice in Indiana. Plus, I'm leaving tonight, remember?" She scrubs a hand down her face. "But we can drop by the station and check on him before heading to the hospital if you want."

I nod. "Let's get ready then."

I really need a shower, but I don't think we have time. I pull my hair back up into a messy bun atop my head, exchanging the sweatshirt for an oversized *Animal Crossing* t-shirt, since the day is bound to be ungodly hot and humid again.

I was hoping to go check on Ethan first thing today, but if there was any change, the hospital would've called me.

We can get over to Andy real quick and then pick up breakfast on the way to the hospital. Damien can go stay with Ethan until we get there. Plus, he'll know all the medical jargon they keep throwing at us and be able to translate it into real words we can actually understand.

Once I get my contacts in, I sling my purse over my shoulder and leave the room to go knock on Damien's door. He'll want to come with us, but I need him at the hospital watching over Ethan. In all the crime and murder stories, you always hear about the killer coming back to finish the job. Someone should be with him at all times.

There is no way Andy can be Tamara's kidnapper. But why was he detained? What happened last night?

Or what if he's being framed? After that video from the diner was posted, everyone knew he was with her right before she disappeared. He would be an easy target.

Then there's still the question of why this person would target Ethan. Maybe he saw something or figured something out. Perhaps we are getting close.

He needs to stay safe. I *need* him to stay safe.

It takes a few knocks before Damien finally opens the door, I assume because I'm waking him up. Suddenly, I'm faced with the sight of a bare, olive brown chest. It's not like I haven't seen him without a shirt before, but there's something about the sleepy look in his eyes, the messy bed hair and dark stubble, and strong arms that look like they could throw me around a little, that's really doing it for me right now.

His grey sweatpants ride low on his hips, the thin material—

Look up now, Elsie. Stop staring, you absolute psycho.

My eyes dart up to Damien's face and see that he's grinning at me. Leaning against the doorframe, arms crossed, with one foot casually propped over the other, he one hundred percent caught me staring at him. Again.

I may never live this down.

My face heats as I press on, eyes averted from his amused expression. "Hey!"

Well that came out way too chipper. *Tone it down.*

"Umm...hey, so Jade and I have to go down to the police station. They've taken Andy in for questioning."

His smile drops instantly as he uncrosses his arms and pushes off the doorframe. "Oh shit. Okay, no problem. I'll come with you."

"No, no," I blurt out as I put up my hands. "I actually came to ask if you'd go stay with Ethan until we get there. I'm worried that he might not be out of the woods yet, or you know..."

"The bad guy is going to come back and finish the job?"

"Right? You get it."

There's that amused look again. "As long as you and Jade are okay on your own, I'm more than happy to go on Ethan duty. I'm going to pack up our stuff in my car first, just in case Ethan needs anything. Plus, we don't know when he could be discharged."

Right, because Damien drove Ethan out here this weekend, and he probably has work in the morning. I can't think about all that right now.

"Okay, so we'll meet you back at the hospital a little later? We'll pick up breakfast."

"Can't say no to that."

I almost go in for a hug but get flustered and settle for an awkward wave. I see him smiling as he closes his door.

I'm walking back to my room when I get another text. This one from Greg, the photographer.

GREG (7:08 A.M.)

Morning Elsie! Sorry for not getting back to you last night. So many photos to get through.

Didn't find a whole lot but thought this one might be of interest to you.

[photo attached]

Take care, I hope to see you around today!

I click on the attachment and stare at the photo. "Holy shit."

<h1 style="text-align:center">32</h1>

The photo Greg sent me must have been taken early on that first day. The main subject is a cosplayer, Princess Peach, posing for the camera, but just behind her in the background is Tamara, talking on a shiny green phone, being led through a crowd by some random guy dressed in black — a con worker...or handler — followed by Andy, whose eyes are trained on Tamara.

There's a lot going on here.

The handler...I wonder if this is the real handler or if the switch has been made already. I don't recognize him, but this will be good to have in case there are any new suspects.

I click off my phone screen with a sigh.

"Why would they take him in for questioning?" I ask Jade as she drives us to the police station. "Do you think he actually has something to do with her disappearance?"

"I wouldn't worry too much yet. The fact that they haven't arrested him means there's not enough evidence to do so. They might just need more information, or..."

"Or what?"

"Well, it's possible they're starting to feel some pressure to handle this quickly now that it's becoming such a high-profile case."

In the past twenty-four hours, news of Tamara's disappearance and possible kidnapping has spread like wildfire. Supposedly, a few camera crews have been set up around the hotel and convention center since yesterday afternoon. People are hungry for news about what happened to her.

The ambulance last night must have gone to a side entrance of the building, because I don't remember seeing anyone. Although my memories of last night are hazy at best.

"What do you mean, what kind of pressure?" I don't like the sound of that.

Jade twists her mouth, trying to find the right words as she focuses on the road ahead. "There could be pressure from higher up to solve the case quickly...regardless of whether it leads to the proper conclusion."

"You mean they're going to try and pin it on Andy?"

She shrugs. "I don't know, babe. All I'm saying is don't worry just yet. We're going to go see what we can do to help."

We pull up to the Glenville Police Department around seven thirty a.m. I'm surprised when I don't see any news vans or camera crews here, which means Andy being taken in was kept under wraps. Maybe Hawthorn did that as a courtesy to his friend, so speculation of his involvement wouldn't go public just yet.

Jade climbs out of the car wearing a stunning purple pantsuit and matching stilettos, her short natural curls swept perfectly to one side. From out of the trunk, she procures a fancy black leather briefcase.

As I come to her side, she begins flawlessly strutting towards the building, spine straight as steel, but I stop her with a hand on her elbow.

"Okay, I just have to know. Do you always pack a work outfit with you wherever you go? On the off chance your incredible lawyer services will be needed?"

She levels me with a stare and a quirk of her brow. "Seriously? You don't recognize it?"

I look her up and down, confusion lining my face. "Recognize what?"

"It's my Joker suit, babe."

My eyes go wide.

"Without the green vest, wig, and makeup, it's actually quite a respectable outfit, don't you think?"

God, I love her. "Incredible. You're incredible, Jade."

"I know," she says with a wink.

Her whole demeanor screams power, and...something like enchantment. I will never cease to be amazed by her.

Jade opens the door to the small brick building, and we walk inside with as much confidence as we can muster. Easier for some of us than others. Maybe I should've changed into my Serafina costume for this, but I guess I'll just cosplay as Put-Together Elsie for now.

Jade's heels click on the grey linoleum floor as a uniformed young woman with a kind face pops her head over the reception desk.

"May I help you, ladies?" she says, pausing her typing.

Jade steps up to the desk, resting an arm casually on the ledge and says to the woman who appears to be a rookie, "Yes, I'm Attorney Jade Crawford, I'm here to see Mr. Andrew Locke. I believe he is being detained here."

"Oh...umm..." Her eyes go wide as Jade continues.

"I would like to know exactly what time he is being released."

The rookie gets to her feet and nods, her blonde bob swaying. "L-l-let me go check, Ms. Crawford." She nearly stumbles to the hallway, anxious to leave this conversation like she knows she could be Jade's next meal if she so much as breathes wrong.

I give Jade a wink and decide to text Damien to see how Ethan is doing.

ME (7:42 A.M.)

hey we're at the station. let me know if there are any updates with Ethan

DAMIEN (7:43 A.M.)

of course. I'm here but visiting hours don't start until 8

not much longer now

ME (7:44 A.M.)

thanks MeeMee

DAMIEN (7:44 A.M.)

oh there's a throwback

thought I told you to stop calling me that years ago ;)

ME (7:45 A.M.)

I dunno, I think it's making a comeback

I can't help but smile. Talking like this with Damien feels as natural to me as breathing. We're just picking back up like no time has even passed.

I'm grateful he is there, but it's killing me not to be with Ethan right now. Hopefully this won't take long, and we can head back to the hospital soon. After picking up some breakfast, of course.

I still don't understand why they would detain Andy though. I reread my texts with him from last night, trying to understand what happened between the time he messaged me and when Hawthorn called.

It doesn't make sense.

His texts asking for updates on Ethan spanned from about three to three thirty a.m., and the voicemail from Hawthorn was at 3:56. I first texted Andy from the hospital around one a.m., and he said he was with Hawthorn, and that Hawthorn had just picked him up.

What did they do after that? What happened?

I try not to think too much about it. Jade says they don't have enough to arrest him, but if the cops are feeling pressure to wrap this up, and they've picked Andy to take the fall, we need to move quickly. We have to find Tamara and get this solved before they find a way to pin it all on Andy.

I mean, there's no way that Andy, of all people, could be behind this. I know I may not have the greatest track record when it comes to trusting men, but the thing that always brings me back is the fact that Ethan was targeted too.

He was like a little brother to Andy, and Andy would never cause Ethan harm. I refuse to believe he has anything to do with this.

I look at Jade. My best friend. The kick-ass, smart as hell lawyer.

Our very own Defender of Justice.

She will help get Andy out. She will get to the bottom of all this.

No one is more driven or determined than Jade. She knew she wanted to become a lawyer nearly a decade ago when her uncle was wrongfully convicted of armed robbery. She saw the injustice of it all and decided at just sixteen years old that she would do something about it. She made it her goal to help overturn the conviction.

Unfortunately, he passed away in prison a few years later, before she even got her law degree. Since then, she has never stopped fighting for others and standing up for what is right.

A text from Damien comes through at the same moment the rookie cop returns to her desk.

DAMIEN (7:52 A.M.)

He's awake

They're moving him out of the ICU now and
they'll let me see him soon

I can't even hear what the rookie is saying to Jade.

I don't even care.

My heart is fluttering in my chest, and I can't contain the grin overtaking my face.

Holy shit, he's awake.

I breathe a long sigh of relief, tipping my head back. We need to get out of here. I need to get to Ethan. To see with my own eyes that he's awake and that he's okay.

"…nothing more I can say at this time, Ms. Crawford."

"Is Detective Hawthorn here? I'd like to speak with him."

"He went home a few hours ago. He won't be back until later."

"I see. And what is your name?"

"M-my name? Um, my name is Ruby—I mean, Officer Campion."

"Well, Officer Ruby Campion, please tell your superiors that if he is not released soon, I will be sending word to the media that this police department is illegally detaining a citizen and cannot be trusted to handle a case of such importance."

The rookie officer just stands there, frozen in place, unable to respond.

"Have a wonderful day," Jade says sweetly as she turns on her heel, nodding her head towards the doors in a request for me to follow.

I wait until we are past the front doors to say, "Holy shit, that was incredible. She looked like she was going to puke back there."

Jade flings on her sunglasses and smiles towards the morning sun warming her face.

I add, "Ethan is awake. He's being moved out of the ICU now."

She stops walking and grabs my arm, eyes wide. "What? That's incredible! Let's fucking go!"

I wrap my arms around her. Finally some hope, some good news to celebrate.

"But first..." I start as we pull apart, and we both respond at the same time. "Food."

We get in the car to make the short drive to one of our favorite spots for breakfast burritos. I pull out my phone again to let Damien know we're leaving the station.

ME (8:02 A.M.)

we're on the way

want your usual burrito?

DAMIEN (8:03 A.M.)

you know it!

ME (8:07 A.M.)

how is he? what's he doing?

ME (8:08 A.M.)

???

DAMIEN (8:12 A.M.)

sorry! was talking to the doc

he's a little out of it but talking

doc said he made great improvements overnight

cognitive function is good minus some short-term memory loss

My heart picks up. I don't like the sound of that.

ME (8:14 A.M.)

memory loss?

DAMIEN (8:14 A.M.)

he doesn't remember anything from yesterday

ME (8:15 A.M.)

fuck

DAMIEN (8:15 A.M.)

but he's good Els. really.

we should know more after they run tests but it looks really good

new room # is 623

I let out a long breath. He's awake. He's going to be okay. Everything else we'll just figure out later.

ME (8:17 A.M.)

thank you Damien

thanks for being there ♥

I see the bubbles come up, meaning he's typing, but it keeps disappearing like he's typing and then erasing his message over and over again.

When Jade hands me the bags of food from the drive-thru, he still hasn't replied, and I just sit there waiting.

Finally, it pops up.

DAMIEN (8:19 A.M.)

Always

33

I'm already diving into my greasy bacon, egg, cheese, and potato breakfast burrito before Jade even hits the main road. She gives me a look that I know means *do not make a mess in my car*.

I can see St. Mary's Hospital in the distance, since this city is small enough for everything to be within just a few minutes of each other.

After washing down the last bite of my burrito with a sip of coffee, I say, "If I'm being honest, I'm not sure we're going to be able to solve all this in time."

Jade just nods.

"I mean, it's the last day of WyvernFest. Most people are going home tonight. Plus, I just want to be with Ethan."

"It's okay to walk away from this, you know."

I look out the window, contemplating everything. I get where she's coming from, I just hate giving up when it feels like we're getting close. Have we really done all we can? Considered every possible suspect? Studied every clue?

Last night, I was all ready to avenge Ethan. To do whatever it takes to find out who did this and make them pay. But in the light of day, the harsh reality is crashing down on me that we can only do so much.

"And there's no way to find out why they brought Andy in for questioning? What they might have found?"

"Not unless he wants to tell us himself."

The only evidence we have right now is the hat from the alley and the notes with those random numbers on the back. We never figured those out. Of course, they're probably a dead end too, just like everything else has been.

Maybe once Ethan is feeling well enough, we can ask him what he remembers before blacking out. If he really was drugged then I want to know why.

Did he see something? Did he find something out about the kidnapper that made them deem him a threat? That's the only explanation I can think of for why someone would try and kill Ethan.

He must know something, and we need to find out what it is before it's too late.

After getting off the elevator on the sixth floor, we quickly walk down the hospital hallways towards Ethan's room. My heart is pounding, antiseptic tickling my nostrils.

I open the door to room 623 and am immediately flooded with relief when I see him awake, but my heart sinks just as quickly at how weak he still looks. My brave and fearless brother, confined to a hospital bed, hooked up to monitors and IVs.

He'll be fine. He has to be.

He pauses his discussion with Damien when he sees me and flashes me a warm, beautiful smile. I run the short distance to him and lean down to wrap my arms around him as best I can around all the wires.

Squeezing him as tight as I can, I laugh softly, but it quickly turns to sobs. One of his arms comes around my shoulders, and to my surprise, he starts crying too. He rarely shows this much vulnerability, not since we were little kids.

"I love you," I whisper in his ear between sobs, making sure he knows for sure. I'll say it every day, so he always knows.

"I love you too, sis," he chokes back.

We stay there, embracing for a minute or so, letting the tears run dry before I pull myself away. Jade and Damien have stayed quiet, giving us this moment together.

I ruffle his hair to try and break the overwhelming flood of emotions, pulling a smile from him.

"So…what's new with you?" he asks casually, making me laugh.

"Oh you know, little of this, little of that," I say with a wave of my hand.

"Doc said I almost died. What the fuck was that about, huh?" He's trying to joke around, but I still sense that very real fear he keeps hidden just below the surface. I could always see right through him, but I'll indulge him in this playful sparring.

"I know, right? Although I wouldn't have minded inheriting all your video games and mint-in-the-box action figures. Those things must be worth a fortune by now."

"Oh fuck off," he says with a smirk.

We both tend to use humor as a defense mechanism and resort to joking when things are tough, but underneath it all, we both know what the other is thinking.

Too close. That was entirely too close.

We'll talk through all the serious stuff in due time, but for now, we just need to get each other through this. Ethan and I have been through so much together, and we'll get through this too.

I affectionately wipe away one of the last tears streaking down his pale cheek before I back away and take a seat next to

Damien, who is already halfway finished with his breakfast burrito.

Jade goes over to Ethan and squeezes his hand. "Hey, E. Welcome back."

"Looking sharp there, J." He gives her a wink. "You miss me?"

She rolls her eyes and ignores his question. "You hungry? Got your fave." Jade waves the foil-wrapped burrito back and forth, but Ethan shakes his head.

"Nah, go ahead and put it on the table, I'm not quite ready to eat yet."

She puts it down on a nearby tray next to a set of keys. Pulling her own food out of the paper bag, she looks around for a place to sit, and Damien jumps out of his chair and motions for her to take his.

The room falls into a heavy silence while Jade and Damien eat their breakfast, and we all try to get a handle on what to say or do.

Is Ethan even ready to get into any of this right now? I don't want to push him, but we're kind of running short on time if we want any chance of figuring this thing out.

Plus, I'm not sure there is ever going to be a right time to tell him that Andy was taken in for questioning.

He'll be released soon, so there's no point in worrying him.

Right now, we just need to find out what Ethan knows.

I pull my chair up next to his bedside, placing a casual elbow on his bed and propping my chin on my hand. "So..." I start, but Ethan cuts me off with a raised hand.

"I know what you're going to ask, but I don't remember what happened."

"That's okay. What *do* you remember?" I ask, placing a hand over his.

"Last thing was visiting Andy at his signing." He pauses as if trying to reach for the missing pieces. "Hey, where is Andy by the way, have you talked to him? Any news on Tamara yet?"

Jade and I exchange a quick look as I tuck a loose strand of hair behind my ear, unsure of how much to tell him. I really don't want to upset him right now.

"No news on Tamara. Everyone is still looking. But we're kind of at a dead end. We really don't have much to go on right now, unless we can figure out what happened last night."

He seems to notice that I didn't really answer his question about Andy — because of course he does — but thankfully, he doesn't push. Instead, he uses his big brain and starts trying to put things together to see the bigger picture.

"So, the docs say I was on Xanax. That I OD'd." He looks around at us nervously. "You all know I didn't take anything on purpose. Someone did this to me."

"We know." I rub slow circles over his hand. "We need to figure out *why* someone did this to you, and maybe that could lead us to who would've wanted you...dead." That last word is barely a whisper.

"Exactly," Jade says, slipping into lawyer mode. "We backtrack, figure out what happened before Kat's party. Maybe you found something out about the kidnapper, or found some sort of evidence or something? Any of that ring a bell?"

He thinks about it, clearly struggling to bring it all into focus, when he angles his head. "Bell...? Wait...There was an alarm, a fire alarm, right?" He looks up at us hopefully.

"Yes!" I squeeze his hand. "We left with a huge crowd, but we got separated. You stayed inside to follow the Mandalorian guy. Then you brought us through the back entrance, and we looked around for a bit before getting caught and had to run back out."

He furrows his brow. "Yeah, I think I remember that. Did we see something or figure something out though? I feel like something else happened."

I look around to the group. "No, honey, we went back to the con and just hung out until dinner and then went to Kat's party."

Ethan twists his mouth to the side and shrugs.

"Damien, how long does it take for memories to return with something like this?" I ask.

"There's no way to know. Could be hours, could be days, if they return at all. Depends on the extent of the damage to the brain."

Shit.

But then an idea strikes me. "E, what about your phone? Were you texting anyone yesterday? Did you take any pictures?"

"Search history?" Jade adds.

We all sit up a bit while Ethan grabs his phone and starts scrolling and searching his phone. "Looks like I took a few pics of the guy I was following."

"Can I see?"

He angles his phone so I can look. There's the Mandalorian cosplayer indeed, looking down at a phone. I zoom in on it to see if I can make out what it looks like.

A shiny green case.

Bingo.

I pull up the photo Greg sent me this morning of Tamara on her phone. The same shiny green phone.

"I was right," I say, grabbing Ethan's phone and holding the pictures side by side. "The Mandalorian is our guy. That's Tamara's phone. He posted that weird message on social media after the fire alarm went off!"

"How do we find out who he is?" Damien asks.

"I don't know." I hand Ethan's phone back to him. "And you don't remember anything else after following him?"

"The only photo I have after that is a selfie I took before the party." He flips his phone around to reveal a smiling, half-naked, mustachioed Walter White, giving a thumbs up in one of the hotel room's full-length mirrors. "I'm guessing Kat had her no-phone rule in place?"

We all nod, and he puts his phone back on his bed before scrubbing his hands down his face.

After a minute or two of silence, he finally says, "What did Andy's detective friend say? They still don't have any suspects?"

"I haven't seen him since the first night when we gave him the notes," I deflect, looking to Damien.

"That wasn't yesterday?"

"No that was Friday. It's Sunday now."

So much has happened this weekend that it's hard to believe we should be off enjoying our last day of WyvernFest.

I doubt Ethan will be discharged today either. I guess if we need to, I can have him transferred to the hospital closer to our house. How long does it take to recover from a benzo overdose anyway?

I really need to find his doctor and get an update on everything so I can start making a plan.

I'm supposed to be at work at ten a.m. tomorrow, so the absolute latest I can stay is eight, but that would be cutting it really close. I know Jade and Damien have demanding jobs to get back to and won't be able to stay any extra days either.

We have to figure this out today.

If we don't see this through, we'll all just have to walk away from it and go home, back to our normal everyday lives. There's nothing more we'd be able to do for Tamara or for Andy, except hope that things just work out for the best.

"When is everyone planning to head home?" I ask.

"Tonight, unfortunately," Jade answers first. "I gotta be up and professional at an ungodly hour."

"I really should leave tonight too. I've got an early shift tomorrow...unless you want me to stay," Damien says. "I can call and see if someone can cover me."

My heart squeezes, knowing he would stay if I asked him to.

Hell, he'd probably do anything I asked of him, because that's just who he is. Who he's always been. Selfless, caring, always looking out for others.

But I don't want to take advantage of that kindness.

"No, no, it's okay. I'll stay with Ethan. We've got one of the hotel rooms for another night, right? We'll figure it out."

I pause.

The hotel rooms…

I suddenly wonder what happened with Tamara's hotel room and if she would still be checked in over there.

Tamara's…hotel room.

What was in there, I wonder? Did the police already search the place?

They did a welfare check when she missed her Q&A on that first day, but have the police officially declared it foul play for their investigation? Surely they checked the room for evidence.

A plan starts to form in my mind.

I turn to Ethan, eyes flashing. "How hard would it be to break into someone's hotel room?"

34

"I'm sorry..." Ethan's eyebrows scrunch together. "Whose room are we breaking into?"

I look around the room at everyone, as if it's obvious. "Tamara's."

"Are you serious? We can't do that!" Jade says, ever the lawyer.

"I agree, I'm not so sure that's a good idea," Damien adds as the protector. "What if the kidnapper is hiding out in there? Haven't we put ourselves in enough danger?"

Ethan hasn't said anything, but the look on his face tells me he thinks I'm out of my mind.

I guess it's three against one.

"Look, it's not like I *want* to do this." *Except I totally do.* "But we're running out of options. You're both leaving tonight. Ethan was almost murdered. Tamara is still missing, and Andy is being detained by the police."

"*What?!*" Ethan shoots up, wincing at the sudden movement. *Shit.*

I turn to him, plastering on a smile. "It's nothing, he'll be out before we know it. They can't hold him much longer without a charge anyway. It's going to be fine."

"They can't possibly think Andy had anything to do with this. There's no way!" He slams his hand down on the bed, his chest rising and falling with rapid breaths. The beeping monitors by his bedside start picking up speed.

"I know, I know, it's okay. We know he didn't do anything." I squeeze his hands again, trying to help calm him down. "I'm sorry, I didn't mean to upset you. We can talk about this later."

"This is all just fucked. I know Andy, he wouldn't hurt anyone. Someone has to be setting him up."

"I know. I think you might be right."

"But who would do that? I..." Ethan stops himself, and his eyes move side to side as the gears in his mind start turning. He's close to figuring something out, but he's struggling to get there.

"E? What is it?"

He narrows his eyes a little and looks to me. "Did we talk about this before? That someone could be framing him?" He keeps searching his mind for the answers that won't come.

I shake my head. "I don't think we talked about it. It's just the only thing that makes sense right now. We know Andy would never do this to you. It's probably some crazy fan who thinks Andy would make an easy fall guy."

He knocks his head with his palm. "Fuck! I can't remember anything! I fucking hate this. If someone is going after Andy, we need to stop them!"

"It's okay, it's okay," I say. "Let's just take a step back. You need to rest. Stressing out isn't going to help anything. We can talk it out later."

Ethan rakes a hand through his messy copper hair and then back down his face.

We both take a breath and try to calm ourselves, leaving a heavy silence between us.

Who *would* do this? Who would take Tamara and then try to kill Ethan? Who would frame Andy, and why?

Ethan looks at his tray with the breakfast burrito on it.

"You want it?" I ask.

He simply shakes his head. It's a little unnerving seeing Ethan like this, not his usual joking self. Not the life of the party or the energetic, joyous center of attention.

"Okay, so…" I clap my hands together as I stand up, looking around the room. "Let's talk about how I can break into Tamara's room. Whatcha got?" I can only hope Ethan's freakish tech knowledge extends to this sort of thing.

"Els, are you being serious right now?"

"Yes, I'm serious. I'm getting in there."

I don't even care that everyone in this room is looking at me like I'm crazy. Like they're all just done with this, the novelty of it having worn off long ago.

"Okay, well, first of all, you can't exactly just break in. Each room has an RFID lock that is tied to its own room key. So your best bet is going to get a key."

"And how am I supposed to get Tamara's room key?" I blink at him. "Oh, is there like a master key? Maybe I could sneak in there and swipe it off some unsuspecting housekeeper?"

"Yeah sure, you go do that. Let me know how it works out." He waves a hand at me.

"Okay fine, then help me out here!"

"*Why?*" he snaps at me. "Why is it *so important* that you get in there, Els? Why can't you let this go? I nearly *died* last night and all you can think about — still — is meeting your goddamn hero, Tamara Jenkins!"

Ouch.

His words land like a punch to the gut. I rarely see this side of him, no one does. His tight grasp on his emotions is slipping, showing us how vulnerable and scared he really is.

The silence in the room is palpable as he looks off to the side, too upset to even look me in the eye.

I take a deep breath to steady myself. I need him to understand. "Ethan. It's *because* you almost died that I need to see this through." I put my hand on his leg. "Whoever took Tamara also tried to *kill you*. You want to help Andy? Then we need to find whoever really did this before it's too late."

I fight the tightness in my chest as I try to finish what I need to say. "I almost lost you, Ethan. I can't just sit around and wait for things to magically be okay again. I'm going to find out who did this, with or without your help."

The stinging behind my eyes gives way to a single tear that splashes onto his hand. He finally turns to me and nods. It's all I need before I lean back down for a hug, pressing my ear to his chest. Still needing that reassurance, to feel his heart beating, reminding me he's still here.

That he'll still be here tomorrow when we go back to our real life.

I pull away, and Ethan's face seems to soften as he stares up at me with those sweet, baby blue eyes. The same eyes as Dad.

"Fine, I'll help you," he starts as he carefully hides all traces of emotion he let slip just moments ago. "But only because I want you to stop ugly crying…you look ridiculous."

That pulls a startled laugh out of me. I nod and pull myself together so we can get through this. "Fair enough," I say with a smile.

"So there's really only one way I can see us getting a key to her room — wait, do you know her room number?" he asks.

I purse my lips and squint, hoping my imminent confession isn't a deal breaker. "No…?"

"Cool cool cool. Great start." He rolls his eyes. "Okay, well if you can get behind the computer at the front desk you should be able to make your own key card pretty easily. Once you figure out her room number, of course."

"Oh yeah, just jump behind the front desk like I work there? You're not suggesting—" I pause to pinch my chin for dramatic effect, "—that I steal some clothes and cosplay as a hotel employee, are you? 'Cause that might be a bit much, although I'm not entirely ruling it out if I have to. For the good of the mission, of course."

Damien is leaning against the wall shaking his head, but smiling.

"I can't give you all the answers here, but I can talk you through the software and how to make the key once you're in."

"You know I'm sitting right here?" Jade says with a hand raised. "I really shouldn't be hearing any of this to keep plausible deniability an option for myself should you get caught."

"*We* are not going to get caught." A smile tugs at my lips.

She raises an eyebrow. "We?"

<h1 style="text-align:center">35</h1>

We decide to wait until noon to commence the plan — a window between guest check-outs and check-ins — hopefully when enough employees will be on their lunch breaks that we can go unnoticed.

Jade is obviously opposed to participating in anything illegal, so her job is to simply distract the front desk employee long enough for me to find Tamara's room number and make myself a key.

I assume it won't be as easy as searching "Tamara Jenkins" in the guest database. It's likely she booked the room under an alias, so I'll have to scroll through the entire guest list and see if I can figure out the name she was staying under. Let's hope my freakish knowledge of the details of her life finally come in handy in this moment. If there was ever a purpose to being a superfan, this has to be it.

You know, to illegally break into her hotel room.

Like a stalker.

When it's time, we walk from the lounge area towards the front desk, trying to look as casual as possible. Easier for Jade, because she doesn't possess the awkward gene like me.

Lord knows what I'd end up saying to someone in a fit of panic.

But Jade? She is practically spellbinding. A real-life mage, capable of rendering even the most powerful men speechless. The tallest and bravest become a groveling mess at her feet.

"You ready?" I ask, as if I didn't already know.

"Are *you* ready, babe?"

That remains to be seen. But ready or not, here we come.

We split off once we're in view of the front desk, grateful that the Graystar Hotel employee I talked to on that first day and told to have a nice stay, has been replaced by a scrawny, twenty-something young man. He will be no match for Jade. Hopefully she can work her magic and lure him away just long enough for me to access the system.

I watch the scene play out from behind the fake plants at the base of the stairs, transfixed by how easily she slips into this role.

From this spot, I can't hear their conversation, but knowing Jade as well as I do, I know exactly what she's doing. Flirting with such ease and magnetism that even I can't look away. He's buying it too. Now I just need her to take this man-child out of view.

After a few minutes pass and he still hasn't budged, I begin to fear our plan won't work. There are no guests in sight right now, but it would just take one trying to check in early for our plan to be foiled.

"Come on, Jade," I say to myself as I continue to wait impatiently.

Finally, she leans over the desk and whispers something in his ear that makes his face flush and the pen fall from his hand. She walks around to his side of the counter and holds her hand out, which he takes after a quick, nervous look around.

Damn she's good.

He fumbles for something under the desk and procures a

little sign that says, "Ring Bell For Service" before following Jade around the corner and out of sight.

Here we go.

I walk towards the front desk and hold my hand slightly over my face, in the event any security cameras will pick up what I'm doing. Hopefully I can get in and out quickly without anyone noticing, or even realizing there would be a need to look at the footage. If the cameras are even working again.

We probably should have had Ethan break into the security system remotely from the hospital like the little hacker he is, but it's too late now. Security cameras be damned.

I try to steady myself, standing in front of the computer, remembering that I only have one shot at this. Luckily for me, in the kid's haze of being under Jade's spell he forgot to log himself out and just left his computer on, open for anyone to peruse.

And peruse I shall.

I follow the directions Ethan gave me earlier and locate the directory of guests staying here. I try my luck real quick searching "Tamara Jenkins," knowing in my heart it won't be that easy.

Zero results, of course.

So I start speed scanning down the list.

There has to be some way to tell which name she used…right?

Ava Wilson
Mackayla Anderson
Brian Kim
Logan Price
Jamie Ortiz

Nothing out of the ordinary. Nothing tying them to Tamara. Shit, I need to hurry. More and more names fly past.

Jamal Jackson
Sam Beaumont
Benjamin Warden
Jennifer Taylor

Wait.

Something snags at my memory.

Benjamin is her dog's name.

Could be a coincidence, it's a fairly common name. But Warden? Is that anything?

I close my eyes, trying to scan my brain for all the Tamara Jenkins knowledge I possess, but nothing clicks. It's not her dad's name or her mom's maiden name.

Quickly, quickly.

I go ahead and select the name to open the guest profile, hoping there's another clue in here to confirm that this is really her. It's my only shot, and I need to be sure.

Let's see, Benjamin Warden. Home address in Los Angeles, that's a good sign. I won't even try to memorize the address like a crazy stalker, which takes great restraint.

What else, what else.

Checked in Thursday, supposed to check out tomorrow.

Housekeeping came Friday morning…but a hold was put on cleaning Friday afternoon for the rest of the stay. I scan the rest of the profile for any more information. At the bottom under "Notes" there's a strange set of letters and numbers, probably some code used by the hotel. But also:

****Glenville Police Department****
Possible crime scene
Room has been held until further notice

Bingo. Room 509.

I find the option to *Create Room Key* and follow the prompts just like Ethan explained. Looking under the desk, I fumble to find a blank card. Once I locate them, I slide one into the machine, waiting for it to flash red.

The screen says "Successfully Created Room Key" and I close out of everything as fast as I possibly can, looking around to make sure the coast is still clear.

509? Her room was on the same floor as ours this entire time?

I can hear Jade in the distance, but her voice is unnaturally loud, as if warning me that they were coming back. I grab the key card and shove it into my pocket and crawl away from the front desk in an attempt to look like I was simply tying my shoe.

Nailed it.

Natural 20 roll for stealth.

Thankfully, the ensorcelled young man comes around the corner a moment later, never seeing or suspecting a thing, still engaged in his conversation with Jade. I can tell that she has him looking at photos of her best cosplay on her phone.

"...and you *made* this? Wow."

I stand up and pull out my phone to fake scroll, passing without a trace towards the elevators. I take one last glance back at Jade, who is still stuck in conversation with the young man, as I step into the elevator alone.

When the doors begin to close, her warning glare cuts straight to my heart as I mouth, *Sorry.*

She'll be furious with me for going up there without her. Absolutely furious. But I can't put any more of my friends in danger for my reckless ideas. She can't be involved in this anyway; I won't put her career or her safety at risk for this.

No, this is a solo mission.

I'll be in and out of there quickly, and if someone is in the room, I'll just run away. How bad could it be?

I realize I'm shaking.

I start to second-guess this plan.

Should I really be doing this?

What if the police are in there, or the kidnapper?

When the elevator doors open, I have to force my legs to start moving.

I need to do this. All it takes is one thought of Ethan and my gut clenches.

The image of him dressed as Walter White, unconscious on the floor of Kat's hotel room is seared into my memory. The possibility that he could've died, ripped away from me by some monster. That's all I need to keep going.

I pray that when I get into her room, I can finally get us some answers. All we need is just one clue to breathe new life into this investigation.

It's the last day of WyvernFest, and most people are busy living it up across the street for as long as they can before returning to their real lives. I just hope everyone is distracted enough that I'm not seen breaking into Tamara Jenkins's room.

My feet bring me to room 509.

I look around and take a deep breath.

I can do this.

With shaky hands, I wave the key card I made over the black panel until the green light blinks and the lock disengages, and slowly push the door open. It's dark inside, so I feel around for the light switch.

When I step into Tamara's room and the lights come on, I find the last person I expected to see.

36

A familiar figure kneels by the window on the opposite side, amid a mess of bed sheets, papers, and women's clothes. His head whips in my direction once the door slams shut and the lights fully illuminate the room.

"Andy?" I gasp.

I'm struggling to comprehend what I'm seeing right now and take a few steps into the room.

"What...what are you doing here? What are you doing in Tamara's room?"

Andy looks at me, pain and guilt written all over his face. "How did *you* get in here?"

I take another deep breath, needing to steady myself.

This betrayal...it feels all too familiar.

"*Answer me!*" I shout. "What the fuck are you doing in here?"

He flinches and puts his hands up in defense, still sitting on his heels. "I know how this looks. Just let me explain. Please. This is not what it looks like."

"Bullshit! Don't tell me what it looks like, Andy! What the actual *fuck*?"

"Elsie, please. Look, there's something you don't know." He pushes a hand through his disheveled hair as he looks off to the side, avoiding eye contact.

He's shaking, rubbing his arms. Panicking.

He's finally been found out and can't come up with any more lies to tell.

"Tamara and I were…we were staying here, together. It's *our* room." He reaches into his pocket and holds up a room key and waves it around erratically. As if that proves anything.

I narrow my eyes and slowly shake my head. "I don't believe you. Do you even hear yourself?"

He's frantic, like he's losing his mind. I don't even recognize this man anymore.

"Look, I have to fix this, okay? This is all my fault."

Holy shit. He's admitting it.

He really did this.

"I put her in that car. She's gone because of me." His voice is strained. Pleading. I don't even understand what he's saying.

All I know is my world is closing in on me.

I barely even notice that I'm biting down on the inside of my cheek. My whole body feels like it's on fire.

I can't even look at him right now. At this man I thought I knew, and trusted. Who was practically family. Like a big brother to both me and Ethan.

Oh God. Ethan.

Andy shakes his head and covers his face with his hands. "I fucked up."

I'm finally starting to see the truth.

He was using me, using us. Keeping us close this whole time to throw us off the investigation, so we wouldn't suspect him. So we would defend him and help him. He used our trust and our friendship against us to get away with taking Tamara and doing…lord knows what with her.

But why? I still don't understand why he would do all this.

My stomach is roiling, and I think I'm going to vomit. I begin scratching at my throat.

"Andy…what did you do?" I can barely get the words out, the quiver in my voice betraying the bravery I'm trying to project.

Fear seeps in at the realization that the man sitting before me is way more dangerous than I ever believed.

Never underestimate someone.

You do not know what they are capable of.

"Elsie, please. You don't understand." He runs a hand through his hair once again, panic flaring in his eyes as he registers my full understanding of the situation. "I love her! We're supposed to be together!" His voice cracks on that last word.

Jesus.

He's completely lost it.

He sounds like…an obsessed, crazy stalker.

What has he done?

I'm not safe in here with him. I have to get out of this room. This is not the man I once knew. He's dangerous, capable of so much more than I ever realized.

I should never have come up here alone. If he was okay with killing Ethan, there's no question he would do the same to me. Or worse.

I back away slowly towards the door, not taking my eyes off him, until I trip over a hard object on the ground and bump into the nearby desk. Something tips over on its surface with a rattle. I look down and my blood runs cold.

An orange prescription bottle.

I know what it is before I even read the label, but I have to see it. I need the proof.

I roll the bottle to its side with a shaky hand.

Andrew Locke
Alprazolam [Xanax]

Terror sets in. I need to get out of here now.

Then I notice next to the bottle of Xanax is a WyvernFest guidebook.

Slowly, I grab both the bottle and the con guide and clutch them to my chest as I look back up at him, forcing myself to breathe.

"I can explain," he says as he slowly stands up. "I never meant for Ethan to get involved in this. For any of you to get involved. You have to believe me."

I shake my head.

A single tear runs down my face as I continue backing away towards the door. I make the mistake of sparing a glance to the floor to see what I had tripped over, and another wave of dread hits me like a bucket of ice water.

What's left of my cold, broken heart shatters.

On the floor is a large red brick.

He was there. He followed Damien and me up to the roof and locked us up there.

All so he could get Ethan alone long enough to slip Xanax in his drink, knowing he was drinking enough alcohol that it could be lethal. And it nearly was.

I force my eyes back up to his, but I'm frozen in place. "How could you do this, Andy? How...how could you?" I can barely speak, the words so low I'm not even sure he heard me.

My feet manage to move me back the remaining few steps, my free hand finding the door handle, but I fumble, filling the silent room with a loud metal *clunk*.

It snaps him out of his trance. His face contorts into panic, and he suddenly starts moving towards me with an outstretched hand. "No, wait!"

After what feels like an excruciating amount of time, I finally get the door open and rush out of the room just before he can reach me. I make a run for the stairwell, since the elevators are too far away, not willing to risk getting stuck waiting for them.

I hear him yelling after me, but I don't dare slow down or look back.

My heart is pounding. The bottle of pills in my hand rattles loudly, echoing through the concrete stairwell along with my thunderous steps, but all I can think about is getting as far away from him as I can.

Tears stream down my cheeks as I flee from a man I once trusted.

Was it all a lie? Was this just the inevitable end to yet another failed relationship in my life? I thought I had hit rock bottom already and was finally starting to climb back out of the darkness.

But this? This feels even worse, because I had allowed myself to feel hope again and trust someone, but it was all a lie. Again.

I blink and suddenly I am in a wedding gown. Tearing down another flight of stairs, unable to breathe, clawing at my throat. Trying not to trip over the tulle of my obnoxious white dress as I flee from the life I thought I wanted.

Betrayal.

My feet hit the landing, and now I'm eight years old. The sound of his old car rumbling to life downstairs. He can't be leaving. He can't leave us. I run down the stairs of my childhood home, Ethan close behind, opening the garage door to beg Dad to please just stay. Only to find it already empty.

Betrayal.

I make it to Level 2, stopping here just in case I need to make a run across the skybridge towards the convention center. The crowd of people there should give me enough cover to escape. Luckily, I don't see or hear him behind me, so I take a moment to catch my breath once I open the door.

I have to find Jade so we can get to Ethan and Damien before Andy does, and I need to call the police. I need to call Hawthorn.

I turn into a corner by the ice machine and roll up the bottle inside the con guide, stuffing it into my purse. I pull out my phone with shaky hands to call Hawthorn, ignoring the several missed calls and texts from a very angry Jade.

First, I need to get him here to arrest Andy for real this time, and maybe they can find out where he's taken Tamara. I only hope we're not too late.

Hawthorn isn't answering.

Goddammit!

I start to walk towards the grand staircase as I dial Jade, who picks up immediately.

"What the hell were you thinking—"

"Jade. Listen to me," I cut her off. "Get back to the lobby, I'm coming down. It was Andy. I just found him in her room, and he was tearing the place apart. He's guilty as hell, yelling stuff about loving her and needing to be together. He did it."

"Fuck, are you serious? Are you safe?" I can hear the alarm in her voice.

"I'm fine, but we need to get out of here. I'm coming down. I'll be there in a few seconds."

"Okay, be careful."

I sprint down the stairs to the lobby where I see Jade waiting nervously at the bottom. I grab her hand and yell, "Let's go!" nearly knocking over a small group of young cosplayers on our way out the sliding glass doors.

I keep looking over my shoulder to make sure we're not being followed. All I see is a handful of news reporters sitting down by the entrance, bored out of their minds. They're about to have a field day with this.

We reach Jade's car in the parking lot when I recognize the silver Mazda parked across from hers. It's Andy's.

I remember it because it has a bright yellow Amoeba Records bumper sticker on it that he told me all about years ago. The memory makes me roll my shoulders into my ears to suppress a shudder.

I open the passenger side door of Jade's car, aiming for the glove box, knowing exactly what's waiting for me in there. Squeezing the handle of the five-inch blade, I stride over to Andy's car and bury the knife deep into each of his four tires. The soft hiss of the escaping air echoes around us.

Neither of us says a word as I jog back to her car. We both climb in, and she quickly peels out of the parking lot.

I let out a long breath as I place the knife back in the glove compartment. "This is so fucked up."

"Don't you *ever* pull that shit again, do you hear me?"

I wince. "I know, I know. You have every right to be mad at me. I just—"

"You just what?" She whips her head in my direction, eyes flaring. "You just thought you were trying to protect me and keep me out of harm's way? Is that it?"

"I'm sorry—"

"You don't get to decide that. You don't get to make that choice for me. Elsie, if anything ever happened to you..." She trails off and shakes her head.

Doesn't she see that's the exact same reason I didn't want her to come up there too?

I look at her, but she won't meet my gaze, pretending to be concentrating on the road in front of her.

"I can't have anyone else getting hurt because of me. I got us all into this, it's my fault. For once, I just wanted to fix things and keep my friends safe. I'm sorry."

The silence is deafening, until she finally says, "This is not your fault. It's Andy's." She sighs. "Let's just get back to the hospital and come up with a plan. You're in for a big disappointment if you think you're doing the rest of this all on your own. It doesn't fucking work like that. Okay?"

I nod. "Okay."

The Con

We don't speak for the rest of the ride to the hospital. My forehead pressed against the window, I simply watch the city pass by, wondering how I'll ever be able to tell Ethan that one of the only people he's ever looked up to in his entire life tried to murder him.

37

We arrive at the hospital to find Damien scrolling on his phone, slumped in a chair in the waiting room.

"Hey, what are you doing out here? Everything okay with Ethan?" I ask, an edge of panic to my voice.

He stands up quickly, putting his phone in his pocket. "Yeah yeah, he's fine. They're just running some tests to see the extent of any damage and get an idea of what his recovery is going to look like. But everything is looking really good, Els." He rubs a hand up my arm to my shoulder. "He got really lucky."

I nod and lean into his side. I'm grateful Damien is here to ask them all the right questions and make sure they're acting in Ethan's best interest.

"So what happened at the hotel? You okay?"

I look over to Jade, her expression still hard as stone. Yeah, she's pissed. I don't blame her, but at the same time, I can't help but think about what could have happened if she went up there with me, and Andy had managed to grab her or something.

I know she can handle herself, but the man I saw in that hotel room was not the Andy I thought I knew. It was like the mask had finally come off and I was seeing him for the first time, for who he really is. I guess with enough time, everyone's mask falls off eventually.

I recount what happened when I got into Tamara's room, reaching into my purse and extracting the bottle of Xanax with Andy's name on it, along with the con guide I took from his room. I hadn't even told Jade about that part yet.

Damien takes the bottle and studies it as he rubs the back of his neck. "Fuck. I just can't believe this."

I hold up the con guide and wave it around. "How much you want to bet if I open this baby up, we're going to find a page missing?"

Sure enough, the first page has been ripped out. The page that would've shown the map of the convention center and surrounding buildings. Ripped out to be used as threatening notes for me and my friends.

I just shake my head as I run my finger over the torn edge. "Fucking Andy…"

"What do you want to do now?" Jade asks.

"We need to stop him, and we need to find Tamara before he does something crazy. I've tried calling Hawthorn, but he's not answering."

I look at Damien, who's leaning forward in his chair, hands clasped and elbows propped on his bouncing knees.

"What? What are you thinking?" I ask.

He turns to face me. "Doesn't Andy live around here? He talked about going home at night. Do you know where he lives?"

I rack my brain for any memory of Andy talking about his house or where he lives. "I don't know, we've never been there. The only thing I remember is when he was introducing us to Hawthorn, he mentioned that he built his house here to stay close to his parents."

"I'll see what I can find. There's got to be some public

record," Jade says, always thinking like a lawyer. "I can send an email to my guy right now."

"Wait!" My mind snags on something.

Sending mail...

Ethan sent Andy something a few years ago. He was building Quantum Protector models on his 3D printer and mailed them to Andy that summer.

I jump out of my chair and jog towards the reception desk before I can explain my revelation to my friends.

"Ma'am, ma'am," I wave politely. "Hi, can I get an update on Ethan Graham, please? I need to see him right away."

The woman nods and replies, "Of course." She begins typing, while I nervously tap on the desk with my nails.

Damien and Jade appear behind me, Damien's brows pinched. "What is it?"

"We have to talk to Ethan. A few years ago, he sent Andy some packages. If he still has the address, maybe we could go check it out." I look to both of them. "What if Andy took her to his house, and she's been there this whole time?"

Like he's keeping her locked up in some basement or dungeon or something. The thought makes my stomach churn.

"If she's even still alive," Jade says, her voice low.

"Yes. If she's still alive," I nod in agreement. "But it's all we've got. And we're running out of time. Now that Andy knows we're on to him, he might act out and do something dangerous."

The receptionist looks back up at me. "Ma'am, it shouldn't be too much longer. If you'll have a seat, we'll let you know when you can go back."

Ugh. More waiting.

We head back to our seats. "Okay, so we don't think Andy would go back to the con right? Like for any more signings or events or anything?" I ask, trying to cover our bases. I want to make sure we're not missing anything.

"Doubt it," Damien replies. "He already missed his signing at ten today. Word is the con organizers are pissed, and it's just chaos over there."

Damien did say he had a signing every day this weekend.

Wait a minute.

Three days of signings.

The third one was at ten o'clock.

I open the con guide to the missing page and run my finger over the torn edge again, as my mind starts putting the pieces together.

"Hey guys, what time was his signing yesterday, do you remember? Was it at noon?"

Damien looks at me curiously. "Yeah, that sounds right. We ate breakfast and went there after getting in costume. Why?"

I pull out my phone to check the photo of the notes that were slipped under our doors that first night. "And the first day? Do you remember what time?"

Jade sits back in her chair. "God, that feels like so long ago. It was right after we split up to go find clues, but before dinner. Damien and I were in our Star Wars getups walking the floor. So like…what, five o'clock?"

I angle my phone around so they can see the picture of the map, and those numbers scribbled along the side.

5

12

10

The times of Andy's signings this weekend.

He must've written the times in his con guide as a quick reminder of when he needed to be downstairs. In Exhibit Hall C.

Before we can talk about what all that means, I hear the woman at the desk say, "Miss Graham?"

I whip my head in her direction and quickly stand up, fumbling over my own feet. "Yes?"

"You can all go see him now."

I turn around to Jade and Damien as they stand up alongside me. I clasp Jade's hand in mine and say, "Let's go. He's going to hate us for this."

38

He's been through so much, and I'm about to drop a bomb on him. Obliterating his trust in the one man he's ever looked up to in his entire life besides Dad. Maybe I can do this without divulging the whole truth.

I just need him to give me the address. Everything else can come later.

After getting off the elevator on the sixth floor, the three of us walk quietly down the empty, sterile hallways. My mind is racing, trying to figure out exactly what to say to him.

I place my hand on the door handle to Ethan's room, pausing to look back at my friends one last time. They give a reassuring nod as I knock softly on the door, opening it slowly.

Stay strong.

Damien and the doctors said his tests looked good and that he got really lucky.

But what if our luck is running out?

"Hey, E. How you feeling?" I say brightly, trying to hide how nervous and worried I really am.

The others follow behind me with small waves and quiet

awkward greetings. He picks up on our strange behavior immediately, of course.

"Why are you guys being weird?" he says with a scowl.

"What? We're not being weird," I scoff, waving my hand around like any normal person would do in this situation. "What do you mean?"

"God, you're such a terrible liar, Els. Spit it out, what's going on?"

At our silence, he sits up straighter, scooting himself back on his bed. "What is it?"

I force an inhale, steeling myself for this conversation. I'll only reveal what I absolutely have to, otherwise he's going to freak out.

"It's really nothing! We just...wanted to ask you something." I already sound suspicious, and he knows it, but I power through. "So...super random...but do you remember a few years ago when you sent Andy those packages of 3D printed models? For his comic?"

He thinks for a second, trying to figure out where I'm going with this. "Yeah, why?"

I cross my arms and smile. "You don't happen to still have his address, do you?"

"I'm sure it's still in my email somewhere." He narrows his eyes, assessing me. "Why?"

"He doesn't live far from here, right?"

"Stop bullshitting me, Els. *Why?* Why do you need his address? Please don't keep me in the dark here, I've missed out on enough already."

"It's nothing, we just...thought if we had his address, we might stop by and check things out real quick."

He pauses and cocks his head. "Do you think whoever is framing Andy might be there? Or that they might've taken Tamara there?"

I could go with that line of thinking, except he's right, I'm a terrible liar. I glance behind me at Jade and Damien, who have remained silent throughout this whole interaction.

Thanks for the help, friends!

"Yeah, maybe. Good to just make sure, right? Cover all our bases?"

"Or…" He waves his hand for me to continue. "What? What aren't you telling me?"

Fuck.

I really don't want to have to do this. Why do I always have to be the one to deliver bad news?

It's just like when we were eight and I learned first that Dad was leaving us for another woman. Of course, Mom was too hysterical to explain things to us rationally. I had to grow up way too quickly that year, telling my twin brother that Dad wasn't coming back and that we weren't enough to make him stay.

The look on Ethan's little face when I told him the truth and stole his innocence is burned into my memory. The moment everything changed for us.

"Elsie." He reaches a hand out to me. "Tell me. Please."

I ignore the stinging behind my eyes and look to my friends behind me for strength. They nod at me to tell him, to push forward.

I grab his hands, inhaling a deep breath. "Okay…It's Andy."

He tilts his head again. "What's Andy?"

"Ethan," I urge. "It's *Andy*. It was him this whole time."

His eyebrows pinch together, as he tries to make sense of what I'm telling him. He looks to Damien and Jade before pointing at them, bursting into laughter. "Ahhh okay, you got me. That's a good one."

I close my eyes and keep going. "I'm sorry you had to find out like this, really. A lot has happened since you were…since you got here last night. And I promise I'll explain everything soon, but for now, we really need his address."

His smile slowly drops as he realizes that I'm not joking.

"What?" He scoffs. "No, that…that doesn't even make any sense."

Behind me, Damien says, "E, I'm so sorry."

"If there's a chance he took Tamara there, we have to go check it out. We have to go see." I squeeze his hand. "It's our last chance."

"He's being framed, remember? Someone is setting him up, why can't you see that?" He pulls his hand out of my grasp and looks away, crossing his arms. "Stop making him out to be the bad guy. He would never do this."

He's in denial. Holding on to any shred of hope that it isn't true. I hate this for him.

"Ethan, I know this is hard for you to hear—"

His head whips back to me. "Then stop. Just stop, Elsie!"

I huff out a breath. "Ethan, I found him in Tamara's room, okay? And…I found these." I reach into my purse and pull out the bottle of Xanax along with Andy's con guide and toss them both unceremoniously on his lap.

I could mention the brick too, but he doesn't even know we were locked up on the roof last night. It doesn't matter now.

Ethan stares at the back of the bottle for what feels like an eternity before turning it over slowly. The moment he glimpses Andy's name, he drops his hand and looks back at the wall, tears forming in his eyes.

The only sound in the room is the quick beeping of his heart monitor.

"I'm so, so sorry, Ethan. I trusted him too. But he's been using us this whole time. He took advantage of that trust and has been hindering the investigation from the start. We need his address."

His face is angled away from me, but I can still see the scowl, so menacing he's practically snarling. "This doesn't prove anything. Someone is setting him up."

The room falls silent once again.

Beep-beep-beep-beep

Dammit. How else are we going to get that address? Jade says she has a connection that could dig up some records, but today being Sunday, we probably wouldn't get any information back until tomorrow.

We need it now.

After a moment, he says, "I'll tell you what. I'll look up his address for you, but only so it can prove that he didn't do this. You want to go see if he's got Tamara locked in the attic or some shit? Be my guest. But you're wrong. He's innocent." He extends his hand. "Give me my phone."

I was wrong, this isn't like when we were eight, watching his little face crumple with devastation. No, this is something different. He's angry...with me. And that is not a feeling I'm used to.

He's not ready to face the reality of this situation, and maybe that's my fault for revealing too much, too soon. He's been through so much already, and maybe he just wasn't ready to hear the truth.

Damien steps up and hands Ethan his phone from the table beside him. Ethan snatches it out of his hand. I try not to let his anger deter me from what needs to be done.

After scrolling and typing for a minute or two, I feel the buzz of his text in my back pocket as he slams down the phone at his side.

"There. That's his address. Now if you don't mind, I'd like to be alone."

"Ethan, I'm—"

"Goodbye, Elsie." He crosses his arms, looking off to the side.

Nodding, I slowly turn towards my friends already standing by the door. I steal one last glance at my brother before leaving him once again.

Feeling like absolute shit, again.

As we head towards the waiting room, I pull out my phone to copy and paste the address Ethan gave me into my maps app. It's only a seventeen-minute drive.

"Let's go," I say to Jade. Putting a hand on Damien's arm, I tell him, "We'll let you know when we get there."

"Whoa whoa whoa." He twists his arm out of my grasp. "Are you kidding me right now? You're not leaving me behind again. I'm coming with you."

"Look, I appreciate you trying to help, but—"

"But nothing, we're all going. End of discussion."

"I'll drive," Jade says, walking towards the doors. Leaving no room for argument.

Damien starts to follow.

"Wait! What about Ethan? I don't like the idea of leaving him here alone."

"He made it pretty clear he doesn't want us here right now, Els," Damien says. "He'll be fine."

"Plus, you slashed Andy's tires," Jade adds, earning a startled glare from Damien. "I don't think he's going to make it here any time soon."

"I would just feel a whole lot better if someone was here watching him," I insist.

"Maybe the detective can send one of his guys over?" Damien suggests.

"Good idea, I'll try calling him again." Even though I haven't been able to get ahold of him all day. Probably still sleeping after working so late.

After four rings, it looks like I'm still out of luck. I decide to leave him a voicemail this time though. Maybe he'll be able to check it soon and send someone here. Then he can meet us out at Andy's house.

"Hey, Hawthorn. It's Elsie. We need to find Andy right away. It looks like he, uh…might be behind this after all. We saw him at the hotel, but we're headed over to his house right now. Um, is it possible for you to send one of your guys here to St. Mary's Hospital to watch Ethan? He's in room 623. And then can you meet us out at Andy's house? We're not sure what we're going to find out there, but if we're right, then maybe we can find Tamara too? Please call me back. We'll be there in about twenty minutes. Okay bye."

Also, for good measure, I fire off a text to Andy.

ME (3:10 P.M.)

> Let's talk. Can you meet in the hotel lobby?

Let's hope that keeps him there, distracted long enough to let us do what needs to be done.

39

The drive to Andy's house is torturous. It's mostly silent, except for Jade's usual roadtrip playlist of '90s and early 2000s rock.

I need to get a handle on my emotions before we get there, but for now, all I can think about is how mad Ethan is at me. I hope for his sake that I'm wrong about Andy. I hope there's a perfectly reasonable explanation for all this, and it's just one big misunderstanding.

But I don't see how that's possible.

Resting my head on the cool passenger side window and closing my eyes, I think back on what we've learned so far and try to put all the pieces together.

I need to understand. I need it to make sense.

Andy said he and Tamara were friends, but I'm pretty sure he was harboring feelings for her. We know that they were together at the diner just before her disappearance, the video online confirming she got in the car, but he didn't. So Andy must have been working with the driver.

I put her in that car.

Andy knew he would be seen with her beforehand and that

she definitely would've been recognized out in public this weekend, so he needed undeniable proof that he wasn't the one to drive her away.

An alibi.

With witnesses.

Whoever he was working with could have brought Tamara to his house, maybe tied her up in a basement or a shed or something. Meanwhile, Andy would appear distressed in front of thousands of people at the con. With his old detective buddy heading up the investigation, Andy could steer him in whatever direction he needed to.

Then, he slipped us threatening notes once we got nosy, trying to scare us away, knowing we would figure it out eventually if we kept pressing.

But he made some mistakes.

I fucked up.

Whatever he was doing to "help" the investigation, must have helped a little too much and Hawthorn started getting suspicious. He got sloppy, and Hawthorn found something or learned something last night. It wasn't enough to arrest him, but he knew he was getting close, and took him in for questioning in the hopes he could get Andy to confess where she was and find her before it was too late.

Maybe Jade was right in that there was pressure from higher up in the department to solve this case since it was starting to get national attention. Hawthorn already knew it was Andy and did what he could to put pressure on him to confess.

Then, when Hawthorn couldn't hold him any longer and he had to be released, Andy went straight to her hotel room — at some point, I guess he had to have taken her room key — to destroy or hide any evidence that could've pointed to him.

I have to fix this.

He wasn't expecting that I would catch him in the act. That I would go to these lengths to try and find her.

I have to admit, I'm a little surprised myself, but I'm glad I'm still here, trying to help her. That I can be that one person who's looking out for her.

Sometimes all it takes is one person.

My only regret is that I've put my friends in danger, and that Ethan was hurt too.

I sit up in my seat and clear my throat. "I still don't understand something though…"

"What's that?" Jade asks from the driver's seat next to me, turning down the stereo volume.

"Why Ethan?" I turn in my seat to face both Jade and Damien, who is lying down in the back seat. "That's the part I can't get past. What did he find out that made him such a threat to Andy?"

Damien sits up and chews on his lip. "He must've figured out he was behind it, or found something that would've pointed to him, but can't remember just yet. That's the only thing that makes sense."

"Yeah, but when? He never mentioned anything to us last night. We all went to Kat's party right after dinner, after talking to Andy over at the hotel. He would have told us right away. It just doesn't make any sense."

Damien leans forward and puts his hand on mine on the center console. "I know. Sometimes these things just don't make sense. Not when you're dealing with someone dangerous and unhinged. I'm really sorry."

"I hope we're not too late finding Tamara. What do you think he even did to her?"

No one answers. I guess there's no telling what we're about to walk into. What we've already involved ourselves in. I turn in my seat to face the front, pulling out of Damien's grasp.

What was the whole point of taking Tamara though? Did he confess his feelings for her and she rejected him? Causing him to lash out? I guess it's possible, but this seemed planned out in advance, with the handler and everything.

Perhaps they weren't friends at all, just acquaintances, but he became crazed and obsessed. He got her to agree to meet somehow, so he could commence his sick plan and they could be together.

I love her! We're supposed to be together!

A shiver runs down my spine at the memory of him shouting all that nonsense in Tamara's hotel room.

And who is he working with? Someone had to impersonate the handler and drive her somewhere. Perhaps this person also had knowledge of the security systems that mysteriously went down everywhere at just the right times.

So many questions we need answers to. For now, I just hope whatever is at his house is enough to help us find Tamara.

And that we're not too late.

We finally turn onto the street of our destination around three thirty. We roll past Andy's house at a slow pace, all of us looking out the windows to assess the area as best we can. We talked through a rough plan just before we arrived, but it's really hard to anticipate what's about to happen.

This could be a really, really stupid idea.

It's a modest-size, two-story house, with a cute white brick exterior, bordered by a garden bed of assorted, colorful flowers. An enormous front yard and a long gravel driveway lead up to the home. There are no neighbors in sight, and according to the map, only three other houses exist within a half-mile radius. I would guess this house sits on at least five acres of land, probably more.

Large oak and maple trees line the edges of the yard, secluding the home from any prying eyes. No one around to see anything suspicious...or hear *anything*.

Jade parks her car down the road, just in case he's nearby, hopefully passing for a visitor of one of the neighbors. Though he wouldn't necessarily know what Jade's car looks like, it's probably best not to advertise to anyone that we're here to break into a crazy kidnapper's house to save a missing Hollywood actress.

We start walking towards the house through the yard, and I can't help but wonder, will this be a simple rescue, or are we heading into a final boss battle situation? We are without any weapons, and woefully unprepared, but let's fucking go.

The stifling heat is already too much, the humidity going straight to my frizzy hair as I pull it away from my face and tie it back off with a scrunchie.

As we approach the side of the house, I can now see the land out back. In the distance, the yard leads into a dark, eerie forest. A beautiful pond spreads out underneath a large willow tree with hanging branches skimming the surface. Unkempt bushes and creeping ivy line the property, which at some point, I'm sure used to be beautiful. Now it's just unsettling.

"Wait, so we're not even waiting for Hawthorn?" Damien whispers as we round the corner towards the back of the house. "How are we even going to get in?"

"I have my ways," I reply with a wiggle of my eyebrows. "Besides, he hasn't been answering, so I don't know what else to do. If Tamara is actually here, we need to get to her before Andy comes home."

I just hope I've bought us enough time before he finds a way to get back here.

Jade stops walking. "So, I know we said we should probably stick together, but legally, I cannot be a part of a breaking and entering. How about I stay out here as the lookout and keep you both informed if anyone arrives."

"Good call. We'll be quick. In and out in two minutes flat."

"Just how Damien likes it," Jade mutters.

I snort, slapping a hand over my mouth in an attempt to stay quiet, but I'm laughing so hard I need a minute to compose myself.

Damien shakes his head, trying and failing to suppress a smile. "Lead the way, m'lady."

Jade gives a salute as Damien and I approach the back door. I don't see any security cameras back here, thank goodness. I pull out my favorite lockpick set from my back pocket: a skeleton key multi-tool that can hold up to nine picks and a tension wrench.

Damien huffs a laugh. "Since when do you know how to pick a lock? And...wait...is that like, a Swiss Army knife lockpick set?"

"Cool, right? Ethan taught me when we were kids. He was always getting into trouble and rebelling any way he could, but I guess you met us after that particular phase in his life. He was a straight-up menace, but he did happen to acquire some useful skills." I raise the two pieces I need and get to work.

"He should be here with us. Our crew isn't the same without him," he says softly.

"*We* shouldn't even be here. We should be enjoying the last day of WyvernFest, drunk off our asses and dressed in the costumes we've worked on all year! I mean, what the hell did we get ourselves into?"

What did *I* get us into?

I keep working until I hear that familiar, satisfying *click* and open the door to Andy's house.

40

I close up my tools and put them away in my back pocket as I stand up. Before I can walk through the door though, Damien gently grabs my arm.

"Hey. Are you sure you want to do this?" His chestnut eyes are wide and pleading. "It's not too late to turn back."

"It *is* too late to turn back. We're close. This is it." And with as much conviction as I can muster, I say, "I'm not scared. We can do this." I honestly believe it now, that we were supposed to be here to help.

I can feel it in my bones that we are close.

"Okay. Then we stay together," he says as he takes my hand.

I try to ignore the way his touch sends heat creeping up my neck.

Focus, Elsie.

We walk through the back door into a dimly lit kitchen with dark wood cabinets and cream appliances. Next to the kitchen is a small eating area with a round wooden table and matching chairs with floral cushions. The entire house is very...plain, and completely ordinary, with very little artwork or decorations.

I can't put my finger on it, but it just feels...off.

"This is Andy's house?" Damien asks as he looks around. "It's definitely not what I would have expected."

"I know, right?"

We continue to tiptoe through the main level, looking for any clues, but there's not much to see. To the right is a simple, country-style living room with a small sofa and a recliner in front of a small television.

I come to a glass shelf on the side wall by the front entrance, holding a handful of photos in golden frames. Older photos, from the looks of it. Family photos, grandparents...but I don't recognize anyone from them. I suppose one of these younger boys is Andy as a little kid.

Then I see a picture with two men I definitely recognize. Andy and Hawthorn. They look about ten years younger, standing on a boat with huge smiles on their faces, each holding up a fish they caught on the lake.

I pick up the photo to get a closer look. Now *this* is the Andy I remember, and whom I haven't seen this entire weekend. His face is bright and full of life, like he's just been cracking jokes with his best friend.

I can't help but wonder when everything changed.

Did something happen to him to turn him into such a dangerous psychopath, or was he always that way? Wearing a mask and hiding his true self from the world. Cosplaying as Andrew Locke, the upstanding citizen and successful comic book author.

When did Hawthorn realize who Andy really was?

The thought makes my stomach drop. I guess we really don't know anyone. Not really.

I put the photo back down and continue looking around. Maybe there's a basement or something around here.

We need to move faster.

I turn a corner into a small, narrow hallway with an old hutch at the end. There are two doors on either side of the hall, each opening to medium-sized, empty bedrooms. No signs of Tamara, or anybody else.

"Hey." I nudge Damien in the ribs and point down the hallway. "Does that hutch look weird to you? Like it's a little skewed or something?"

He shrugs but follows me down the hall, squinting at the antique furniture. We both startle when the buzz from my pocket breaks the unsettling silence.

JADE (3:56 P.M.)

Leave now

Car.. Someone here

Shit.

Shit shit shit.

I show my phone to Damien to read the texts as I put a finger to my lips. When we hear a car door slam, he takes my hand and leads me into one of the empty bedrooms and opens a set of closet doors for us to hide inside.

I freeze when I see what's hanging up. A Mandalorian costume.

I forgot all about that.

Except...wait, that can't be right.

Something about this feels wrong.

Damien pushes on the small of my back for me to get inside the closet. I take a seat on the floor, pulling out my phone to look at my photos as he quietly shuts the doors and sits down beside me.

Other than the costume, there are just a few banker's boxes in here and only a little bit of space to move around. I'm suddenly very aware of just how close Damien and I are in this tiny closet, scrunched up together on the floor, thighs touching, but I force the thoughts away as I search for the pictures that will confirm my suspicions.

I think about how I've always had to get up on my tiptoes to give Andy a hug, which means he is probably about a foot taller than me, putting him at eight inches or so above my twin brother.

Sure enough, I find the photos from yesterday at the con of the Mandalorian standing next to Iron Man — Ethan.

They're the same height.

I swipe to the one with me, dressed as Daenerys Targaryen. Whoever is in that Mandalorian costume is just barely taller than me.

We were right there...standing next to...whoever this person is. The thought sends a shiver down my spine, and I roll my shoulder to ease the discomfort.

I angle my phone to Damien and whisper, "This can't be Andy in the picture. This guy is too short."

His eyes widen with realization. "Then it must be the other person Andy's been working with, the one who picked up Tamara from the diner."

There's a faint thumping sound coming from further inside the house. Damien puts a finger to his lips as my heart starts pounding in my ears.

Do they know we're in the house? We didn't leave anything out of place to give us away, did we?

I shoot off a text to the lookout.

ME (4:01 P.M.)

did you see who it was?

is it Andy?

JADE (4:02 P.M.)

I couldn't tell from this angle. They went straight into the garage

Placing the phone down in front of me, I hug my knees to

my chest and squeeze my eyes shut. I can't believe this is happening.

Damien takes my hand and laces our fingers together. "It's gonna be okay."

I just nod. I don't believe him, but it's still nice to hear.

"Hey." He takes my chin with his other hand and turns my head toward him, his face barely visible in the dim light. "I'm right here. Whatever happens, I've got you."

He said the same thing last night, right before taking me up to the roof to help me through my panic attack. The roof, where he drank alone last year after I got engaged and didn't show up to the con. He said he didn't want to be that guy who told me what to do or who I should be with.

I had to let you go.

Suddenly, it feels very hot in here, the side of his body pressed up against mine.

My heart pounds even harder.

In this moment, sharing the same breath as him, I can't move. I can barely think. He breaks our eye contact, his eyes darting down to my mouth as I lick my lips.

Time slows down as his hand brushes along my jaw and tucks a few strands of hair behind my ear. Goosebumps erupt along my skin. When our eyes meet again, I suddenly forget what we're even doing here. It's just me and him alone in this tiny space, in this moment that's just ours.

All those years of dancing up along that line between friends and *more*, but never actually crossing it.

But right now? Right now, it feels like everything has led us to this point, this moment. Like the stars aligned, and we are the only two people left in the entire universe.

I lean towards him ever so slowly as he runs a strong hand behind my head, tangling in my hair. Our breath mingles, and my heart is trying to leap out of my chest. He pulls our intertwined hands to rest on his own chest so I can feel his heart pounding too.

We inch closer and closer until our lips are mere molecules apart, when a buzz from my phone startles us both, breaking our trance as we pull away.

JADE (4:06 P.M.)

Where are you?? Can you get out?

I untangle my fingers from his grip to reply.

ME (4:07 P.M.)

we're hiding in a closet

I take a deep breath and run a hand down my face, looking to Damien, who shares the same curious expression.

Maybe this isn't the time for all that.

In fact, it's probably too soon to be making romantic moves with *anyone* so soon after my failed engagement-almost-marriage, to a man who left me a shell of my former self.

Especially while our lives are still in immediate danger.

I shake my head to clear my thoughts, forcing myself to focus on the task at hand. We can continue this later…if we survive, that is.

I use the nearest box to leverage myself up slowly, trying to peek through the sliver of an opening between the closet doors. In my attempt to be quiet and stealthy, I lose my grip and fumble forward, taking the top of the box to the ground with me with a loud *thud* as my head crashes into the door.

My hand instantly presses to my head, trying to dull the sudden throbbing pain.

Dammit!

Could someone have heard that?

We freeze in place as the sound of footsteps slowly approach along the hardwood flooring of the hallway. I swear I'm not even breathing.

Is this it? Are we about to be caught?

I hear nothing for the next minute or so, then finally the footsteps recede. We both blow out a breath at the same time, after what feels like an eternity. Once we hear a door close in the distance, we know this is our chance.

We have to get out of here...*now*.

Damien slowly opens one side of the closet doors and peeks out, making sure no one is near. As the light spills into the closet, something catches my eye from within the open box to my side. From what I can tell, it's a collection of printed pages and small photo prints.

Lots and lots of photos.

I lean in closer to get a better look, shining my phone's flashlight on them. What I see knocks the breath out of me.

Photos of Tamara. Hundreds of them. Many of them part of a sequence, like they were all shot throughout the same afternoon.

Jesus, Andy, you psycho.

Tamara walking down the street.

Tamara shopping.

Tamara sitting down at a café.

Tamara sharing a meal with...Andy?

I squint and pull this one particular photograph closer. Tamara and Andy are sitting at a cute little café with no one else around, eating and drinking together. They look...happy.

I shove the photo at Damien while I reach back into the box for the rest of the stack.

A whole series of images with Tamara and Andy together. They are laughing, smiling, and sitting *very* close to each other. Then, one photo stops me in my tracks.

Tamara and Andy...kissing.

Like, really kissing. One of his hands is snaked around the back of her neck, gently cupping the base of her head. Fingers twining in her hair. Her hand rests on his forearm in a familiar and comfortable way.

I flip through the next few photos. Between deep, passionate kisses they are smiling and gazing into each other's eyes.

Damien looks over my shoulder at the photos I'm holding.

"Whaaaaaat the fuck?" he whispers. "So they're…together? Like *actually* together? He said they were just friends."

My head is spinning. This doesn't make sense. Were they really together and then something happened to make him want to kidnap her and stage this whole thing? But why do it during con weekend, out in public, where it would receive so much attention?

No…something is wrong.

We've gotten this all wrong.

Another buzz from my phone jolts me out of my dizzying thoughts.

JADE (4:16 P.M.)

Hello?? You okay???

ME (4:16 P.M.)

coming

"Els, we have to get out of here right now."

I take the stack with me as Damien grabs my hand and leads me quietly out of the room. He looks around each corner before motioning that it's clear for me to follow and lets my hand drop.

As we tiptoe towards the back door, I can't help but look more at the stack of photos in my hand. So many photos. Like the photographer just kept clicking away at the scene in front of him.

Andy and Tamara making out. Holding hands.

Lovers. Not just friends or acquaintances.

Wait…the photographer?

If Andy didn't take these, then who did? A private investigator? Paparazzi? Or…a stalker?

When we reach the dining area, I grab Damien's arm for him to stop as everything comes together all at once.

With clearer eyes, I stop and really *look* at this house.

A house with older, outdated furniture and appliances. Floral prints and country quilts. A house that must be at least forty or so years old.

"Holy shit," I whisper. "This isn't Andy's house."

"What? What do you mean?" Damien looks around as I hand him the stack of photos.

I walk back over to the fishing picture I saw earlier, grabbing it as I scan the wall next to it, leading up a flight of stairs. A second level we never got a chance to check.

Come on, come on.

Then I see it.

A family photo of an older couple and a young man probably in his late twenties. I pull it off the wall and show them both to Damien side by side, his eyes going wide.

Before he can say a word, the front door bursts open, and in walks Jade, handcuffed and gagged.

Being led inside by the real owner of this house.

Detective Michael Hawthorn.

41

Hawthorn already has his gun trained on me as he holds Jade's bound hands behind her back. Damien and I put our hands up, the stack of photos still in his grasp.

"Well, well, well. Looks like y'all are having a party in here," Hawthorn drawls with a sadistic smirk.

"Hawthorn. What are you doing? Please...just put the gun down."

I'm frozen in place, but my mind is still reeling. It was Hawthorn this whole time.

But how?

We got the address from Ethan because he sent Andy all those packages a few years ago. Why would he have them sent to Hawthorn's house?

Wait...

He even let me stay with him when I was building my house out here.

Andy was living here with Hawthorn at the time.

We should've realized the moment we set eyes on this house that it wasn't new, but we were so focused on getting inside in case Tamara was here. Oblivious to what was staring us in the face the whole time. Never questioning that this wasn't Andy's house at all.

But...does that mean they're working together?

What is Andy's involvement in all this?

Hawthorn pushes Jade into the living room and towards the sofa, nearly stumbling over her own feet before she slowly lowers herself down. Never taking her eyes off him.

I need to get to her and make sure she's okay, but Hawthorn is still pointing that gun in my face.

For a moment, I consider playing dumb and trying to convince him that we only suspect Andy in all this and that this was just an innocent mistake coming to his home. But I see it in his face. It's over. He knows that we know the truth.

How are we going to get out of this?

"What the fuck, Hawthorn? What have you done? Why are you doing all this?" I ask with a surprisingly steady voice.

I ball my hands into fists and keep myself planted in place, so I don't do something stupid like charge him and knock the gun out of his hand and point it right back at his stupid face.

He quietly studies me for a bit and angles his head, like a predator sizing up its prey, before he suddenly bursts out laughing, startling us all.

Dropping the gun to his side, he says, "So many questions! Come on, relax. I see you've already made yourself at home. Can I offer y'all something to drink? Water? Coffee?"

He says it so casually, so completely untethered from reality, like we're all just friends hanging out, not a care in the world.

Does he even realize what he's done? Is this all just a game to him?

I'm waiting for him to take his eyes off us, just for a moment, so I can discreetly reach into my pocket and dial 911. Even if I can't talk, maybe they can ping my location or something.

I slowly drop my hands, but he notices it instantly. In three quick strides, he is at our sides, pushing both Damien and me towards Jade, shoving us onto the couch alongside her.

"Empty your pockets. Hand them over." He lifts an eyebrow in challenge.

"Hand what over?" I ask sweetly with a fake plastered smile.

Before I can even gauge his reaction, I'm blindsided by a sharp pain in my temple.

Everything fades away in a blur.

I force my eyes open and find myself slumped against Jade. I think I hear Damien's voice, but just faintly, like he's shouting across a football field.

Fuck, what just happened?

I lift my hand to my throbbing head and am met with warm, red liquid coating my fingers and trickling down my face.

Still disoriented, I manage to look up at Hawthorn who is holding a gun, the butt end having been used to shut me up.

Point taken. Don't antagonize the crazy guy with a gun.

"Empty your pockets. And hand...me...your...phones," he says again, slower this time.

I reach into my pocket and hand mine over. Damien throws his on the coffee table along with the stack of photos.

Jade notices the photographs of Andy and Tamara but doesn't react, doesn't move. Hawthorn likely already patted her down and took her phone after finding her outside keeping watch. All while Damien and I were getting cozy in a closet.

Fuck, this is all my fault. Again.

I made us all come here, and then, when we didn't leave the house fast enough, we got trapped in here with an unhinged psychopath with a gun.

There's no way Hawthorn is just going to let us all go now that we know he's involved in Tamara's disappearance. Or worse...her death.

I'm just grateful that Ethan is safe and far away from here.

At least he'll survive.

Hawthorn sits himself down in the worn-out, maroon recliner across from the couch, staring us down with a demented smile on his face. Daring us to talk first.

I'm still recovering from the last time I spoke up to him, so I decide to stay quiet for now. Taking in as much detail of our surroundings as I can, I try to come up with a plan to get us all out of here before he kills us.

Damien is the first to speak. "Why are you doing this, man?"

Such a simple question. We haven't actually done anything — aside from breaking and entering, I suppose — so why does he have it out for us?

"Oh, I do apologize for roping you kids into this. You see, it really had nothing to do with y'all except...well, you just kept poking your noses where they didn't belong. I asked you all to drop it, to mind your own business, if you remember."

My mind flashes to the notes left in our rooms.

"But you wouldn't leave it alone. So I decided maybe you could be some use to me instead."

"How?" Damien asks.

Hawthorn's head rears back slightly, and he chuckles. "I'm sorry to have to break it to you, but our dear friend Andrew Locke is not all he's cracked up to be." His gaze lands on me. "I understand he's like a big brother to you, but you really don't know anything about him at all, do you?"

"What's that supposed to mean?"

"Don't worry. I think we'll all find out just what kind of man he is here soon enough." He checks his watch with a smile. "I do believe the show will begin any minute now."

What the hell? What show?

Are they working together? Or has Hawthorn orchestrated some kind of...revenge? It almost sounds like he's setting a trap for Andy.

Are we the bait, or is Tamara? Is she even alive?

"Where's Tamara? Is she here?" I need to keep him talking while I figure out how to get us out of this mess.

Hawthorn stares me down with the most unnerving look in his eye. "Oh right, Miss Hollywood. I know you came all this way but, I'm so sorry. As they say, 'our princess is in another castle.'" He laughs way too hard at his own joke.

"This isn't a game. You're not going to get away with this."

"Oh, I think that I will. I've had enough practice, and I think I can handle a bunch of kids." His bored expression gives nothing away.

"What practice?" Jade's tone is even, but there's an edge of fear to it. "What are you even talking about?"

"You don't think this is my first time, do you? I certainly didn't intend for it to happen the way it did with her, but she ended up teaching me so much. I would've never known how much I enjoyed it."

With who?

"Wait…" I whip my head to Jade, who seems to be thinking the same thing. "The woman who went missing a few years ago?"

"That was *you*?" Jade gasps, eyes wide.

Holy shit. No one ever found her.

What the fuck did he do to her?

Any hope of getting out of this alive feels like it just evaporated.

"By the way," Hawthorn looks me dead in the eye. "I never asked…how's your brother?"

My stomach plummets to the floor as my hands clench into fists. I know he's just trying to get a rise out of me, so I try my best not to take the bait. I breathe in slowly to steady myself. "He's fine now. No thanks to you."

"Is he now?" He taps his chin. "St. Mary's Hospital, room 623…right?"

The world stops moving. I can't move. I can't breathe.

He continues in a mocking tone, *"Can you please send one of your guys over to watch Ethan?"* putting his free hand to his cheek and batting his eyelashes.

Oh my God. I told him exactly where Ethan was.

"You really wanted to make this easy for me, didn't you?" He shakes his head.

I led him straight to Ethan.

He's not safe at all.

"I miscalculated the dose last night," Hawthorn continues. "I thought with the amount of alcohol he was drinking it would be enough. Ah well. No matter. It's all taken care of now."

No.

I slowly shake my head. "No…no, please."

"It's already done, my dear," he says as he stands up, looking down on us with contempt.

But I can barely see him. I can barely see anything as tears blur my vision and I lose the strength to keep my emotions in check yet again. I can't do this.

Damien lays a strong hand on my knee, a gentle reassuring squeeze to help keep me grounded as my mind begins to spiral.

Ethan…no. It's not true. He can't be gone, he just can't. He must be lying.

I rub the inside of my wrist. My Princess Leia tattoo, matching the Luke drawing adorned on Ethan's wrist, reminding me of our unbreakable bond. We said we would always be there for each other.

But…I failed him.

Hawthorn walks a few steps away as he taunts, "We wouldn't be in this mess if y'all had just stayed out of it. Your dear brother was getting a little too close to figuring out what was going on, and he could've exposed my plan, compromising everything and…well, I just couldn't have that."

"Why? Why are you doing all of this?" I shout at him. I can

barely think straight. I need to get to Ethan. We need to get the hell out of here.

"You'll do well to shut your fucking mouth. Once our honored guest arrives, we can get started. Our noble hero, searching for his sweet, lost princess." His eyes darken. "He's about to get a rude awakening."

"What happens when Andy gets here?" I ask on a shaky breath.

"Oh, I wouldn't want to spoil the surprise. Y'all have been so helpful up until now, and I guess you won't be around much longer, so...let's just say, he's going to get what's coming to him. For the choices he's made, he's going to pay."

"What's that supposed to mean?" Damien asks, his hand still steady on my knee.

"Are you...?" I narrow my eyes at him. "Are you *jealous* of Andy? Is that what all this is all about? A woman? Because Tamara is with him and not you?"

I know I'm pushing too hard, but I can't stop myself. Everything is coming to the surface, and I'm powerless to stop it. I'm so tired of holding everything in all the time. I'm a volcano ready to erupt.

He killed my brother...and is probably about to kill us, too. There's nothing left to lose.

I snap. "What is wrong with you? You pathetic piece of shit!"

I feel Damien's grip tighten in a silent warning. But I ignore it.

"Just because a woman chose your friend over you, you think you can mess with people's lives like this? Because you didn't get your fucking way? No wonder she never wanted you, you psychotic...worthless...*asshole!*"

Hawthorn closes the distance between us in one single step as he rears back the gun again, and everything goes black.

42

My head fucking hurts.

I can't move my hands.

Where the hell am I?

My thoughts are thick and syrupy. Everything moves in slow motion, like trying to run in a swimming pool.

I gain enough control over my mind and my body to sense that I'm sitting upright...on a cold, hard floor. My hands are bound tightly behind my back, and I'm leaning against some sort of metal pole, which is putting too much pressure on my shoulders.

But I realize I'm not alone. I feel the warmth of another person behind me. No, two others.

Jade. Damien.

Thank God they're here.

I can barely muster the strength to pry open my heavy eyelids, fighting to bring my vision into focus. Why do my eyes hurt so much?

It's dark, but there is just enough light trickling in through a short, narrow window near the ceiling to make out the space around me.

A basement, I guess.

It's dank and musty, the air stale. To my right, shelves filled with storage bins and boxes line the far wall next to a set of stairs. Turning to my left, I see brownish-red stains on the floor just past Jade.

Is that blood? Is it my blood? I can still feel it on my cheek, hard and sticky.

My friends are behind me, bound to the same pole as I am. We are all propped up against each other, back-to-back, like a pyramid, and both of their heads are slumped forward.

"Hey…" I manage to croak, nudging them both with my shoulders. Nothing. "Come on…We've gotta get up."

I can feel them both breathing, so I know they're alive, but they must be unconscious. My mind slowly focuses enough to begin thinking clearer, but with that, my new reality hits me like a boulder to the chest.

Ethan.

Hawthorn sent someone to my brother's hospital room to kill him. To finish him off. And I told him exactly where he was. We should have never left him alone.

My eyes sting with fresh tears, and this time, I don't fight them. I deserve to feel this pain, this anguish. This is all my fault.

From the beginning, I was the one who insisted we go find Tamara, like it was all just some fantasy quest full of adventures and games. I put us all in danger for my own selfish reasons. I just couldn't stay out of it.

I put my friends in this situation.

I got my brother killed.

I deserve to feel every ounce of this agony, for the rest of my life, however long that may be.

Maybe I should just stop fighting it. Hawthorn will be back down here any minute to finish us off anyway. To finish whatever sick plan he came up with to get back at Andy, or whatever the fuck is going on.

I don't even care anymore.

It's not worth fighting it anymore.

I just hope it's quick.

I don't want to live in a world where Ethan isn't there.

Adjusting my position, I wince at the sting from sitting on this bare concrete. But that's when I realize, my back pockets are empty.

Where's my lock pick set?

I didn't hand it over with my phone earlier, but Hawthorn must have patted me down before bringing me here. Of course I would never get that lucky. Handcuffs are the simplest lock to pick, since all you really need is a…bobby pin.

Holy shit. I know I still have some in my unruly hair — the reality of being a cosplayer. But how the hell am I supposed to get one out if my hands are bound?

Think think.

I thrust my head forward, hoping by pure luck one will fall out.

Nothing.

I shake it left to right, trying to loosen this damn bun.

Nothing. Dammit!

I can do this.

I lift up my knees and lean my head forward in between them. If I can press enough on either side, I may be able to slide one out. Except…*owww* this really hurts.

Shit. I don't think I can do this. One more thing to add to my list of failures.

"What are you even doing right now?" Damien's soft voice makes me jolt up.

"Hey! You okay?"

He squeezes his eyes shut before saying slowly, "Yeah. I think so. You?"

"I'm fine. Trying to get a bobby pin out of my hair. Any ideas?"

He looks over at my tangled mess. "Turn your head. I can see one on this side. Maybe I can get it out."

We lean towards each other at the same time, and his mouth is suddenly at my temple. His warm breath sends a shiver down my spine as his teeth grab hold of the bobby pin above my ear, pulling it out with ease.

"Vhutt now?" he says around the pin in his mouth.

My bound hands are positioned between him and Jade so I scoot around and try to get my open palms as close to him as I can. "Can you see my hands? Drop it if you can."

He does what I ask, and for a split second I worry it will miss my hands completely, bounce away, and ruin any chance we have of getting out of here. There's suddenly so much riding on this one action.

But he doesn't miss.

"Yes, got it!"

For the first time since entering Hawthorn's home, I allow myself to feel a glimmer of hope. Hope that I might be able to get us all out of here after all. That I'm not a complete failure.

I have to push my feelings about Ethan aside for now. There will be time to think about him later...and to grieve.

Then I can fall apart.

Then I can succumb to the pain.

It's too late for Ethan, but maybe it's not too late for us.

For Jade and for Damien, I will try.

In this moment, I have a new mission, a new purpose: to save my friends.

I straighten out the bobby pin as I try to twist my head enough to see what I'm dealing with. The three of us are woven together, our handcuff chains criss-crossing with each other's around this metal pole.

"Can you get it?" Damien asks.

"Should be pretty easy. Handcuffs were one of the first locks Ethan ever taught me to pick." I resist playing back the memory.

The mention of Ethan seems to affect Damien, too, as he turns his head away and clears his throat.

I try pulling my hands to the side so I can see what I'm doing, but it's straining my neck and shoulders. Instead, I close my eyes and relax my arms, picturing the mechanism in my mind so I can find the opening to the cuffs on my left hand and jam in the pin with my right. It takes two clumsy tries, but I finally get the right angle and maneuver the bobby pin in between the metal teeth of the lock, finally getting one hand free.

"Got it."

I slip the cuffs, still attached at my right wrist, through the tangled mess of my friends' hands and try to stretch my shoulders back out. I take a few extra seconds to work out a cramp in my neck as Damien looks on impatiently.

"Come on, you're killing me here. Let me out!"

"I don't know, I was thinking of letting you stay there. Seeing you in handcuffs unlocked a kink I didn't even know I had," I tease, trying to lighten the mood.

The corner of my mouth lifts when he closes his eyes and just shakes his head. I twist to his side, leaning down to free him from his handcuffs. Once he's out, we both turn to Jade.

She is still unconscious, so Damien takes her shoulders and gently lays her down on her side once I get her hands free.

"Are you sure you're okay?" he asks again as he surveys my head, fussing over the spot where Hawthorn clocked me. Twice.

"I'm fine, really." *Physically, sure, but everything else, no.*

He seems to read my thoughts as he tucks a strand of hair behind my ear and lowers his forehead onto mine.

"We're going to get through this."

I know he's not just talking about escaping. I shut my eyes and nod. I want to believe him, I really do.

First, we need to come up with a plan to get out of this house.

I assume Hawthorn is still upstairs, or at least he probably won't stray too far from here. He has our phones and probably Jade's car keys too. So we're essentially stranded out in the middle of nowhere.

I look around the basement to assess whether there is anything down here we can use to escape and possibly defend ourselves with. Or even better, do some serious damage.

Damien places a quick, gentle kiss on my forehead before standing up and walking towards the high window. A smile plays on my lips as I head over to the shelf of storage bins, opening up a few to take a look inside. Surprisingly, they are mostly filled with costumes, materials, and props.

Whoa. Is Hawthorn into cosplay?

I guess it makes sense if he was the Mandalorian this whole time, but I thought whoever it was just did it to keep an eye on us. From the looks of it, he actually enjoys this stuff. Or *did*, at least.

I rummage through another bin and find a bright, stretchy superhero outfit with the letters QP on the front. Quantum Protector?

No way. This thing is kinda badass.

Did Hawthorn *make* this? Was he out here supporting his buddy Andy with a homemade Quantum Protector costume?

What the hell happened between those two?

"Fuck," Jade croaks from the ground as she brings a hand up to her head.

Damien and I both run over to her and kneel down. "Are you okay?" we say at the same time. Damien looks her over for any injuries.

"Fucking fabulous," she says as she pushes herself onto her elbows. "Do you two have a plan to get us out of here yet?"

I shrug, looking to Damien.

"Well, is Hawthorn still here?"

"We haven't checked yet, but I would assume so. Who knows what the hell he's planning up there when Andy arrives."

Jade looks around, jabbing a thumb towards the storage shelves. "What's in those bins? Anything we can use?"

I love that we're all on the same page here.

"I started looking through a few, mostly costumes and props." I stand up and cross my arms over my chest. "Turns out Hawthorn was a cosplayer. He even made a legit Quantum Protector costume."

"Wait, for real?" Damien asks. "So...hold on. They were friends, but now he's taken Andy's girlfriend and set a trap for him? How do you even get to that point?"

Jade starts to climb to her feet with a grunt as I offer her a hand. The moment she's standing, she pulls me in for a hug. A silent reassurance.

Ethan would have wanted us to keep going.

I squeeze my eyes shut. We need to focus.

"I'm not sure there's really anything in these bins we can use though," I say as I pull away from her and walk towards the shelves. I open another storage bin full of fabric and foam pieces. "But it's three against one. Maybe if we can take him by surprise, we can overpower him, right?"

Jade opens a long, rectangular box from the bottom shelf and pulls out a huge wizard staff at the same time that Damien holds up a round golden shield.

She says, "Okay, but having these couldn't hurt, right?"

"Nice. What else is in there?" I peek over her shoulder and find a crazy-looking contraption. It looks like some kind of sword but with long pointed rods framing its sides, and a round piece surrounding the hilt, all painted in bright colors.

This could do some serious damage, actually. It would not have been approved by the con's Weapons Master.

"Oh wow, a Quantum Construct!" Damien gasps as he comes up behind us.

"Is that what this is? Oh hell yeah, I'm keeping it," I say as I swing it around and flip it over my wrist. "Let's go kick some ass."

43

We slowly climb the rickety wooden stairs, armed to the teeth with fake weapons, armor, and shields.

Reaching the top, I turn the knob ever so slowly, and to my surprise, it's not even locked. I guess with all three of us handcuffed together, he didn't imagine there was much of a chance that we could escape. Or he wasn't planning on keeping us down here much longer.

We have to hurry.

I peek through the slim opening and see nothing. Nudging the door open, I'm suddenly met with resistance. We must be at the end of that hallway with the antique hutch. I knew it was covering something.

I lean into it with all my weight, being careful not to make too much noise. All it would take is one squeak from this old, worn door — or worse, the entire hutch tipping over — to give us away and lose the element of surprise.

My heart is in my throat as I reach my arm through the narrow space and manage to grab an edge of the hutch, helping me push it out of the way, so, so slowly. Once the door is open wide enough for us to squeeze through, I look back at my friends and nod.

Taking the final step through the door, I listen for any sound of Hawthorn. The hardwood floor creaks softly under my feet as I pad through the hallway past the two bedrooms.

The moment I turn the corner, I'm violently grabbed from behind, arms pinned to my sides, as a strong hand clasps over my mouth, muffling my scream.

It's all over.

"Stop! It's me, it's me! Shut the fuck up, Els!" he says harshly in my ear.

I freeze.

That voice.

It can't be.

I spin around to look at the person holding me and find those familiar baby blue eyes staring back at me.

Ethan.

"Oh my God!" I throw my arms around him, squeezing with everything I have. Tears are already streaming down my face.

Is this even real?

"How? How are you here?" I continue to sob into his neck as Damien and Jade approach us with wide eyes, Jade clasping a hand over her mouth.

"It's okay," he says gently. "I'm fine. Long story. My memories of yesterday started coming back when Andy came to visit me at the hospital. He busted me out once we figured out what Hawthorn did and where you all went. He took an Uber for some reason, so we had to drive Damien's car here."

Damien pats his own pockets and looks up incredulously at Ethan.

"Hey, it's not my fault you left them in my room," he says with a wink.

I wipe my face. "I thought you were dead. Hawthorn sent

someone to your hospital room and..." I can't even finish that thought, as I lean back in and hold him tighter.

"You're insane, you know that?" Jade says with a shake of her head, unable to suppress a smile. "Good to see you, E."

"Welcome to the party, my man," Damien adds as he slaps him on the shoulder.

I finally manage to extract myself from his arms and wipe at the wet spot I leave on his shirt.

"He busted you out? Please tell me you didn't dramatically rip the IVs out of your arms like they do in the movies. You know how much I hate that."

"Yes, I'm very aware, you tell me every single time it happens. You'll be pleased to know I *gently* pulled them out... and they still hurt like hell."

I shudder at the thought. "I still can't believe you're here. Where's Andy?" I look around and lower my voice, remembering where we are. "And where's Hawthorn? He's got a gun, we need to be careful."

"Andy's over at his house. I assume you all figured out by now that this is Hawthorn's place?"

"Yeah, we got that much. Thanks for the address, by the way," I tease with an elbow jab to his side.

He winces in mock pain. "Hey, I didn't know! Look, I came here to help, but I see you all have everything under control here. So maybe I'll just see myself out."

We just stand there watching him pathetically walk away, pretending he's going to leave like he did all those times as a little boy, desperate for attention. One time, he even packed his suitcase and marched out the door, only making it as far as the mailbox before giving up and turning back around.

He stops at Hawthorn's front door and looks back at us with a pout.

"Are you done?" I ask with my hands on my hips. "We've got a princess to save."

He rolls his eyes when we refuse to engage in his antics. "Fine. Grab your phones and let's go." He points to the coffee table. "Found them all out back. Thought you might want them. *You're welcome.*"

Ethan picks up a familiar contraption off the floor by the entrance and straps it to his back.

"You can't be serious," I say to him as he fiddles with the mechanical arms of his Doc Ock costume.

I forgot Damien packed all their stuff in his car this morning before going to the hospital. I'm only now realizing he's even wearing his regular clothes and not a hospital gown, or the Walter White outfit he was admitted in.

"What do you plan to do with that?"

He looks at me with a raised eyebrow. "What do you plan to do with *those*?" He waves a hand at the Quantum Construct holstered at my waist, the viking-style helmet on Damien's head along with the shield he's holding, and the enormous wizard staff resting in Jade's hands.

I nod. "Fair enough."

"Come on, we need to get over to Andy's. Hawthorn is probably already on his way there, and we're wasting time."

The three of us look at each other and then back to Ethan.

"Where's Andy's real house?" Jade asks.

Ethan levels us all with a glare. I don't need our twin telepathy to translate this familiar look. The one that says, *Are you stupid?*

"He's next door."

The four of us start the trek across Hawthorn's property towards Andy's house. Ethan explained it's about a three-minute walk after I told him the term "next door" was a bit misleading.

How many acres does he own anyway?

It's still light out, but in the sky, the edges of soft clouds are dusted in a faint orange glow. I check my phone to confirm that it's just after seven p.m.

I'm only now realizing how hungry I am, and the fact that we haven't actually eaten anything since breakfast. Not since we brought food to the hospital after trying to visit Andy at the precinct, which feels like forever ago.

"Are you okay, man?" Damien asks, assessing Ethan's slight limp and heavy breathing. "Should you be up walking around like this so soon?"

"Psh, I'm fine. You know I can't sit still for that long anyway."

I shake my head and turn to look at him. I still can't believe he's here. I really thought I lost him. Twice.

Clearing my throat, I aim to change the subject. "So explain to us how they're next-door neighbors?"

"Els, I know you're the slow twin, but try to keep up."

I roll my eyes as he continues.

"Hawthorn's family owns his house and all this land. A few years ago, they sold a couple acres to Andy so he could build his new house. They've been buddies since they were kids and their families are super close. He stayed with Hawthorn during those months it was being built, but we hadn't really talked about any of that at the time. He never even mentioned Hawthorn."

"I still don't understand what happened between them," Damien says. "If they were such good friends, then why is this all happening? What does Tamara have to do with any of it?"

"Andy didn't say much about it on our drive here. He was more focused on getting to Tamara than trying to understand how his friend could do this. But it sounds like it goes much further than his relationship with her."

"You said your memories started coming back. What did you remember?" I ask.

"So, when I followed Mando after the fire alarms went off,

there were a bunch of locked rooms back there. I didn't think much of it at the time, but after we got back to the con floor, I realized one of them might actually be the server room where they keep all their security camera footage."

"But when did you…?" I stop myself, thinking back to that moment. We met up with Kat, and…Damien said Ethan left to go get something from the rooms.

I swat at his arm. "You went back down there alone? Are you crazy? We were almost caught the first time."

"Do you want to hear the rest of this or not?" He swats me right back. "I went outside towards the back of the building to see if I could find a way back in without a key card, but I stopped in the alleyway when I saw Detective Hawthorn walking out, dressed in his normal clothes and holding some bag. He saw me, but I didn't know what to say to him, so I just waved and walked back to the front entrance."

"And you didn't tell us this when you came back inside?"

"There wasn't much to tell. At the time, I had no idea he was actually involved in anything. I just thought he was back there investigating or whatever. He must have seen me following him dressed as the Mandalorian, and then once I saw him leaving the building through those back doors, assumed that I had figured it all out."

"So he thought you would expose him, and then he tried to…" I trail off.

"Take me out?" He shrugs. "I guess. But, again, I didn't make the connection that he was the one dressed as the Mandalorian at the time, or that he had posted on social media from Tamara's phone, *or* that he was messing with footage in the server room like some hacker. I didn't put it all together until Andy showed up."

We all continue walking in silence as I grab his hand and squeeze. Letting him know just how much I need him, and that I'm glad he's okay. He squeezes back.

A house begins to come into view about fifty yards away, partially obscured by more tall oak trees.

Ethan lets go of my hand and signals for us to slow down. "Okay, here's the deal. On the drive over, Andy told us about a secret entrance he built into his house that no one, not even Hawthorn, knows about."

I pause for a moment. "Wait…'us?' Who's 'us?'"

Ethan just grins and raises his eyebrows. "You'll see. Follow me."

What the hell? Who else came here with them? I think back to who we've even seen this weekend and suddenly I remember that goofy-ass grin. There's only one person I've ever seen have that effect on Ethan Graham.

Right as I'm about to call him out on it, a tall, gorgeous woman peeks her head out from a modest shed just up ahead.

Kat.

I hardly ever get to see her out of costume, but of course she looks stunning in a plain white t-shirt and ripped jean shorts. Her chocolate brown hair is pulled up out of her face in a high ponytail.

I run to meet her halfway and embrace her in a big hug. "What are you doing here?"

Jade and Damien wave.

She pulls away with a smile. "I came to visit E at the hospital just before Andy showed up. We figured out what this Hawthorn guy was up to, and I wanted to help."

This is incredible. The five of us should easily be able to take down Hawthorn. I only hope Andy and Tamara are both okay and can hold on long enough for us to get to them.

"I'm so glad you're here," I say to her with a smile. "So… what exactly are we doing in the shed?"

Ethan brushes past me, and I notice he's still moving a little slower, holding his side. "Check this out. Andy had a secret underground entrance built during construction. Total spy shit.

The entry point is here through the shed. Down some stairs, through a short tunnel, and it puts you in his basement behind a fake wall."

Whoa.

We enter the small shed, the exterior matching the house just across the yard. Closing the doors behind us, we begin our descent down a tiny flight of stairs.

"Have you already been inside the house?" Damien asks Kat.

"Only to the basement, which is hidden behind a wall. No one is down there, so we should be okay for now. As long as we're quiet."

"So what's the plan?" Jade asks the group.

We all look to Ethan since he seems to know more about the current situation than any of us.

His eyes dart back and forth between all of us and, with an innocent shrug, he says, "Don't die."

44

This is a bad idea.

Like, really bad.

Once we reach the base of the stairs, I put a hand up. "I know this might sound hilarious coming from me, but…should we really be doing this? Shouldn't we call the cops?"

Ethan answers, "Andy didn't want to call the police just yet. Any one of them could be in on it with Hawthorn, and he didn't want to risk tipping him off. We know he has at least one person helping him. Andy wanted to get to Tamara first."

We make it through the tunnel and approach a door leading into the basement. Inside is a small, enclosed space, barely enough room to fit all five of us. There's a small rectangular cutout along the wall, just big enough to see through to the other side, giving a full view of the basement.

Just like Kat said, there's no one there.

"The opening should be over here," Ethan says as he fumbles in the low light, feeling around before pushing on a small section of the wall. The entire partition hinges open.

"Badass," Damien and I say together as we all walk into the

basement, past the fake wall. The two of us trade quick glances, and my heartbeat cranks up a notch.

Stop. Focus. Breathe.

"And Tamara is *here*? At Andy's house?" Jade asks. "I wonder why Hawthorn wouldn't have just kept her at his own house."

"Maybe she was there but he moved her here as part of his plan?" I offer. Waking up in his basement, I'm pretty sure I saw blood on the floor. Maybe it was hers.

"Did Andy say anything else? Anything that might help us out here?" Jade is certainly not one to like going into a situation without knowing exactly what she's up against. And right now, we can use all the help we can get.

"Not really. I think he's still having a hard time dealing with the fact that Hawthorn was behind all this. That he was even capable of it."

Never underestimate someone.

You do not know what they are capable of.

"We really have no idea what we could be walking into up there," Ethan says as he points to the stairs leading up to the main house.

"Ethan, you don't even *know*. He's extremely dangerous. He's the one who took that woman who went missing a few years ago. We need to be careful," I say as I start up the stairs ahead of the group.

"Wait, what?" he and Kat say at the same time.

"Yeah. We'll have to talk about that later. We're out of time." I let out another breath. "Okay. Moment of truth. We stay together, no matter what."

"Wow," Ethan whispers, still standing at the base of the stairs.

"What?" I ask, ready for him make fun of me or tell some inappropriate joke.

Instead, he says, "Nothing, just…look at you taking control, leading us all into battle." He nods proudly.

I can't help but smile. I realize in this moment that I'm not afraid. I'm ready to stop this asshole. I'm determined to save Tamara Jenkins.

Ethan is okay. We're all in this together.

"Let's do this."

I turn the handle and peek through the opening to assess our surroundings. Luckily, there's no one around. The basement door opens into a wide hall near the front of the house. To the left is a soaring two-story foyer, with large, wooden, double doors at the entrance, and a tall sweeping staircase leading to the second floor.

On the other side is an enormous living room with a stone fireplace and a TV mounted above it, framed by built-in book-shelves. Dark wood beams sweep across the high ceiling, and a long glass coffee table sits before pristine white furniture. Just beyond the living room is a gorgeous open kitchen with stain-less-steel appliances, bright white cabinets, and an island with dark marble countertops.

Mounted on the walls are framed photos and plaques, along-side a small shelf of various awards. An impressive collection and a testament to all of Andy's achievements throughout the years.

Movement catches my eye, and I look back at the TV, which I didn't even realize was on. The dark image on the screen makes my heart stop.

Tamara.

She's tied to a chair, with duct tape over her mouth, directly facing whatever is being used to record her. It's like some fucked-up live-stream.

But she's alive.

She looks...relatively unharmed, from what I can tell, except for a gash across her cheek. Who knows what else he's done to her though.

But *where* is she? And where are Andy and Hawthorn?

The rest of the group file into the living room, their gazes falling on the disturbing image on the TV screen. Gasps and whispers fill the room.

It's one thing to think in hypotheticals and what could have happened to her, it's something else to see it with your own eyes.

"Where is she? Is that a bedroom?" Kat whispers.

Jade moves closer to the screen, angling around the large sectional sofa. "That looks like a bed over there, but she's surrounded by…candles or something. What the fuck is he planning to do with her?"

Suddenly, there's a loud *bang* from a closed room off to our side near the basement door, but Tamara didn't flinch. She must be further away, or on a different floor entirely.

Ethan walks over to where the noise came from and holds up a finger to his mouth before motioning to the door with his other hand.

We all ready ourselves.

This is it.

If Hawthorn is behind that door, we need to act now. We need to make our move before he realizes we're here, while we can still catch him off guard.

Ethan gently puts his hand on the knob and slowly turns it clockwise, careful not to make any noise. The entire house goes eerily silent as we collectively hold our breath.

Then, several things happen at once.

The door Ethan is holding on to flies open, pulled fiercely from the other side, knocking him forward right into Hawthorn's broad chest. Ethan's Doc Ock arms catch on the doorframe, giving him just enough resistance to maintain his balance, as Hawthorn wraps an arm around Ethan's waist to stop himself from falling back.

In the split second it takes to get his footing, Hawthorn points his gun through the door frame and a tangle of Doc Ock arms, towards the living room, sending everyone to the ground for cover. I watch in slow motion as Damien instinctively raises the shield, trying to protect himself, along with Jade and Kat, at the same moment Hawthorn pulls the trigger.

The noise is so deafening, I clasp my hands over my ears, but it does nothing to block out the scream that soon fills the room.

Jade.

"Fuck!" she cries out. The bullet may as well have pierced my heart.

She's kneeling on the ground, holding the top of her arm, blood trickling out between her fingers. Her face is contorted in pain...and the next moment, rage.

The shield — being made of foam — allowed the bullet to go straight through, piercing Jade in the shoulder. Damien drops the shield, jumping to her side in a flash as he rips off his helmet and begins tending to her wound.

Without thinking, I sprint towards Hawthorn in a blind rage, reaching for his gun with one hand and trying to pry his grip off Ethan with the other, while we both fight to gain control of the weapon.

Ethan braces his hands on the doorframe and pushes back with all his strength, taking Hawthorn and me with him into the living room. The movement is enough to throw Hawthorn off balance, and I take advantage of the split-second distraction to knock the gun out of his hand with my fist.

The gun goes sliding across the floor at the same moment Hawthorn pulls himself out of Ethan's grasp, backing away towards the fireplace. Damien finishes tightening a strip of fabric over Jade's bleeding arm just as Kat lunges for the gun and points it at Hawthorn.

Damien helps Jade to her feet as we all approach Hawthorn slowly. Ethan and me on his right, with Jade, Damien, and Kat rounding the sectional couch to come up on his left side.

He's surrounded. We've got him.

"It's over, Hawthorn," I say. "You're done."

He faces us calmly, too calmly, his lips curling into the most unsettling, soulless smile as he reaches a hand behind his back.

Shit!

We all advance on him at the same time, not stopping to think about what he could be reaching for, only that we have mere seconds to act before it's too late. Before any one of us could be killed.

Jade launches her wizard staff towards him like a javelin, which he narrowly avoids by ducking away at the last second, the staff clanking to the floor. Kat aims the gun towards Hawthorn's knees, not to kill but to incapacitate, but when she pulls the trigger the hollow *click* from an empty chamber seems to echo throughout the entire house.

Hawthorn pulls his arm out from behind his back, producing another gun, at the same moment I release the Quantum Construct out of its holster at my waist. Before he has a chance to aim, I shove the bright, colorful contraption with all my weight straight at Hawthorn's face, the end of the hard plastic tube jamming into his left eye socket with so much force I hear a wet popping sound.

He lets out a piercing shriek that rings through my skull as he stumbles backward, dropping the gun to the floor.

He grabs his face, whipping his head back so hard it cracks on the wall, and he crumples to the ground.

I take the opportunity to kick him right in the balls and watch with immense pleasure as he curls up and writhes on the floor with another blood-curdling scream.

From my side, Ethan lunges at Hawthorn, straddling him and grabbing both of his wrists with impressive speed before rolling him facedown onto his stomach.

Damien kneels down and presses his knee on Hawthorn's neck, while extracting the pair of handcuffs from his pocket that bound his own hands just an hour or so earlier.

A noise from the room at our side has me sprinting. There, I find Andy tied to a chair with a blindfold over his eyes and duct tape over his mouth as he tries to scream for our attention.

I nearly trip over my own feet to get to his side and quickly remove the blindfold and duct tape. "Are you okay, are you hurt?" I ask as I kneel down and work to untie him with shaky hands.

"I'm fine, I'm fine. Tamara's upstairs!"

I untie the last knot and pull the ropes free. He offers me a hand to stand up, and I take it as we run out of the bedroom together. I glance behind me to see Ethan and Damien, who have Hawthorn detained on the ground. The TV screen above them shows Tamara leaning over, being untied by Kat and Jade.

Andy releases my hand to sprint to the stairs in the foyer that lead to the top floor. I race to keep up with him, but he's so damn fast. His long legs are a blur as he disappears behind the corner.

I finally get to the top landing, rushing to the open bedroom ahead, and watch as the last of the ropes fall off Tamara's hands.

Andy scoops her up in his arms, off her feet, burying his face in her neck as she wraps her legs around his hips, and her arms clutch his neck. Andy clings to her as he lowers them down to the ground, never breaking their embrace.

I can't take my eyes off them. The whole thing is surreal.

My chest tightens as I watch their beautiful reunion. I can only imagine what they must be feeling right now. A tear cascades down my cheek, realizing in this moment, that I'm actually witnessing true love for the first time in my entire life, and it's almost too much for my heart to bear.

Kat and Jade appear at my sides, and Jade puts a hand on my shoulder.

"Let's give these two a minute, yeah?" She runs the hand from my shoulder down my arm, pulling me into a side hug as we walk back towards the stairs.

45

Jade, Kat, and I descend the staircase and come around the corner to find Hawthorn in a dining room chair, handcuffed, ankles tied with rope, and facing the couch where Ethan and Damien are sitting.

The interrogation begins.

"I'm gonna make some calls," Jade says as she pulls out her phone. "I'll have my contacts make sure we get the right people over here, since we don't know who we can trust in his department yet." She points at the guys on the couch. "Do not touch him. This asshole is not getting off on a technicality."

They put their hands up in mock defense.

Jade gives me a nod to proceed with the plan we hashed out if it ever came to this.

"While we wait, it doesn't hurt to have a little chat, does it?" I say sweetly as I walk into the living room and take a seat next to Damien on the couch, casually placing my phone face down on the coffee table between us. I lean forward and prop my elbows on my knees, clasping my hands.

"Fuck you, Red." Hawthorn spits at me.

I smile. "Aww, that's not very nice. Come on, Mikey, I thought we were friends."

He looks off to the side with a scowl. I need to get him talking. Get him to confess what he did, and why. For myself especially, I really need to understand the "why" in all this.

"Just like you and Andy were friends," I continue. "You know, before he went off and landed that hot Hollywood girlfriend of his, am I right?"

His head snaps in my direction and the look in his eyes is lethal. "You don't know what you're talking about."

My head tilts to the side, my smile never faltering. I know I can get him to talk if I just push the right buttons. People like him are so predictable.

"You're right. It wasn't all about Tamara, was it? Not really."

I pause, relishing in the silence, as his full attention is now on me. I decide to go for it and see if my suspicions are correct.

Never breaking eye contact, I continue, "No, this all started way before her, didn't it? Right around the time when Andy found his well-earned success writing that...award-winning, *hilarious* comic book series and catapulted himself into fame." I motion towards the awards and accolades mounted along the wall behind me. "Don't you think?"

His chest rises and falls, his breath picking up as his face turns a pale shade of red, clearly at war with himself to try and keep calm.

But I've hit a nerve.

I let the silence marinate for just a moment, as the final piece clicks into place in my own mind, and I realize...I've got him.

I know exactly what happened.

I steeple my fingers under my chin. "It really is incredible how he created The Quantum Protector...*all on his own*. I mean, he's always been so—" I wave my hand around dramatically, "—ambitious. So talented. So...successful."

"*Bullshit! Bull-fucking-shit!*" he screams. "He fucking stole my ideas, and he took *everything* for himself! Just like he's been doing ever since we were kids!"

The room falls deadly silent, and I try to contain my grin.

Bingo.

He huffs out a breath. "So I decided to take something from him. He deserved to know how it felt to lose something he cared about for a change."

I fight with everything I have not to glance down at my phone, which has been recording audio this whole time. Let him dig his own grave.

Jade explained that we don't need his consent to record him in the state of Indiana, and that he'll want to brag about how smart he is. So I just let him talk.

"He really made it too easy when he convinced her not to bring a bodyguard with her on this trip, thinking *he* was enough to keep her safe."

The image of Andy kneeling on the hotel room floor flashes in my mind.

She's gone because of me.

He wasn't admitting he did it. He was blaming himself for not having any security with her. Between him, the con handlers, and the WyvernFest security guards, she should have been perfectly safe at our scrappy little convention. They couldn't have imagined anything like this would ever happen.

But Hawthorn knew she would be vulnerable, and he saw it as an opportunity. But to do what with her, I still don't understand.

Hawthorn can't help but keep talking. "And it was *really* a big mistake on his part, not even checking whose car he was putting her in. Having one of my rookies act as the handler, using a car from the impound lot, texting her at the number I swiped off his phone when he wasn't looking."

"How did they keep her in the car once she realized something was wrong?" I try to sound interested, fascinated with how brilliant his plan was.

"They stopped in some alley. A rag full of chloroform was all that was needed before moving her to the trunk." He shakes his head. "Fucking idiot didn't realize her damn hat fell off though. But I do thank you both for bringing it right back to me so no one else had to know about it."

Chloroform. That must also be how he got Damien and Jade down to the basement without any injuries.

"Yeah, you really got us there," I say with a chuckle.

Keep talking, asshole.

His gaze shifts from me to Ethan, and that evil smile returns. "You would've been an added bonus in all this too, you know. Dear, sweet Andrew playing mentor to a sad, broken delinquent, only to find he couldn't save him either? It would have been more than enough to break his spirit. It was just too perfect. Especially after I caught you following me yesterday."

Ethan doesn't give him the reaction he so desperately wants. He simply crosses an ankle over his knee and casually picks at a piece of lint from his pants, smiling right back at him.

He said he hadn't actually figured it all out before Hawthorn drugged him, but he doesn't need to know that.

Instead, Ethan says, to state clearly for the audio recording, "Did you really think I was that much of a threat that you had to kill me? You were that scared of me?"

"I honestly don't know how you survived, kid. The amount I put in your drink should've been more than enough with how much alcohol you were drinking."

Jade returns from outside, moving behind the sofa to join Kat, who asks, "How did you get into my party, anyway?"

"Oh, that part was easy. I have plenty of costumes and masks to help me blend into any situation. And no one ever pays much attention to the dull, frumpy loner…isn't that right, Andy?"

We all whip our heads around to see Andy and Tamara

standing at the entrance to the living room holding hands. I'm not sure how long they've been standing there, or how much they heard, but the look on Andy's pained face tells me he heard enough.

He unlaces his fingers from hers as he slowly approaches Hawthorn, stopping behind the short side of the sectional couch. "All this? Because of the *comic*?" He's so angry. But...he's also hurt.

Betrayed by his best friend. The man he considered a brother.

Hawthorn looks up at Andy with pure contempt. "You know I helped you create it. We came up with it together!"

"Oh sure, except you never wanted to put in any real work! We came up with one idea together — *one* — and you never wanted to actually *do* anything with it." He rakes a hand through his hair and takes a step back. "So yeah, I ran with it, but *I* was the one who put in all the work."

Hawthorn shakes his head and scoffs.

"I would have loved to do all that together," Andy continues. "But you were so focused on girls, and wanting to fit in, and pissing your life away behind your computer screen—"

"You *stole* my girlfriend, remember?"

"—all the while blaming *me* that your life wasn't going the way you wanted it to. Well guess what? It doesn't fucking work that way! And I never stole your girlfriend. She never even knew you existed. You obsessed over her and created some fantasy in that fucked-up head of yours."

"Fuck you," Hawthorn says bitterly.

"No, fuck *you*, Hawthorn." Andy slams his hands on the back of the couch. "You pissed and moaned that life wasn't fair, and that I always got what I wanted and you didn't, rather than actually getting up off your ass and doing something about it."

"Well I did something about it now, didn't I?"

Andy crosses his arms and scoffs, "You always took things

too far, man. What were you even going to do here anyway? You're not a murderer."

We all look at each other. He doesn't know about the missing woman.

"You don't know half of what I can do, or what I have done, *Andrew*."

Andy walks a few steps closer and looks down at him, shaking his head. "What happened to you, man? You're a fucking waste. I just feel sorry for you."

"What happened to me? What happened to *you*? You were my brother. As soon as you had the chance, you went off to be with all your fancy Hollywood friends, and you left me behind!"

"No. That was your choice. I surrounded myself with people who supported me and actually wanted me to succeed. You never wanted that for me. It was always about *you*."

He looks away from Hawthorn to Tamara, standing there alone, with her arms wrapped around herself. He walks back over to her and takes her hands in his, kissing her knuckles and staring into her eyes.

"Then I met someone who I could be myself around, and who made me laugh. I hadn't laughed like that in so long." He chuckles, dropping his forehead to hers, a tear splashing on her cheek. Talking more to her than to Hawthorn now, he continues, "I never knew love like that was even possible. That you didn't have to put on a show or pretend to be something you're not. But that someone could just...love you exactly the way you are."

He wipes the tears from her face as she wraps her arms around his neck and kisses him with so much passion and longing that it makes my breath catch.

I've never known a love like that could exist either.

My entire life I've been trying to be who others wanted me to be, so they might love me. So I might actually feel worthy of it.

My love for my father wasn't enough to make him stay.

But that wasn't my fault.

My love for my mother wasn't enough to make her show up for her children.

That wasn't my fault.

My love for Jared wasn't enough to make him love me back.

And that wasn't my fault either.

I assumed that "true love" was just a fairy tale and that no one ever *really* felt like that. But I'm seeing it now with my own two eyes. It all seems so…unlikely, the two of them. She is a Hollywood star, and he's the goofy comic book writer. I was too blinded by my own experiences and judgments to see it.

"I love you," she says softly. It's the first time I'm actually hearing her voice in person.

"I love you so much," he says in return.

I love her! We're supposed to be together!

Those words from last night, which I assumed were laced with hysteria and malice…instead, it was true love all along.

"Ugh, give me a break!" Hawthorn yells, absolutely ruining the moment. "She doesn't love you, she's just using you. People like her look down on people like us. She's nothing but a spoiled princess, slumming it for a good fuck."

Tamara lunges out of Andy's arms before he can stop her, and it's Ethan and Damien who jump up and have to hold her back before she reaches Hawthorn.

Damn, I suddenly really want to watch her beat the crap out of him.

"He is nothing like you, you bastard!" she spits at him. "Tell him about all the photos you took, and how you were stalking us for months! All the gross, obsessive shit you've done? Keeping me locked in your basement like that? I hope you rot."

Andy comes up to her and releases her from Ethan and Damien. She turns to bury her face in his chest while he wraps his arms tightly around her.

I stare at Hawthorn. "What was the point in all this? What were you hoping to get out of it?"

He keeps his eyes trained on Andy. "I wanted Andrew to *watch* as I took it all away from him. His girl...his career. Planting enough evidence along the way to pin it all on him in the end. I really did enjoy watching y'all turn on him."

Shit.

We played right into his hands.

Taking him in for questioning. The Xanax. The brick. The con guide and the notes. He turned us against Andy and would have had us believe he was the one behind Tamara's kidnapping, and ultimately, her murder.

Ethan was the only one who never believed any of it.

"Of course, when y'all wouldn't leave it alone, I had to... modify the plan. The rest of you showed up here, and it would've been so easy to prove that Andrew was responsible for your deaths. That these poor kids witnessed him murdering the girl who broke his heart, so he had no choice but to kill them too. He would've spent the rest of his miserable life in prison, blaming himself for *everything*."

He leans back in his chair smiling, proud of himself for being so clever.

Before anyone can say anything else, the front door bursts open.

46

Suddenly, it's chaos.

Several police officers file into the house in a rush, shouting commands to each other. We all instinctively put our hands up as they flood into the room, most of them heading straight towards Hawthorn.

We lower our hands as one of the officers calmly approaches Jade.

"Ms. Crawford?" he asks as he extends a hand. "Captain Gutierrez."

"Yes, sir." She shakes his in return with her good arm as I come to her side.

"I must say, you've got some impressive connections around here. The chief has filled me in as best he could, but do you mind answering some questions for me?"

"Of course, anything you need."

I watch as the officers finish removing the ropes from Hawthorn's ankles and haul him up out of the dining room chair, still in handcuffs, as they read him his Miranda Rights.

We all wave as he is escorted out of the house. EMTs file into the house asking if anyone needs medical attention. I wave one over to Jade to check her arm. She insists she's fine and that the bullet just grazed her, but I won't rest until she's taken care of.

I exchange contact information with Captain Gutierrez, so I can forward him the audio file of Hawthorn's confessions. Another officer approaches Andy and Tamara, who is also being checked out by an EMT, but I can't quite hear what they're saying. No doubt they will want statements from everyone, but especially from Tamara.

"Sir, what about the person Detective Hawthorn was working with?" Jade asks, hissing as someone cleans the wound on her arm. "We believe they're in his department."

Captain Gutierrez nods his head. "Officer Ruby Campion has already turned herself in and is cooperating."

Jade and I look to each other in shock.

"Wait, Ruby Campion?" Jade asks. "I spoke with her at the police station when Andy was taken in."

"That explains why she was so nervous around you. She must have already known who we were at that point."

After what feels like hours of answering questions, the last of the police officers finally file out and close the front door. Apparently, word has already gotten out about Tamara being found, so they let us give our statements here without having to go in to the station, which, understandably, is a madhouse right now.

"Hey Andy, what's your wi-fi?" I ask as I approach him at the kitchen island putting out plates of snacks. "The signal out here is terrible."

Tamara is on the other side of the kitchen washing her hands. They've both gone into hospitality mode, like they've just invited us over for a Sunday hangout.

"It's the one named Warden."

He rattles off the insane password of random letters and

numbers as I try desperately to keep up, but when he's done, I pause.

My head pops up. "Warden. What is that?"

"It's an anagram for Andrew. I use it sometimes as my username or alias."

I can't help the smile spreading across my face. "So like… Benjamin Warden?" I say with a raised eyebrow.

Tamara whips her head to me from across the kitchen, eyes wide, and Andy just grins. "Yeah, you know at some point we're going to need to talk about how you broke into our hotel room."

I purse my lips.

"And—" his grin widens, "—how you slashed my tires?"

My eyes go wide, and I shake my head. "Hmm…no, I think you must have me confused with someone else."

I shoot him an apologetic smile, and he reaches out to ruffle my hair before pulling me in for a hug. Total big brother move.

He leans away and says, "It was actually kinda badass. You were looking out for her, and you did what you thought was right. So thank you…for everything."

"Any time," I return with a smile, backing away before Tamara comes over and I no doubt say something embarrassing.

I walk up to Ethan, who's standing by the fireplace. Desperate to remind myself that he's really still here, I put my arm around his waist. He pulls me in to his side.

"Told you," he says, lifting his wrist with the Luke Skywalker tattoo. "Nothing in the galaxy can keep us apart."

I squeeze him even tighter.

With Hawthorn and the rest of the police gone, the reality of the situation begins to weigh heavily on each of us, and the room falls into silence.

What do you even say after something like that?

"So…" Ethan starts, desperate to break the silence, but coming up short of any actual words. Instead, he just waves his hand around.

Jade shakes her head from over on the couch with a smile.

"Well, I guess introductions are in order," Andy says to us, as he and Tamara take a few steps into the open living room. "Everyone, this is Tamara."

We all wave awkwardly, like we don't already know who Tamara Jenkins is.

"This is Kat, Damien, and Jade," Andy says as he gestures to the three of them sitting on the couch.

He pauses and puts his hand gently on the small of her back, coaxing her closer to me and Ethan. "And this…you may have already guessed…is Ethan and Elsie."

Tamara looks at us and flashes a bright, genuine smile. My heart nearly stops when I realize this is the moment I'm finally meeting my idol.

Play it cool.

Before either of us can say anything, she pulls us both in for a group hug. With an arm slung over each of our shoulders, she says, "It's nice to finally meet you both. I've heard so much about you."

Me? Tamara Jenkins knows who I am?

"Uhh…you too. I mean…umm…I love your hair."

Seriously? I shouldn't be allowed to talk to people.

Ethan says, "It's so nice to meet you," like a normal person. Show-off.

She pulls away but keeps her hand on my elbow and chuckles. She's…gorgeous. Radiant. Even with a little bit of dried blood still caked on the side of her face and her slightly disheveled hair, she's breathtaking. Her dazzling aquamarine eyes reminding me of that necklace I lost a lifetime ago.

She lets go of my arm entirely too soon and walks back over to Andy, the two of them embracing once more.

God, they look so…happy.

I'm still processing it.

This whole time, I mistakenly took his erratic behavior for

something threatening and unhinged, but it all makes sense now. The woman he loves was taken from him. Of course he would be upset and agitated and losing his mind.

She wasn't just a friend. Clearly, she is *everything* to him.

My cynical ass couldn't possibly fathom true love between such an unlikely pair. I was projecting my own insecurities and trauma onto him and everyone around me. It wasn't fair to judge him so quickly, because of what happened to me.

But the truth is, I'm so happy to be proven wrong.

I take a seat next to Jade on the couch and lean my head on her shoulder, Damien and Kat looking on from her other side.

"So...we're gonna need some details here," Ethan says to Andy with a grin as he takes the chair that Hawthorn had been sitting in and moves it next to Kat.

"Okay. What do you want to know?" Andy takes Tamara's hand and leads her over to the only spot left on the couch, the one next to me. I sit back up.

Wow. She's really here.

She's here and she's alive, and I helped find her.

I still can't get over how stunning and...ethereal she looks up close. Her red hair is actually more of a caramel brown with a reddish tint, and it's shorter than I'm used to seeing on the show. I realize now that was a wig.

My eyes are wide as I look over at Ethan.

Pull it together, he says telepathically.

I clear my throat, trying desperately not to embarrass myself any further.

"How did you two meet?" Ethan asks. "How long have you been together?"

Andy does a cute little hand gesture to Tamara that says, *go ahead you tell it,* like they've had this conversation with others enough times that they have their whole story routine down. He casually rests his arm behind her over top of the couch.

"We met back in LA. One day, I was out walking my dog—"

"Benjamin, yep," I say before I can stop myself. Mortified, I close my eyes and nod for her to continue.

"Anyway," she says with a sweet smile. "He got loose just before we entered the dog park, and he took off. So I'm chasing after him like a lunatic when I round the corner and see him sitting like a perfect little gentleman, while some *strange guy*—" she looks to Andy with a sparkle in her eye, "—is petting him and ruffling his ears. Both as happy as can be."

Andy jumps in. "He came right up to me like he already knew me. It was the sweetest thing."

"We had a good laugh and got to talking and found out we had several mutual friends and a lot in common."

"I asked her out for coffee."

"And coffee turned into dinner."

"We talked so long that we closed down the restaurant and then kept the night going at a bar downtown."

"Since then, we've been inseparable. Talking and texting every day. And…the rest is history," she ends with a smile at Andy, interlacing her fingers with his as he plants a light kiss on her temple.

The whole thing is so damn cute, I kind of want to puke a little.

"How long ago was that?" I manage to ask.

"Ten months," they say together.

Ugh, they're so adorable.

Ethan stares longingly at them, like he's fallen under a love spell. "I'm so happy for you both, truly."

He would never admit it, but he's a hopeless romantic at heart.

I can see why Tamara likes Andy. He really is a great person. Funny, smart, nerdy, genuine. He's already back to being his old self around her, and she loves him for it. They can both just be themselves, neither one demanding that the other change or act a certain way.

With Jared, I felt like he wouldn't love me if I was "too nerdy" or "too" anything, so I toned it all down. I whittled down my entire self until it was something palatable enough for him.

And in the end, he still didn't love me the way I needed.

Andy and Tamara have shown me that love can exist without sacrificing pieces of yourself or changing who you are to suit the other person. What I see before me is hope. Hope that true love really is possible, but it starts with loving yourself first.

I turn to Andy. "So, one thing I don't quite get is why you didn't just tell us from the beginning that you two were dating? When she first went missing, you only referred to her as a friend. And on top of acting all strange...I'm sorry, but it made you look suspicious as hell."

Andy huffs out a quiet laugh, and Tamara looks up at him. "Would you have believed me if I told you the truth?" He shrugs. "Maybe, maybe not. I know what people think when they first find out we're together..."

My stomach twists, knowing I was guilty of that same judgment.

"...but we both agreed that we didn't want our relationship known to the public just yet, and when all this happened, it didn't seem like the right time to announce it. Not while she was still missing. We had been planning to go public at the end of the year, on the advice of our agents."

"We wanted to keep it quiet for as long as we could." Tamara squeezes his hand. "Once the media picks it up, we'll get hounded. Although, I guess the cat might be out of the bag now."

"I told the police everything over at the station this morning though. I had no idea Hawthorn already knew about us. I guess he used it as an excuse to take me in for a few hours. Planting those seeds of doubt for everyone else." He shakes his head, still coming to terms with everything his best friend has done.

I shoot him a sympathetic smile.

"Elsie, I wanted to tell you, especially once you found me in our hotel room. I've been so delirious and sleep-deprived, and then you looked at me with such...devastation. I just panicked. I'm sorry."

"You don't have to be sorry. I get it." I reach over and put a reassuring hand on his knee.

"So...what now?" Ethan asks.

We all look around at each other.

I take a moment to marvel at these incredible people before me.

We really did it.

We saved the princess. The good guy got the girl. The bad guy has been defeated.

We worked together, and our individual strengths put together made us unstoppable. A force to be reckoned with.

Jade puts her arm around me, leaning her head on mine.

Ethan and Kat look to each other, unblinking, as he laces his fingers with hers. She smiles and playfully jabs her elbow into his side.

Then I look over at Damien, those dark eyes piercing straight through me.

I want so badly to go to him.

This would be that perfect moment where we leap into each other's arms, my hands running through his raven black hair as we kiss passionately, and everyone gets to live happily ever after.

But...

I can't do it. Not yet.

This whole time I've been trying to find my old self again. Thinking I needed to go *back* to who I was before all this happened, before Jared broke me apart, and then everything would be okay.

But I'm not that person anymore.

While searching for Tamara, I found myself.

I needed to figure out who I really am, and now I get to decide who I want to be.

I'm close.

But I'm not quite there yet, and I refuse to dive into a relationship with Damien before I can truly love myself first. I couldn't do that to him, and I won't do anything to jeopardize what we could have together.

Because it's there, the potential for a happy life with him. We both know it.

We've just been waiting for the right time.

He seems to read my thoughts, as a slow smile spreads across his handsome face.

I return the grin with a wink before saying to the rest of the group, "Who's ready to book rooms for next year?"

Epilogue

Four Months Later

Ethan puts his famous cheeseburger casserole in the oven as the clock ticks down to our guests' arrival. His shiny gold hat tips back as he takes a swig of beer and the bells on his ugly sweater jingle.

This will be the sixth year of our Friendsgiving tradition, where our group gets together sometime between Thanksgiving and Christmas for an epic night of food, drinks, and games.

The house is decked out in silver and gold decorations. A small Christmas tree takes up space in the corner of the living room, adorned with bright multicolor lights and various sentimental ornaments.

Ethan and I don't see our parents much anymore and have no desire to spend holidays with them, so we cherish this time with our chosen family every year.

Jade had to miss Thanksgiving with her family but will be leaving next week to drive back to our hometown and spend

Christmas with them. Every so often, we go back with her, since they've always welcomed us as part of their own family.

This year, however, Ethan and I weren't feeling up for much traveling and wanted to stay grounded here.

Damien keeps busy at the hospital and usually has to work or be on call around the major holidays, so he won't be able to see his family until spring. He has a good enough relationship with his parents nowadays, and his sister, Sasha, plans to visit him on her way back to school for the spring semester.

We always make sure to have our Friendsgiving on a night when all four of us can be here.

Our doorbell rings, and Ethan jogs over to open the door, revealing our first guests of the day and the newest addition to our annual celebration: Andy and Tamara.

They are the picture-perfect couple. Andy is in fitted black trousers and a bright red button-up shirt, holding out a bottle of wine. Tamara, gorgeous as ever, is wearing a cute black dress and long overcoat, hair curled by her shoulders, and is balancing some sort of pie in her palms.

"I'll take that, thank you so much!" I say as I approach, taking the pie in one hand and pulling her in for a quick hug with the other.

A gust of cold, brisk air hits us just as Ethan closes the door.

I still can't get over the fact that I'm on a first-name — and hugging — basis with Tamara Jenkins…I mean *Tamara*. We've kept in touch since WyvernFest and have actually become, dare I say, friends.

She and Andy officially announced their relationship to the world shortly after the night we found her. The Glenville Chief of Police held a press conference that night, once Hawthorn was taken into custody, and it was all but confirmed once the details of the case were made public.

Andy bends down for a hug. "Thanks for having us, Elsie," he says softly.

"Are you kidding me? Any time." I usher them both inside and place the pie — pecan, my favorite — on the dining room table.

Like good hosts, Ethan and I take their coats, offer drinks, and help get them all settled into our cozy, little home.

It's been a whirlwind since WyvernFest ended, and Michael Hawthorn and Ruby Campion were arrested. Hawthorn himself has been charged with a handful of felonies for his actions against Tamara, including false imprisonment and aggravated assault. As well as attempted first-degree murder on Ethan.

Ruby flipped and made a deal to reduce her own charge of abduction in exchange for testifying against Hawthorn. She claims he abused his position of authority and threatened to fire her if she didn't participate in the kidnapping.

After we told them about the missing woman from a few years back, they searched his property for days and eventually found her remains buried within the forest behind his yard.

So yeah, Hawthorn will spend the rest of his sad, miserable life in prison.

Jade is the next to arrive, not even bothering to ring the doorbell, since she's essentially an honorary roommate at this point. She is wearing a sparkly silver jumpsuit, her curly black and burgundy hair flawlessly styled to one side. She holds up a bottle of champagne after kicking the door closed behind her, to laughter and applause.

Ethan immediately helps pour glasses for everyone.

Kat couldn't come, unfortunately. She lives about three hours away, but she and Ethan talk and video chat all the time these days. He still won't divulge many details about their relationship yet, but I don't press. He's obviously happy, so I'm happy for him.

I take a sip of my champagne, but we're still missing one person.

My stomach flutters as I anxiously wait for Damien to arrive, my fingers drumming on the kitchen counter.

I've spent the last four months working on myself and really focusing on taking care of my body and mind. I started seeing a new therapist, one who I felt comfortable enough with to be truly honest about what I was thinking and feeling. She put me on medication after our second session, which is helping immensely. She couldn't believe my old therapist hadn't even suggested it.

I also found out through friends that Jared had gotten Tegan pregnant. Poor girl. I texted him "Best wishes" and then promptly blocked his number. In that moment, I imagined him disintegrating into dust like a Thanos snap and blowing away in the wind, no longer feeling anything for him.

After WyvernFest, Damien and I talked about that near-kiss in the closet of Hawthorn's house. I've been open with him about what I needed to do and told him I didn't expect him to wait for me, since I couldn't promise how I would feel after taking this time for myself and working to heal my past traumas. The last thing I ever want is to hurt him or lead him on.

But just last week, I realized that I *am* ready, and that I really do want us to be more than just friends.

It happened randomly while I was out shopping and came upon a section of scented oils and candles. The newest product they were selling had me bursting out laughing right there in the store aisle, and I immediately bought it and had it wrapped up for him.

Presents are certainly not required at Friendsgiving, but small ones are often exchanged anyway. Sometimes you just come across the perfect gift for someone and you can't pass it up.

So now I'm standing here in my kitchen, holding this wrapped box in my slightly shaking hands, wondering now if this was the stupidest idea I've ever had, when the doorbell rings.

I walk to the front door, smoothing out my gold cocktail dress, while Ethan and Jade eye me curiously, and I shoot them the *don't say a word* glare.

I open the door to the sight of Damien, dressed in a fitted black button-up shirt, black trousers, and a long charcoal grey trench coat. I take in the sight of this amazing man I'm lucky enough to call one of my best friends, but with whom I now want to be so much more. My heart flutters in my chest.

"Hey, come on in," I say nervously as I motion inside. Why am I nervous?

He tenses. "Actually, can I talk to you about something outside real quick?"

Oh. My fluttering heart plummets to the floor.

Shit.

He met someone.

It's my fault.

I told him not to wait for me.

I'm too late.

I fucked it all up.

But I force a smile and say, "Sure, of course."

I follow him out on the front porch, sucking in a breath as the biting cold air hits my face and I close the front door behind me. I probably should have grabbed my coat first, but since I'm on the verge of a panic attack — which usually makes me all hot and sweaty — I should be good without it.

I'm still holding his present behind my back, but now I think I'll just throw it in the trash, along with my heart.

Good riddance.

He holds out a wrapped gift the size of a large shoe box. "I just...wanted to give you this."

My head snaps up to meet his gaze. "You got me something?"

"Did you get *me* something?" He points behind me with a grin.

"Maybe," I say as I reluctantly hand it over to him and I take mine.

He nudges my arm. "You go first."

I take a breath as I tear open the wrapping, balancing the box on one hand and tip open the box to find a gorgeously detailed 3D printed baby dragon — well, a baby wyvern, if we're being technical. The brown scales cascading down its body contrast beautifully with its red, leathery wings.

"I had E teach me how to use his printer. I thought you might like it for your Mother of Dragons costume."

It's the perfect size and shape to drape across my shoulders, the final missing piece to my costume. One that no longer sends my blood pressure soaring, but one that I love with my whole heart.

It's gorgeous. Breathtaking.

I can't help the huge smile spreading across my face. "It's… perfect. Thank you, Damien. Truly."

I look up at him, and those chestnut eyes have my heart pounding again.

"Okay, my turn," he says.

But suddenly my gift feels so inadequate, so stupid. That familiar feeling of dread seeps into my gut as I remember another moment when I gave someone a gift they didn't appreciate.

"No wait, never mind, it's stupid. Give it back." I grab for it, but he expertly blocks me with an elbow.

"Not a chance!" he says as he continues to open it out of my reach.

I fall back on my heels, defeated, and put a hand up to my forehead, covering my eyes as I place my own present on the wooden porch swing. Waiting for this mortifying moment to be over.

God, this is so stupid.

What was I thinking?

A flush creeps up my neck as he opens the box and looks inside.

But he doesn't scoff or make me feel stupid. Instead, he chuckles. I look up and he's smiling brightly at me, those dimples pulling my attention away from his eyes for just a second.

He pulls out the candle and holds it up reverently.

"Cherry-infused Chocolate Guava and Honey," he reads off the label of the scented candle, before bursting into hysterical laughter. "Unreal. That's a good one."

I huff out a breath. "I know, right?" Relief flooding through me.

We stare at each other for a long moment in completely comfortable silence, grinning from ear to ear, before he sets down the candle and takes off his coat, wrapping it around my shoulders. I lean into the warmth as I push my arms through the large sleeves.

This is it. This is the moment I have to tell him.

I know that I need to make the first move. He's always respected my boundaries and looked out for my best interests. I may have doubted it before, but the way he's looking at me now, I'm pretty sure he would wait for me forever if I asked him to.

But I don't want to wait any more.

I'm done waiting.

I slowly close the distance between us and reach up to wrap my arms around his neck. For a second, he doesn't move, and I worry I've read this all wrong. But the next moment, his arms are around me, clutching me tightly to him.

I press up on my tiptoes to bury my nose against his neck as I loudly breathe him in, then whisper, "I've missed your cherry chocolate guava honey scent, Damien."

He turns his head and smiles against my lips, his forehead

pressing against mine. "And I've missed *you*, Elsie. Just you. It's always been you."

He brings his hand up to my cheek, and I swear I stop breathing. The rest of the world falls away as our breaths mingle, and his lips finally meet mine.

It was all worth the wait. All of it, for this kiss.

The type of kiss that rattles the heavens and moves mountains. That time itself slows down to witness.

A kiss so true, so powerful, it could be written into legend.

Acknowledgments

This book would not be possible without the support of my amazing family. My husband, Frank, for always believing in me, even when I doubted myself. Thank you for being my #1 fan. Olivia, Emma, and Isabelle, for assuming that, simply by writing this book, I would become a famous author. I can't wait to watch you achieve your own dreams.

My brother and beta reader, Mark, for reading this and sharing your thoughts and suggestions to make this story the best it could be. Thanks for all the childhood memories and helping shape me into the nerd I am today.

Jenny and Rachel, my other incredible betas, thank you for going on this journey with me, and for your thoughts and encouragement.

Toby, an OG member of the DragonCon crew. Thanks for letting me pick your brain about con stuff, and for your encouragement early on when this was all just an idea.

Jenny H. for helping me understand the writing and publishing processes and letting me bug you with a million questions. Billy Block would be so proud!

Keith, another D*C member and the real Tony Stark. Thanks for all the cosplay info and helping me understand the community a little better.

Dessi-Desu, for your incredible work bringing Elsie's cosplay to life! I'm so honored to have you on this journey with me.

Shannon, my editor, I tried to make your job as easy as possible, but those commas are a beast! Thank you for working with me on this. I appreciate all your words of encouragement throughout this project.

And to all my friends and family who have been cheering me on, you know who you are! I love you!

About the Author

Rachel Rosato is a debut author with a passion for storytelling. *The Con* marks Rachel's debut into the world of fiction, combining her love of all things nerdy and fun. Currently residing in Virginia, Rachel can usually be found writing, reading, listening to music, and spending time with her family and friends.

RachelRosato.com

9 798990 289703